How the Finch Stole Christmas!

A Meg Langslow Mystery

Donna Andrews

St. Martin's Paperbacks

This is a work of fiction. All of the characters, organizations, and events portrayed in this novel are either products of the author's imagination or are used fictitiously.

HOW THE FINCH STOLE CHRISTMAS!

Copyright © 2017 by M. C. Beaton.
Excerpt from *Lark! The Herald Angels Sing* copyright © 2018 by M. C. Beaton.

For information address St. Martin's Press, 175 Fifth Avenue, New York, NY 10010.

ISBN: 978-1-250-19040-6

Our books may be purchased in bulk for promotional, educational, or business use. Please contact your local bookseller or the Macmillan Corporate and Premium Sales Department at 1-800-221-7945, ext. 5442, or by e-mail at MacmillanSpecialMarkets@macmillan.com.

Printed in the United States of America

Minotaur hardcover edition / October 2017
St. Martin's Paperbacks edition / October 2018

St. Martin's Paperbacks are published by St. Martin's Press, 175 Fifth Avenue, New York, NY 10010.

10 9 8 7 6 5 4 3 2 1

Acknowledgments

I continue to be grateful for all the great folks at St. Martin's/Minotaur, including (but not limited to) Hector DeJean, Jennifer Donovan, Paul Hochman, Andrew Martin, Sarah Melnyk, Talia Sherer, and especially my editor, Pete Wolverton. And thanks again to David Rotstein and the art department for another beautiful cover.

More thanks to my agent, Ellen Geiger, and the staff at the Frances Goldin Literary Agency for handling the business side of writing so brilliantly and letting me concentrate on the fun part.

Many thanks to the friends—writers and readers alike—who brainstorm and critique with me, give me good ideas, or help keep me sane while I'm writing: Stuart, Elke, Aidan, and Liam Andrews, Chris Cowan, Ellen Crosby, Kathy Deligianis, Suzanne Frisbee, John Gilstrap, Barb Goffman, David Niemi, Alan Orloff, Art Taylor, Robin Templeton, and Dina Willner. Thanks for all kinds of moral support and practical help to my blog sisters and brothers at the Femmes Fatales: Dana Cameron, Laura DiSilversio, Charlaine Harris, Dean James, Toni L. P. Kelner, Catriona McPherson, Kris Neri, Hank Phillippi Ryan, Mary Saums, Joanna Campbell Slan, Marcia Talley, and Elaine Viets. And thanks to all the TeaBuds for two decades of friendship.

And of course, Meg's adventures would not continue without the support of many readers. I continue to be delighted and humbled by how many of you tell me that Meg's adventures often prove to be a comfort in dark and trying times. Thank you!

Chapter 1

"Shakespeare was right. 'The first thing we do, let's kill all the lawyers.'"

"I wish I could hear you say that in person," I said.

"Yeah, over the cell phone you miss all my dramatic gestures." Michael's voice sounded more exasperated than angry. And since I knew my husband wasn't usually prejudiced against the legal profession, I was puzzled instead of worried.

"Are you someplace where you can talk?" he asked.

"I'm not at the theater, if that's what you mean. Reverend Robyn wanted to see me about something. At the moment, I'm over at Trinity, sitting in her office, waiting for her to solve a Christmas pageant prop emergency, so until she comes back, I'm at your service."

"Hang up if you need to," he said. "I'm just venting to you so I can be cool, calm, and collected when I go into my meeting."

"What meeting?" I made myself more comfortable in Robyn's guest chair and snagged a Christmas cookie from the red-and-green plate on her desk. "And by the way, all the lawyers would include Cousin Festus and my brother. I know Rob can be annoying at times, but I'd miss him if you did him in, and I thought you agreed that Festus was highly useful and a credit to his profession. Can we settle for bumping off whichever particular attorney has gotten your goat this morning?"

"One or more members of the college legal department," he said. "Possibly the entire department if I can't get them to admit who signed off on that miserable, washed-up prima donna's contract."

"Ah, then it's really Malcolm Haver you need to kill." Robyn walked back into her office as I was saying it, and a puzzled frown crossed her face. I held up my hand with two fingers raised, to signal that I'd be off shortly, and returned to my conversation with Michael. "What's he done now?"

"Showed up drunk for rehearsal. Again." Someone else might have thought his voice sounded calm, but I could hear the anger below the surface. And I took a few deep breaths to cool my own anger. I'd actually been relieved when the college proposed hiring a big-name actor to play Scrooge in this year's charity benefit production of *A Christmas Carol,* because I knew how exhausting it would be for Michael to direct and star. I'd been less than impressed when a board member pushed through hiring his old college buddy Haver—the whole point of casting someone from outside was to help with ticket sales, and I didn't think Haver was a big enough name to do that. And Haver had been a major pain from day one, even before he started drinking. Instead of halving Michael's workload he'd at least doubled it. I was starting to worry about Michael's health and I intensely resented how Haver had turned what was normally a festive, joyous, family-oriented season into one long headache.

"If you want him to disappear, I'm sure Mother can find someone to do the dirty work." I'd almost be willing to do it myself. But I didn't want to say so in front of Robyn, who had taken up her knitting, and would probably have finished another set of mittens for Trinity's Christmas scarf and mitten drive by the time Michael and I finished our conversation.

"I'd settle for figuring out where the hell he's getting his booze."

"None of the businesses here in Caerphilly will serve or sell to him," I said. "Randall Shiffley made sure of that."

"I'm still amazed that so many people agreed."

"They all know that your production is one of the main attractions of this year's Christmas in Caerphilly festival," I reminded him. "And that having a well-known actor like Haver will help boost the ticket sales, a big portion of which will go to things that might otherwise cost tax dollars—all those social service programs we can't otherwise afford. Enlightened self-interest."

"Still, it only takes one rebel to supply him," Michael grumbled. "Or one starstruck private citizen. Or he could be sneaking over to Clay County—they'd love to sabotage anything Caerphilly does."

"Which is why I think it's time to call in Stanley." I'd already talked unofficially to Stanley Denton, Caerphilly's leading—and only—private investigator about whether he'd be willing to shadow Malcolm Haver as part of our efforts to keep the visiting star sober.

"Exactly what I was thinking," he said. "In fact, I'm just venting to you before going into a meeting with the Dean of Finance to get it approved."

"Awesome," I said. "And good luck. I should go; Robyn just got back and I'd better explain our homicidal musings to her before she reports us to Chief Burke."

"When you leave Trinity, can you head over to the theater and keep an eye on things there until I finish arguing with Finance?"

"Can do," I said. "Love you."

"Back at you."

I hung up and returned my phone to my pocket.

"Sorry," I said to Robyn—who had been listening with un-abashed interest as her knitting needles flew through her red and green yarn. "Michael's having a tough day and needed to vent."

"So I gathered. What's he angry about?"

"He was calling more in sorrow than in anger," I said.

"That's from *Hamlet,* right?"

"Yes," I said. "Quoting Shakespeare's an occupational hazard when you're married to an actor."

"Especially one who's also a drama professor."

"Michael was calling to vent about Malcolm Haver," I explained. "The actor the college hired to play Scrooge in the stage version of *A Christmas Carol* that Michael's directing."

"He and Michael aren't getting along?" Even the thought of disharmony seemed to sadden her.

"Michael tries," I said. "But Haver doesn't get along with anyone. He's a nasty, self-centered jerk. Sorry—I know how uncharitable that sounds, but there's just no getting around it: a nasty, self-centered jerk. Walked into the first day of rehearsal with a bad attitude and that was the peak of his popularity in local theatrical circles. But Michael's a whiz at handling difficult performers, and no one would really care how unpleasant Haver is offstage if he did a good job in the show. Unfortunately, he seems to have fallen off the wagon."

"Oh, dear. You know, we have several very active twelve-step programs meeting either here or at the New Life Baptist Church," she began.

"I know. We've got the flyer prominently posted on the cast information board," I said. "I even tried talking him into it once, which wasn't a good idea. He exploded at me and stormed out of the rest of the rehearsal."

"He sounds like a troubled soul."

"I'm sure he is." Or maybe just trouble, but I knew better than to say that aloud in front of Robyn. "But don't try to sympathize with him unless you want to get your head bitten off. He was doing fine at the start of the rehearsal period, but lately he's started tippling earlier each day. Michael doesn't have much hope that it will get any better when the show opens. Unfortunately, the way his contract is written, as long as he can stumble onstage, Michael can't fire him. And although I don't know how well it would hold up in court, the contract still calls for Haver to get most of his fee even if he's fired for cause."

"Didn't anyone question the contract before signing it?" Robyn looked surprised. "I may be in an unworldly profession, but even I know the value of consulting an attorney before signing legal documents."

"If Michael were in charge of Santa's naughty-and-nice list, the college legal department would be getting nothing but coals and switches this year," I said.

"Why were they the ones reviewing the contract anyway?" Robyn asked. "I know the play's a joint project of the college and the town, but I thought the college was mainly donating use of the theater."

"And for some reason they also insisted on being in charge of Haver's contract," I said. "I suspect the same board member who got him the part in the first place. If only I'd known to insist that the town attorney handle it—because she'd have run it by Randall and me when Haver's agent came in with a whole bunch of changes that he claimed were standard Actors' Equity requirements, which was a complete lie. Michael could have told them that if they'd bothered to show him the contract—Randall and I would have. But they didn't. In fact, whatever lawyer the college had handling it didn't do any research, didn't try to negotiate—just caved. And now Michael is paying the price."

"And then there's the whole question of whether Haver is really worth all this trouble," Robyn said. "Wouldn't it have been easier just to have Michael play Scrooge? I've seen his one-man *Christmas Carol* show the last few years and loved it. He was brilliant."

"He'd be light-years better than Haver if you ask me. Of course, I'm biased. The theory was that getting an actor with a national reputation would increase ticket sales enough to more than offset the cost of his salary."

"That makes sense." Robyn held up her knitting to inspect

the green Christmas tree that was taking shape on the back of the red mitten. "But I'm not sure I'd have picked Haver. I mean, I know who he is, but just barely."

I quite agreed. And I thought it was particularly ironic that they picked Haver instead of Michael, who still had a rather active group of fans himself, in spite of having abandoned television for academia more than a decade ago. Not something I could say in public, of course.

"Haver was nominated for a Tony once," I said aloud. "And he was in a reasonably popular TV series for a few years. As a young man he was quite handsome—a B-movie heartthrob."

"Yes." Robyn nodded. "I remember my mother used to like him."

"A lot of people's mothers did," I said. "Let's just hope enough of them are still around to buy tickets."

"And that there's a show for them to see." Robyn paused and thought for a moment. Or maybe she was just listening to the choir down in the parish hall, harmonizing beautifully as they rehearsed their Christmas carol program. "Have you considered getting him a keeper?"

"A what?"

"A keeper. A minder. I don't know what you'd officially call them, but I know they exist, because I know of a diocese that hired one once for one of their employees—not a priest, of course, but a key employee, very capable, even very spiritual in his own way, but with an unfortunate weakness for alcohol. They sent him to a residential rehab program, and when he got out they hired someone to follow him around and keep him away from temptation for the first few months. Of course, you might have trouble getting your actor to agree to a keeper. In the case I'm talking about, it was either that or lose his job with the parish."

"Haver might not agree," I said at last. "But maybe the agent who drew up that contract could force him to accept a minder. Agents don't get paid unless their clients do, and it's still possible that Haver could drink himself into a stupor and breach the contract. I'll suggest it. Thank you—that's a great idea."

I stood up, trying to decide if I should call Michael with the suggestion or head over to the theater and talk to him in person when he got back from his meeting. Then I realized that Robyn was looking at me.

"I'm sorry." I sat down again. "You asked me to drop by to talk about something—I almost forgot. What is it?"

"I received a rather curious request this morning," Robyn said. "That we host a Weaseltide ceremony in the parish hall."

Weaseltide? Robyn was gung ho on reviving old traditions and minor Episcopal celebrations, but Weaseltide rang no bells. Which meant it obviously wasn't something in the Book of Common Prayer. And I could have sworn after several years of helping out in the parish, I'd gotten pretty familiar with the Book of Occasional Services as well.

"That's an interesting idea," I said aloud. Mother had drilled us always to call something interesting when we couldn't think what else to say.

"Yes," Robyn said. "There's just one thing—what is Weaseltide?"

Chapter 2

"Oh, thank goodness." I didn't try to hide my relief. "I thought Weaseltide must be something any good Episcopalian was supposed to know all about."

"You've never heard of it then?" Robyn looked puzzled. "I rather got the impression it was some sort of local custom."

"Not that I've ever heard," I said. "But then by local standards, I'm not from around here. I've only lived here for a decade. You need at least a century before they begin thinking of you as a local. So I gather Weaseltide isn't an Episcopalian festival."

"I'm not even sure it's a Christian one." She frowned slightly. "Not that we'd mind if it wasn't—the congregation is very supportive of ecumenical activities. We've had events with our local Buddhist, Sikh, Hindu, Jewish, and Muslim brothers and sisters. But what if Weaseltide is part of some weird cult? And yet, one hates to upset them by interrogating them."

I began to suspect why Robyn had brought the subject up with me. And of all things: weasels. Why did it always have to be weasels, I found myself thinking. They were among Dad's and Grandfather's favorite animals, so they already played a larger role in my life than seemed absolutely necessary. And now this.

"Let me see what I can find out," I suggested. "If it's something local, the Shiffleys will know all about it. If it's something New Agey, my cousin Rose Noire can fill us in. And if it's not either—"

"I knew I could count on you!"

"Just one question," I said. "Who asked you about Weaseltide—anyone we know?"

"Someone named Melisande Flanders." She read the name from a piece of paper on her desk. "Could she possibly be a new faculty member?"

"Not someone I've heard of, but then I don't memorize the faculty directory. Was she young?"

"Not really. I'd say fortyish. Maybe fiftyish. Of course I'm a terrible judge of ages."

"Probably not a student then."

"Well, there are so many non-traditional students nowadays," Robyn said. "I think half my seminary class was closer to Social Security than high school. But somehow she didn't seem like a student."

"A pity you couldn't have gotten more information out of her." Not only a pity, but downright puzzling—Robyn was normally a formidable though gentle interrogator.

"And a shame I'm dumping it on you, you mean," Robyn said. "I know it sounds ridiculous, but every time I tried to ask her a question she'd sort of dither off in some other direction and we'd never quite get back to anything practical. And she seemed very. . . . well, I know from the name it's tempting to assume it has something to do with actual weasels, but her behavior makes me wonder if Weaseltide could be some kind of gathering for people with an interest in . . . I don't know. Severe anxiety disorder. Or some other mental health challenge."

We both pondered that idea for a few moments. To me, the kind of gathering she was imagining sounded like a fairly normal sort of event for Trinity. But I wasn't sure how Robyn would feel if I said that.

"One more question," I said. "And don't take this the wrong way, but—if she's not a member of the parish, isn't anyone we know, can't be bothered to explain what it is she'd like to do with our parish hall, and didn't leave you any contact information, just how much time and energy do we want to spend figuring this out?"

"A good point." She slumped slightly in her chair. "You and I both have way too much to do already. But what if this is some worthwhile cause that we'd love to support if we knew what it was? Or what if she's a lost soul who needs support and encouragement that we could give her through this? I'd hate to say no without making at least some attempt to find out."

"So I'll make a reasonable attempt and report back to you." I stood and picked up my purse and tote. "And if she comes back—"

"If she comes back, I will tell her I've tasked you with making the decision on whether her event will fit into our crowded schedule and give her your cell phone number." Robyn beamed at me as if she'd come up with a brilliant idea. Of course, from her point of view, she had. "I'm sure you'll have much more luck than I had getting information out of her."

"I'll do what I can." I headed for the door, and Robyn tossed her knitting onto her desk and fell into step beside me. "But for now, I have to head over to the theater and perform my official duties as Michael's assistant director."

"Yes, I heard you were doing that," she said, as she accompanied me down the hall. "I admit, I was surprised—I had no idea you had directing ambitions."

"I don't," I said. "At least for this show, the assistant director's job is as a glorified gofer and organizer."

"You're certainly good at that. The organizing part, at least."

"More to the point, I'm one of the few people other than Michael who can get Malcolm Haver to behave." In fact, I was even better at it than Michael, but I wasn't about to share that with anyone. "And Mother is the best of all. He practically cowers when she looks at him. We try never to leave him at the theater without at least one of us there to manage him."

"So in a sense he already has a keeper," she observed.

"Three keepers, all of whom have other equally if not more important jobs that they'd rather be doing. Not to mention the fact at all three of us are starting to feel homicidal thoughts whenever we spend any time with Haver. Especially Mother. The other night I heard her and Dad having the most alarming discussion about whether it was really possible to kill someone by impregnating one of their garments with a contact poison—and did I mention that she's designing the costumes?"

"Oh, dear."

"I'm sure she's just blowing off steam, but clearly he stresses her. I want him off her hands."

"Definitely—so think about the idea of a keeper. Although, frankly, unless he's really ready to make a change in his life—"

"I know, believe me," I said. "He'll eventually elude even the sharpest keeper, and every time we take a bottle away from him he'll start looking for another. I'm under no illusion that we can fix him. We're just trying to get through the run."

"Does he have any family who could help? Any friends who might be a good influence?"

"He's divorced with no kids," I said. "And any close friends he has would be back in L.A. We're hoping his agent can be the good influence—they've worked together for forty years. He's due in sometime today. Though if the agent can't do anything, Mother thinks maybe it's time to let Haver crash and burn."

"Sadly, she might be right. And speaking of your mother, she's due here in an hour for a meeting of the Christmas Toy Drive, so I'd better let you go. Just one more thing."

I braced myself. Like Columbo, Robyn sometimes delivered

her biggest bombshells under cover of those harmless words "one more thing."

"Why does your grandfather seem to think we should add finches to the church's holiday decorations?"

"Oh, blast," I said. "So he's hit you up, too? Just tell him no thanks."

"I did, but you know how persistent he is. Are finches really part of the traditional Australian holiday celebration?"

"Not that I know of. The finches he's trying to pawn off on you are Australian—they're Gouldian finches. Very pretty birds—they have patches of red, turquoise, green, blue, and yellow—and they sing quite nicely. But they have nothing to do with Aussie Christmas celebrations. Grandfather just happens to have a surplus of Gouldian finches at the zoo and he's expecting another batch any time now, so he's trying to find places to put some of them."

"Expecting another batch?" Robyn looked puzzled. "If he already has too many, why is he getting another batch?"

"He's helping out the U.S. Fish and Wildlife Service—he's a certified wildlife rehabilitator, you know. The finches he's got were seized from an animal smuggling operation, and his contact there has dropped a hint that they could be seizing another big batch sometime soon, so he needs to find a place to put them. Normally he'd just send them down to the Willner Wildlife Sanctuary, but Caroline Willner is off on a cruise with her daughter, and the staff member she left in charge is digging in his heels. I'm sure as soon as Caroline's back she'll figure out a way to help out with the finches, but in the meantime Grandfather's trying to bully everyone he knows into fostering a few."

"I will stand firm, then, and refuse to be bullied!"

Robyn dashed off toward the parish hall, where "Silent Night" had given way to ominous silence—would she have to settle another quarrel over whether to sing "Adeste Fideles" or "O Come All Ye Faithful" to the traditional tune?

I paused to take a few deep breaths, feeling my spirits lifted by the bracing spruce, pine, and fir scents that permeated the church, thanks to all the fresh evergreen wreaths and garlands decking the halls. I made a note in my notebook-that-tells-me-when-to-breathe to have another talk with Grandfather about his attempts to finchify the world. Then I peeked into the sanctuary to check on the progress of the Christmas pageant—and to make sure my sons were behaving.

Josh, who had been cast as the assistant leader of the shepherds, was covertly studying the thirteen-year-old playing Joseph, no doubt with an eye to replacing him in future. I didn't have the heart to explain that it would probably be a few years before he succeeded—as was her custom, Robyn had filled the role of Joseph with a middle-grade boy who'd recently shot up to a gangly six feet. The fact that this year's Joseph couldn't walk three steps without tripping over his newly elongated legs didn't matter, since Joseph was mainly required to be tall and look pious. When the time approached, I would probably advise Josh to angle for a role as one of the wise men. They had better costumes and props, and their dramatic entrance actually allowed some scope for acting.

Jamie, on the other hand, would probably snag the role of First Angel without difficulty. Although I knew I was biased, I couldn't help thinking that he already stole the show as Third Angel. Unlike Josh, he wasn't studying what the two senior angels did—he just threw himself heart and soul into every moment of the performance. When the angels gazed down tenderly at the Christ Child, his eyes brimmed with tears. When they pretended to blow on their trumpets to summon the shepherds, he gave the impression that he was blowing so hard that it was making him breathless. And in his favorite part, when the angels raised their wings and pointed them while the light crew shone a spotlight past them to give the impression that the Star of the East was somehow emanating from the tips of their wings, Jamie closed his eyes and looked so ethereal that for a moment you really could believe he was generating his share of the light. More than his share.

"Yes, he's a ham like me," Michael had said after watching the last rehearsal. "They both are." But he sounded proud, so I refrained from smacking him.

I'd been a little worried about having the boys appear in not just one but two holiday plays, but so far it was working out okay. We'd made sure they knew that any decline in their school grades or the performance of their household chores could result in their understudies taking over the roles. And I was hearing a lot fewer "how many days till Christmas?" questions. Multiple renditions of "How many days till the Christmas pageant?" and "How many days till *A Christmas Carol* opens?" probably took up the slack, but somehow the variety made it all less annoying.

Satisfied that the younger Waterstons were behaving at least as well as their castmates, I slipped out of the sanctuary, quickly donned my winter coat, and escaped from Trinity before anyone spotted me and tried to recruit me for any of the many volunteer projects I knew were going begging.

The whirring of dozens of camera shutters greeted me when I stepped out of the church door, as if I were a celebrity being stalked by paparazzi. It wasn't about me, of course. Trinity Episcopal, with its glossy bright-red door and elegant gray stone walls, was beautiful in any season. In its Christmas finery, with candles in all the windows, wreaths on all the doors, and fairy lights covering all the shrubbery, it was truly magical. And some of the tourists liked to have a human figure in their pictures for scale, so I paused for a couple of moments on the doorstep, buttoning my coat, before stepping aside for the convenience of the other tourists who preferred their church photos unsullied by random strangers.

As I walked I glanced at the sky, which was both leaden

gray and curiously luminous. What I'd learned from the old timers to call a snow sky. I checked the weather app on my phone—yes, we were still getting two to six inches of snow, starting sometime this afternoon and continuing through the night.

"Two to six inches," I muttered. "You'd think this close to the start they could be a little more precise."

Ah, well. It wasn't happening yet, and with any luck I could be safe at home before it got bad. Or if the roads became impassable during rehearsal and I ended up snowbound at the theater, at least Michael and the boys would all be with me.

I set out toward the drama building. My path didn't lie through the town square, thank goodness, but tourists still filled the sidewalks and spilled over into Church Street, making the already congested traffic even worse. Tourists swarmed in and out of the nearby shops and restaurants—fewer shops, and thus fewer tourists than in the very heart of town, but still, it was a mob scene. This close to the town square, all the shops, houses, and—of course—churches had jumped onto the decorating bandwagon with a vengeance. Life-sized nativity scenes vied with life-sized Santa Clauses, with or without sleighs and the requisite quota of reindeer, and the occasional house sporting blue and silver candles and Stars of David. If there was a roof or a bit of shrubbery in this part of town not trimmed with some kind of lights I couldn't spot it, and everyone seemed to have used the overcast sky as an excuse to turn them on early. I had to keep reminding myselef that these days nearly all the tree lights, fairy lights, and candles were LEDs, so my neighbors' electrical bills weren't going to send them into bankruptcy and they weren't likely to burn their houses down. Whole forests had died to provide enough evergreen for the wreaths and garlands festooning almost every house, and there probably wasn't a scrap of tinsel left within several hundred miles.

And copies of the poster for *A Christmas Carol* were in

windows everywhere, in all of the shops and a good many of the private houses. From a distance, the poster's festive metallic red, green, and gold colors added nicely to the glittering, tinseled look the whole town had taken on. And when you looked more closely—as I did while waiting for the driver of a car laden with confused tourists to make up her mind which way to turn and clear the crosswalk—well, Haver did look the part of Scrooge, scowling and shaking his walking stick theatrically at the world. His top hat and high-collared black coat fit in nicely with the festival's Victorian theme.

I didn't so much mind that "starring Malcolm Haver!" was in letters almost as big as the play's title—the town and the college were paying him good money to headline the show, so we might as well get our money's worth out of him. I'd have made "directed by Michael Waterston" a little larger, but maybe that was just me. I'd also have made the figure of Tiny Tim, in the background, a little less tiny, so someone other than his adoring mother could recognize him. Fortunately my son Jamie was charmed to be on the poster at all, and used it to lord over Josh—who was playing what Michael and I were careful to point out was an equally important role, that of Scrooge as a boy. For several weeks now, their lives had been wall-to-wall rehearsals.

The only part of the poster I didn't much like right now was the line that gave the show's run dates. Opening night was only two days away. And Haver was still stumbling through his blocking and mangling his lines—when he showed up at all.

I mentally wished Michael well in his mission to Finance.

I noticed that a trio of female tourists had clustered around the poster in the window of the bakery.

"Malcolm Haver!" one exclaimed. "Isn't that fabulous?"

Chapter 3

Okay, I admit it. When I heard the tourist lady call Haver "fabulous," I inched a little closer so I could eavesdrop.

"Malcolm Haver!" the second lady in the group said. "Wonderful. Oh, Judy, let's go!" she added, turning to the silent third member of their trio.

"Malcolm Haver?" Judy repeated, with an air of slight bafflement.

"Oh, don't pretend you don't know who he is," the first one chided her.

At first glance, the three women were almost indistinguishable. They were all three in their fifties or sixties, well-wrapped against the cold in coats, hats, gloves, and woolly mufflers, and they each carried several red, green, and gold CHRISTMAS IN CAERPHILLY shopping bags in each hand. But the first two wore the starry-eyed expression of true enthusiasts as they studied Haver's picture. As I watched, Judy's expression shifted from incomprehension to mild distaste.

"Isn't he one of those people who used to be on *Hollywood Squares*?" she asked.

"He was Sir Tristan on *Dauntless Crusader*!" Fabulous explained.

"And didn't you see him in the remake of *Now and Forever*?" Wonderful asked.

"What incredible memories both of you have," Judy murmured.

I was starting to like Judy. And to feel a little sorry for her, finding herself saddled with two overzealous Haver fans.

Haver's movie career had been unspectacular and mostly over by the time I was in grade school. His role as the roguish, cynical, yet ultimately goodhearted Sir Tristan was his main claim to fame, but although it lived on as late-night filler on some of the more obscure cable channels, *Dauntless Crusader*'s prime-time run had ended a good thirty-five years ago.

Which made Fabulous and Wonderful—like Robyn's mother—just the right age to be avid Haver fans, I realized.

"The show doesn't even open till the day after tomorrow," Judy pointed out. "And we only have our rooms in the bed-and-breakfast for tonight."

"We could ask to stay on," Fabulous suggested.

"We could," Judy said. "But if you remember, I had to make our reservations six months in advance."

Her two companions drooped with disappointment.

"It's okay," Wonderful said, perking up again. "We could come back down sometime during the show's run. It's only a three-hour drive."

"A much more practical idea," Judy said. And one, her face suggested, that they could carry out without her involvement. "Let's go back to drop this latest batch of bags. We can check to see if there's any possibility of keeping the rooms."

They hoisted the shopping bags they'd set down while studying the poster and headed down a side street. I turned the other way and continued toward the theater.

I avoided the front entrance—although I noted in passing that two students were assiduously polishing the large brass letters that spelled out THE DR. J. MONTGOMERY BLAKE DRAMATIC ARTS BUILDING. Good; Grandfather was in town for the play, and nothing irked him more than seeing his name tarnished. Nearby were mounds of evergreen and reels of red ribbon, so I gathered that when they'd finished the polishing job they'd move on to decorating the façade.

Doubtless Grandfather would like that, too, as long as they didn't obscure any of the letters in his name.

I continued around the side to the stage entrance—and then stopped. Damn. The Fan was there. Sometimes known as the Avid Fan or even the Rabid Fan. She'd been stalking Haver ever since he'd arrived in town. The one time some-one had made the mistake of letting her in the building, she'd dogged Haver's steps until he finally lost his temper and stormed out of rehearsal for the rest of the day. Now we were under orders to keep her out.

Maybe it would be easier to go in the front way.

But no. I was Meg, the assistant director. Even Haver be-haved in my presence, or at least misbehaved more furtively and on a smaller scale. I could cope with the Rabid Fan.

I strode up to the stage door. She turned and brightened when she saw me.

"Meg! How's it going?" Her tone could easily have con-vinced any passerby that we were devoted friends.

"Fine." I paused outside the door and studied her smiling, eager face for a few moments.

She was older than me—fifties? Maybe sixties—and slightly plump in face and form. I wasn't sure whether her glasses were very old or whether they were some sort of retro fash-ion that didn't appeal to me—they were blue with silver glit-ter, made in what I thought of as a cat's-eye shape, with the outside of the frame sweeping up into points. Her features were regular, rather ordinary but pleasant. She was wear-ing a red-and-green sweater festooned with misshapen me-tallic gold reindeer that would be a strong contender in Caerphilly's annual Ugly Christmas Sweater Contest, but I knew better than to suggest this, in case she'd knitted it her-self. At first glance, she was largely indistinguishable from the hundreds of tourists flocking the streets with their shop-ping bags and steaming cups of coffee and hot chocolate.

But I'd seen the glitter in her eye whenever Haver came into view.

"Tell me something," I said. "Why do you keep hanging around here at the stage door? You know we're not going to let you go inside, or even talk to Haver. You know seeing you upsets him. So why do it?"

She was already shaking her head before I finished.

"Seeing me doesn't upset him," she said. "He was just having a bad day. I shouldn't have bothered him when he was trying to focus on his role."

"And he shouldn't have yelled at you just for wishing him a good morning."

"You don't know how hard life is for creative people."

"I'm married to an actor, remember," I said. "I know a lot about how hard life is for creative people. But by and large, no matter how hard it gets, most of them manage to behave decently and civilly toward their fellow human beings. And when they don't they have the good grace to apologize."

"You just don't understand a truly great actor like Malcolm," she said.

Only not-so-great ones like my husband? Clearly she didn't understand how to avoid insulting and ticking off the very people who had the power to grant her access to her beloved Malcolm. Not that I was going to override Haver's oft-stated wish to be left to work undisturbed, particularly by overeager fans.

Though come to think of it, to hear him talk, you could almost believe he had to fight his way through hysterical packs of fans after every rehearsal. I'd run into a few other fans in town—people like the trio I'd seen today, who *ooh*ed and *ahh*ed over the poster. But so far at the stage door the Rabid Fan was also the Lone Fan.

"I should go in," I said. "And before you ask again if you can come in and sit in the back of the theater, I'm afraid the last I heard, Mr. Haver was still adamant about not having any observers at rehearsal."

"I understand." She looked as if I'd gut-punched her, but she was also doing her best to smile bravely and keep her chin up.

I felt so sorry for her that I couldn't resist throwing her a bone.

"And if he changes his mind, we know where to find you."

She beamed as if I'd offered her a front-row seat for opening night.

"Thank you!"

"Are you staying near here?" I asked. "Because in case you haven't heard, it's going to start snowing this afternoon. If you have any kind of distance to go, you might want to start out before the roads get treacherous."

"Oh, don't worry," she said. "I'm at a very nice bed-and-breakfast not two minutes' drive from here. And in case the roads get bad, I can walk—I wore my boots, just in case."

"That's good," I said. "Just stay safe."

I used my key to unlock the door—keeping a close eye on her, in case a sudden irresistible impulse to barge into the theater overcame her—and went in.

I relaxed a little when I heard the lock click shut behind me, and stood for a quiet moment, letting my eyes adjust to the semi-darkness backstage. Somewhere not too far away a radio played softly. A piano, a drum, and a smoky contralto singer were turning "Away in a Manger" into something that sounded more like a torch song.

I pulled out my notebook-that-tells-me-when-to-breathe, flipped it open to today's schedule, and glanced at my phone to check the time. Not quite noon. Rehearsal was supposed to start up again at two. At the moment, the various back-stage crews were hard at work.

"A little to the left," came a voice from onstage. "A little more. That's it."

Our tech director, fine-tuning some of the light settings. Probably making yet another attempt to focus the spotlights so they'd illuminate Haver properly during his grand repentance scene in the final act. It would help if from one day to the next Haver could remember to repent in even approximately the same part of the stage.

"Looks fine from here," said another voice, this time from what I would once have called the audience—though I was getting pretty good at calling it "the house." Backstage, onstage, house, and front of house—the latter being the lobby and box office—those were the cardinal directions of the theater world.

Off on the other side of the stage I could hear some hammering, which I hoped meant that the set crew were rebuilding the bit of scenery Haver had fallen through during last night's rehearsal.

"Okay, let's take that from the top." Gemma, the stage manager. Was rehearsal starting already? I stepped forward and saw that near the other side of the stage, the actors playing Mrs. Cratchit and her two oldest children were sitting in folding chairs, arranged in a semicircle that approximated the positions they'd take around the fireplace in the third-act set. Gemma was holding a script, and Bob Cratchit was hovering nearby. Mrs. Cratchit and the daughter were holding dish towels and pretending to sew. The son was miming leaning against the invisible fireplace. Then Mrs. Cratchit sighed and dropped her dish towel into her lap.

"The color hurts my eyes."

Her daughter wiped her own eyes with her dish towel, and her son took a few steps and put a comforting hand on his mother's shoulder.

"They're better now again. It makes them weak by candle-light; and I wouldn't show weak eyes to your father when he comes home, for the world. It must be near his time."

"Past it rather. But I think he has walked a little slower than he used, these last few evenings, Mother."

"I have known him walk with—I have known him walk with Tiny Tim upon his shoulder, very fast indeed."

"And so have I. Often."

"But he was very light to carry, and . . . and . . . Line!"

The Cratchit son was wearing very anachronistic hipster glasses, Mrs. Cratchit was nursing a Diet Coke, and all three were wearing jeans and sweaters, and yet for a few moments, until Mrs. Cratchit had forgotten her line, I'd been totally caught up in the scene of the family mourning the departed Tiny Tim.

" 'But he was very light to carry,' " Gemma prompted. " 'And his father loved him so, that it was no trouble,—no trouble. And there is your father at the door.' "

"Of course," Mrs. Cratchit said. "Why do I always muff that line?"

"Maybe because it's my entrance cue." Bob Cratchit sounded slightly irritated. "If you do it during performance, I'll just barge in and you can deal with that."

"Sorry."

"Let's take it from 'the color hurts my eyes,' " Gemma prompted.

I slipped away quietly, before I got caught up in the play again. No time for that—I had a million things to do. Sometime this afternoon I needed to drop by the prop shop to see if they'd figured out what was wrong with the Ghost of Christmas Past's torch, and if they'd managed to construct a fake Christmas goose that didn't look as if it had mange. And I should drop by the lobby to make sure the Twelve Days of Christmas hadn't gotten out of hand. In fact, I should do that first.

"Much better," I exclaimed when I stepped out into the lobby. The red-and-gold drums that represented the twelve drummers drumming were now suspended from the ceiling on the left side of the lobby, nicely balanced by the eleven red plaid bagpipes dangling in midair on the left. The life-sized mannequins dressed as lords a-leaping, ladies dancing, and maids a-milking along with the papier-mâché geese, swans, and golden rings had all been fastened to the walls, freeing up much-needed floor space for incoming audience members.

Perhaps I should declare a victory for common sense and learn to live with the four cages of live birds—although together with the many brightly decorated live Christmas trees scattered about the lobby in red and gold ceramic pots, the birds took up at least half the available floor space. The three glossy black Crèvecoeur hens were rather festive looking, and the two turtledoves were adorable. I waved to Rose Noire, who had come in to feed the poultry and appeared to be having a long conversation in his own language with the partridge, who was sitting rather morosely under a potted pear tree much too small to bear his weight. Then I counted the calling (or collie) birds—here represented by Gouldian finches.

"Grandfather's been at it again," I said. "He thinks we won't notice if he sneaks in a couple more finches."

"How can you tell?" Rose Noire said. "There are so many of them."

"I have resorted to counting them," I said. "Last night when I left the theater there were twenty-seven. Now there are thirty-three—which is twenty-nine more than we should have for accuracy. This has got to stop."

"If he's going to sneak in extra birds, I wish he'd bring in another partridge." Rose Noire sighed and shook her head. "I think poor Keith is lonely."

"How can he possibly be lonely with so many other birds around?" I said. "More likely he's suffering from the stress of having too many neighbors."

I heard a door open behind me and turned to see Grandfather, carrying a small cage containing two more Gouldian finches. He stopped when he saw me, and turned as if planning to sneak away.

"No," I said. "You are not bringing another finch into this lobby. In fact, you need to take away some of the ones that are already here. The canonical number is four calling birds, and you have more than eight times that number already."

"But I need someplace to put them," Grandfather said. "Laurencio's counting on me."

"Laurencio?" Not one of Grandfather's usual co-conspirators.

"Ruiz. My friend in the U.S. Fish and Wildlife Service. He warned me last week that they were closing in on the mastermind behind this smuggling ring, and when they catch him they might be seizing a lot more finches."

"And you're finding homes for finches before they're seized," I said. "Isn't that rather like counting unhatched chickens? Just sit tight. Caroline's due home from her cruise in a couple of days—with any luck Laurencio won't show up with the next installment of finches before then. Or if he does, you can put out a call for volunteers to foster them. But the way you're going, by the time you really need their help, people will be as sick of finches as they are of zucchinis by the end of August."

Grandfather heaved a heavy sigh, as if disappointed in my cruel indifference to animal welfare, and strode out, carrying his cage of finches.

"Thank goodness," Rose Noire murmured. "They're very pretty birds, but too much of even a good thing . . . still, I hate to complain to your grandfather—he seems so fond of the finches."

"He's not fond of the finches," I said. "He prefers fierce animals, and there's nothing fierce about a finch. And he's very scornful about their brightly colored plumage. It makes them much easier for predators to catch, since the only place where they'd blend in with the scenery would be a crayon factory."

"Then why is he so obsessed with them? It's very . . . unsettling." Rose Noire had come as close as I'd ever heard her come to criticizing Grandfather. Or anyone else, for that matter.

"He wants to impress the Fish and Wildlife Service," I said. "And help his friend Laurencio. 'You've got more finches than you can possibly handle? No problem! I'll take care of it.' "

"I suppose that's it." She gazed thoughtfully at the finches for a few moments. "I'll tell you who is obsessed with the finches—Mr. Haver. He was in here again reciting poetry to them. And badgering your grandfather about letting him buy one. He doesn't seem to understand that they're not Dr. Blake's to sell. Is that why you had Grandfather put the locks on all the birds' cages?"

"That's one reason," I said. "There's also the fact that for some reason Gouldian finches are currently in such high demand that bad guys can earn a lot of money smuggling them into the country. I pointed out to Grandfather that if he wasn't going to keep them safely out at the zoo, at least he could lock the cages and make any would-be finch thieves work for their loot."

"That makes sense." She took a deep breath and threw back her shoulders. "Well, those cages aren't going to clean themselves."

I'd already made a note to myself to talk to Grandfather. I expanded it to include suggesting that if he was going to foist finches off on people, he could at least pay some of his staff to feed them and clean up after them.

I could tackle that this evening. Right now I planned to drop by the costume shop. Malcolm Haver was supposed to be trying on the latest new and improved costumes. If he was there, he was under Mother's eye, and I could relax until she had to leave for her meeting.

Surely if he wasn't there Mother would have sent out an alert by now. Unless he'd pleaded the need for a bathroom break and snuck out of the building again, leaving her tapping her feet impatiently but too polite to stick her head in to ask what was taking him so long.

I headed for the costume shop.

My immediate anxiety was eased even before I reached the shop door when I heard Mother's voice, in the imperious tone that I'd learned as a child meant that I was treading on thin ice.

"Do try not to writhe quite so much while we're fitting you, Mr. Haver. I have rather a lot of pins in my hand, and Nadja is holding a particularly sharp pair of scissors."

Mother was on the case.

Chapter 4

"How much longer is this nonsense going to take?" Haver's crisp enunciation reassured me that he was, at least for the moment, reasonably sober. Though his grouchy tone warned that he was probably in the throes of a hangover and might at any minute go in search of the hair of the dog.

"A lot longer if you keep squirming," Mother said.

"'I will be the pattern of all patience,'" Haver proclaimed. "'I will say nothing!'"

Probably a quote from Shakespeare, and it irked me that I didn't know which play. But I resisted the temptation to pull out my phone and look it up. I had no time to play one-upmanship with Haver. I retreated to the far end of the hall, ducked into a storage room, and called Ekaterina Vorobyaninova, my contact at the Caerphilly Inn, where Haver was staying. Actually, Ekaterina preferred calling herself my mole. Ekaterina's childhood had been indelibly shaped by her father's claim to have been one of the CIA's most important contacts in Soviet Russia. She'd started at the Inn as a maid to help pay her way through graduate school, and had now risen to assistant manager of the ritzy five-star hotel. But she still had a sentimental fondness for anything that smacked of secrecy and subterfuge, which was why I'd been able to talk her into aiding and abetting my efforts to keep Haver sober.

"I have completed my morning search of the subject's room," she reported. "No alcoholic beverages confiscated. Only an empty vodka bottle."

"Damn," I said.

"Swedish vodka." Her normally faint accent deepened slightly, so the words came out more like "Svedish wodka," and her tone clearly indicated by rejecting classic Stolichnaya in favor of Scandinavian swill, Haver had sunk his reputation to new depths in her eyes.

"However, we have an interesting new development," she went on.

I braced myself. Ekaterina's idea of an interesting development often coincided with my definition of a hideous disaster.

"He appears to have thrown the bottle away in the brown paper bag in which it was purchased," she said. "There is a sales receipt."

"That's great! Maybe we can figure out where he bought it, or who bought it for him."

"Where, certainly—the Clay County ABC store. But unfortunately, whoever bought it paid cash."

Okay, not as helpful as it might have been. There was no love lost between Caerphilly and neighboring Clay County. Caerphilly might be small, quaint, rural, strapped for cash, and off the beaten path, but by comparison, Clay County made us seem like a teeming metropolis at the crossroads of culture and commerce. And the denizens of Clay County seemed fond of blaming their woes on us.

"Somehow I don't think we're going to have much luck talking whoever runs the Clay County ABC store into telling us who's buying vodka for Haver," I said. "And it might be well-nigh impossible for Stanley to stake out the place."

"They know him in Clay County?"

"Even if they don't, they all know each other. Any stranger who shows up will automatically be suspect, even before he starts asking nosy questions."

"I still think the best tactic is to take away Haver's rental car," Ekaterina said. "I could arrange for a staff member to drive him to and from the theater. Or any other place you actually want to let him go."

"It could come to that," I said. "I'll keep you posted. Merry Christmas to you."

"And to you," she said, following the words with a string of sibilant polysyllabic sounds that I deduced must be Russian for "Merry Christmas."

As I ended the call, I glanced at my phone and saw that Stanley Denton had tried to reach me while I'd been talking to Ekaterina. I was about to call him back when I heard Haver shouting.

"What the hell is this? Are you trying to strangle me?"

Probably a good thing to see what was going on. So I hurried down the hall to the costume shop.

I found Haver striding up and down the middle of the room, half in and half out of a starched white Victorian shirt, uttering a stream of semi-coherent abuse liberally salted with unprintable words. Nadja, Mother's chief costume acolyte, had flattened herself against one of the walls and was watching him wide-eyed. Mother was nowhere to be seen. Trust Haver to cause trouble the minute her back was turned.

"Never seen a more ridiculous piece of garbage," Haver was snarling. He tugged at the shirt again and managed to get it over his head and off both arms, but the cuffs were still buttoned tight, so both hands were trapped in the bundle of white cloth. He pulled again, and both Nadja and I winced at the resulting ripping sound.

"Be careful, Mr. Haver." Nadja took a timid step forward. "If you'd just let me unbutton the cuffs for you—"

"Leave me alone!" Haver flailed at her with his fabric-bound hands, and she jumped back with a small shriek, tripped over something, and fell. Fortunately she landed in a box of fabric scraps. Haver didn't even seem to notice what he'd done.

"STOP THIS IMMEDIATELY!" I shouted.

Haver and Nadja both froze. Actually, so did I, because it was astonishing how much like Mother I sounded. And for that matter, how well I'd absorbed Michael's lessons on using my diaphragm for greater volume.

"Mr. Haver." I articulated each word as if it was made out of cut glass. He actually flinched slightly. "Please hold still and allow Ms. Curtis to unbutton your cuffs so you can remove your costume without causing any further damage."

"I'm not wearing this ridiculous thing," Haver said. But he did stand still and hold out his hands toward Nadja.

Nadja shot me an imploring glance. I learned back against one of the cutting tables and crossed my arms to indicate that I wasn't going anywhere. Nadja crept a little closer to Haver and began fumbling with the cuffs.

"Ridiculous piece of garbage," Haver muttered.

"If you have a complaint about your costume, take it up with Mrs. Langslow," I said.

He didn't meet my eye, so I suspected he heard what I left unspoken: that if he didn't have the guts to complain to Mother, he should at least refrain from taking his temper out on poor meek little Nadja.

He settled for glowering in my general direction and making Nadja's job as hard as possible by letting his arms go absolutely limp.

"What seems to be the problem?" I glanced up to see Mother standing in the doorway.

"Mr. Haver seems to have taken a dislike to part of his costume," I said.

"It's monstrously uncomfortable," Haver said. "You need to take off the horribly scratchy collar." From the way he rubbed his neck—to say nothing of the tormented face he made while doing so—you'd think we'd tried to fit him out with a garrote.

"I'm sorry, but we can't simply remove the horribly scratchy collar," Mother said. "*Scrooge* was a *gentleman*."

"And even if he wasn't, you don't want to lose that high collar," I said. "Gives a much more youthful look."

I watched that sink in. Haver was either sixty-four or sixty-seven—sources varied—and in decent shape for his age. But he was a senior citizen in a profession that valued youth over experience. He frowned slightly, his eyes sought one of the nearby mirrors, and I could see him flexing his neck slightly.

Mother and I exchanged a glance. And then, since she was back and had everything under control, I headed for the privacy of the storage room to call Stanley.

"Michael's still in the meeting with the college Finance people," I told Stanley when I'd reached him. "With any luck he'll have approval to hire you by afternoon. But for right now we're still on hold."

"That's great," he said. "But meanwhile I thought of something you can do right now. He's driving a rental car, right?"

"Until and unless one of the chief's deputies catches him driving under the influence, yes."

"One of Van Shiffley's fleet of silver Hondas?"

"What else?"

None of the major car rental companies had a branch here in Caerphilly, so anyone who wanted to rent a car locally went to the Caerphilly Car Rental, owned by one of Randall's cousins. Due to his obsessive-compulsive disorder, Van couldn't stand it unless all his rental stock matched, so if a late model silver Honda Accord didn't meet your needs, you were out of luck. On the plus side, also thanks to his OCD, every one of his cars was cleaner than the average operating room and ran perfectly, so for the most part people found they could live with the silver Accords.

"Good," Stanley said. "Have Randall call Van and get his permission for us to put a GPS tracker in Haver's rental car."

"It that legal?"

"Wouldn't be legal for us to bug Haver's own car, but Van owns the rental car, so he has a right to know where it's going."

"Great idea." I tried not to kick myself for not thinking of it before.

"I've got a couple of devices, so once Randall convinces Van it's a good idea, I'll take care of the paperwork and installation."

"I'll call him as soon as we hang up."

"Then I'll talk to you later."

But I decided to text Randall rather than calling him. If I called, the conversation might take longer. He would ask if I'd found a third camel for this year's holiday parade or if one of the wise men would have to ride in a llama cart like last year. He'd order me to make another call to our heavy equipment distributor to remind them that the county still hadn't received the new snowplow we'd ordered from them in July. He'd remind me that I'd be representing Caerphilly at Temple Beth El's Hanukkah celebration later this week because he had to make an overnight trip down to Richmond to see his grandmother through her cataract surgery. He'd remind me of a thousand things that were already on my list—in some cases, things I'd already done and told him about. December wasn't Randall's most organized season. Texting him would save both of us time.

I fired off an admirably succinct explanation of what Stanley had suggested. Then I headed back down the hall to see how Mother and Haver were getting along.

I was slightly alarmed to find the costume shop empty and silent. Well, not entirely silent—the radio was playing a soft instrumental rendition of "As with Gladness Men of Old." And when I stepped inside, I spotted Mother, sitting in one corner, frowning over her sketchbook.

But no sign of Haver.

"Where is he?" I asked.

"In his dressing room," she said. "His agent barged in and insisted on dragging him off for a conference."

"So his agent has arrived," I said. "That's good."

"Good?" Mother raised one eyebrow. "Clearly you haven't met the agent yet."

"No, and I'm fully prepared to dislike him intensely," I said. "After all, he's the one who suckered the college legal department into accepting those ridiculous provisions to Haver's contract. But the fact that he's here is good. We're going to put pressure on him see if he can get his client to straighten himself out."

"And if that doesn't work?" From her facial expression, I suspected she'd almost said "when" rather than "if."

"Then Michael will be playing Scrooge before the run is out," I said. "Because at the rate Haver's going, Dad thinks he might well end up in the hospital before too long."

In the hospital or dead had been Dad's complete diagnosis, but I was superstitious about mentioning the latter possibility. Or maybe just sensibly wary of mentioning it out loud in a room to which Haver might be returning at any minute.

"That reminds me, Meg—you may need to help me steer your father's conversation into suitable channels for a day or so."

"Why? What's he up to now?" Dad's hobbies and obsessions were almost never suitable for polite company—you'd think Mother would have resigned herself by now.

"You know he and your cousin Horace went over to Clay County yesterday to help them identify that unfortunate soul they found in the woods."

"I still can't believe Clay County asked for our help on something," I said. "We're talking about the John Doe, the hunter who died of exposure, right?"

"Yes. Apparently the deceased gentleman was not an optimal candidate for fingerprinting," Mother said, with her usual delicacy. "He'd been out in the woods for several days. Lying in a stream, I believe."

Yes, fingerprinting dead bodies was exactly the sort of thing Dad was likely to bring up at the dinner table. And exactly the sort of thing Mother would want to squelch—especially if visiting relatives were present.

"And of course, even in Clay County they've heard what wonderful results Horace has achieved with difficult finger-printing subjects." Mother sounded torn. On the one hand, she was always delighted at the opportunity to boast about her family's accomplishments. But she wasn't entirely sure what to make of Horace's growing reputation for being able to fingerprint corpses thought to be too far gone for identi-fication.

"And of course they're both so proud of themselves," she added.

"Both of them? So Horace got some fingerprints? Is Dad taking partial credit?"

"Horace only got a couple, but that might be enough to identify the poor soul," Mother said. "And your father was able to tell them that he hadn't died of exposure at all—he'd suffered a head wound. Probably in the fall—the stream they found him in was at the bottom of a deep ravine."

"I'm not sure how useful Dad's discovery is," I said. "The poor man's still dead."

"Yes, dear, but it was probably quicker than death by ex-posure. It might be of some comfort to the family, to know he hadn't suffered. Still, if they do find out who he is, I really think they ought to wait until after Christmas to notify his family."

"Given the way they usually do things in Clay County, they probably won't get around to notifying them until after Fourth of July," I said. "I'm surprised Dad doesn't suspect foul play."

"Actually, he does, of course," Mother said. "But then he almost always does if there's even the slightest possibility. And even the Clay County Sheriff knows that, so I'm afraid they didn't really pay him much mind. Goodness!" She shook her head slightly, as if clearing out cobwebs. "What a gloomy subject. Let's talk about something more cheerful. More festive!"

"Like how lucky we are that, unlike Clay County, we don't have any unidentified bodies here in Caerphilly, spoiling the Christmas festival?"

"Like how well the play is shaping up," Mother suggested instead. "And—oh dear; I need to be over at the church in a few minutes. I'll leave our wayward charge to you for the time being."

"Have fun. And don't worry. If necessary, I'll let Dad tell me all about his latest body, so he can get it out of his system before the relatives arrive." Or maybe I'd just tell him not to talk about it. Leave Clay County's problems to them.

Mother stayed long enough to survey the costume shop—her temporary domain—and nod with satisfaction. Over the past few weeks, under her supervision, the costume shop had undergone a dramatic change, from utter chaos to a degree of neatness and organization that almost amounted to décor. She'd even brought in a tiny Christmas tree and drafted some of the set crew to festoon the costume shop with fir garlands, giving rise to retaliatory decorating in many of the other backstage areas. Anyone allergic to evergreen would find no haven anywhere in the theater, and I was getting tired of ordering the sound and light crew to take down the mistletoe they kept hanging in unexpected places.

I was under no illusions that the shop would stay the same once the show was over, but it would probably take several years to sink to its previous wretched state. And as Michael and I had already discussed, we could always invite Mother to costume another show whenever we saw that the shop was beginning to get out of hand.

"Although maybe I should have her design a set sometime soon," Michael had suggested. "I'd love to see her work her magic on the scenery and prop shops."

As Mother left, I pulled out my phone and called Michael.

"Guess who showed up," I said.

"Haver?"

"Even better, I think—his agent. You want me to give him the opening salvo and let you come in and bandage his wounds when you get here?"

We'd already discussed how to handle Vince O'Manion, the agent. Our strategy was for me to play bad cop to Michael's good cop. Our only disagreement was on whether or not this was typecasting. I said yes; Michael, gallantly, insisted it was not.

"Go for it," he said.

Chapter 5

So armed with Michael's encouragement, I tucked my phone in my pocket and headed upstairs, where the stage and the dressing rooms were, in search of Haver's agent.

As I stepped out of the stairwell, I saw a tall, stoop-shouldered figure standing in the wings, watching the set crew work and the Cratchits rehearse. Not someone I recognized, so either it was O'Manion—whom I hadn't yet met in person, though I'd seen his picture on his website—or another tourist come to gawk and needing to be kicked out.

"May I help you, sir?" I called.

The man turned toward me, frowning.

"I certainly hope so. I'm looking for Mr. Michael Waterston, the director. The crew members don't seem to know where he is."

Definitely O'Manion. A good twenty years older than the photo on the website, but I could still recognize him.

"He's in a meeting at the moment," I said. "Perhaps I can help you. Meg Langslow. Assistant director."

"Ms. Langslow." He held out his hand and his face took on an ingratiating expression. "Vince O'Manion. Malcolm has told me how much he enjoys working with you."

"How nice of him," I said, in a tone calculated to make it clear that I knew either he was lying or Haver was. "Michael will be back shortly, but in the meantime, he asked me to have a few words with you. Just a moment."

I walked out onto the stage and stood in the spotlight the light techs had been working on.

"Roger?" I called, looking around.

"Right here." Our lighting designer stepped out of the shadows.

"Mr. Haver is—in his dressing room?" I glanced at O'Manion, who shrugged. "Now would be a perfect time to let him show you exactly where he wants that spotlight."

"Won't do any good," Roger muttered to me, too low for O'Manion to hear. "Not as long as he keeps showing up too drunk to hit his marks."

"Just find him and keep him here as long as you can while I have a little chat with his agent," I said.

Roger nodded and ambled back into the shadows. I rejoined O'Manion.

"This way," I said.

I led the way through the backstage area to the lobby. Haver was there peering into the finch cage again. O'Manion and I stopped for a moment to watch him.

" 'Hail to thee, blithe Spirit!' " Haver intoned. " 'Bird thou never wert . . .' "

"Is he reciting Shakespeare to those birds?" O'Manion asked.

"Actually, that's Shelley." I pulled out my phone and began texting Haver's whereabouts to Roger. "Usually it's Shakespeare, though."

" 'That from heaven, or near it / Pourest thy full heart . . .' " Haver continued.

The birds were twittering cheerfully, as if they liked his recitation. Or maybe it was the attention. Rose Noire was watching him with a slight frown on her face.

So was O'Manion.

"They seem particularly fond of 'Sonnet Eighteen,' " I said. " 'Shall I compare thee to a summer's day?' This way."

I led him into the wing that housed the classrooms, and we took the elevator up to the faculty office floor. I could see O'Manion was impressed, although he was clearly trying to hide it. He'd better be impressed. Everything about the Dr. J. Montgomery Blake Dramatic Arts Building was first class and state of the art—Grandfather made sure of that when he gave the college the money to build it. I ushered O'Manion into Michael's office, which was large, comfortable, and right next door to the even larger and more comfortable office of the department chairman—an office that we were guardedly optimistic Michael would be occupying in a few years when the current chairman retired.

I had to move aside part of the mountain of brightly wrapped presents heaped around the foot-high Christmas tree that stood just inside the door. O'Manion glanced at the presents with a small frown—not quite a "bah, humbug," but definitely in the same neighborhood. So I didn't bother to explain that Michael and I were hiding the boys' Christmas presents here—out of the house and thus unavailable for investigation by busy fingers and prying eyes. And since the boys did occasionally visit their dad's office, especially while rehearsing for *A Christmas Carol,* all the boxes were camouflaged with tags that made them look as if they were for his various colleagues in the department.

Michael had left his radio on and tuned to the college station's carol marathon. Much as I loved "Go Tell It on the Mountain," I clicked the radio off. This wasn't going to be a very Christmassy conversation.

"I hope they made you comfortable at the Inn," I said.

"Very," he said. "It's a remarkably nice place."

"You sound surprised."

"I was, a little."

"To find such a nice hotel in a small town like Caerphilly? Or had Mr. Haver given you the impression that we'd put him up in a place a cut or two below a Motel 6?"

He opened his mouth—no doubt to protest that no, of course his client hadn't complained. And then he chuckled and nodded.

"Actually, from the way he's been carrying on, I expected the kind of dump that rents rooms by the hour. You'd think after forty years, I'd have learned to take Malcolm's complaints with a grain of salt. He gets a little hyper when he's working on a role, that's all. Bouncing back and forth between elation and despair—you know the creative temperament. That's why I thought I'd drop in a few days before the opening. Provide a little moral support."

Actually, he'd dropped in because Michael had called and left a message threatening to can Haver, and had then dodged his calls for two days—a tactic deliberately calculated to bring O'Manion running to town to wave the impossible contract at us.

I decided to be blunt.

"Any chance you could also help us keep him sober enough to go onstage under his own steam on opening night?"

He froze for a moment.

"According to Malcolm's contract—" he began.

"I've read his contract, thank you. You put a good one over on the college legal department. As long as he can stumble out onstage and utter some reasonable facsimile of human speech, we can't fire him. But the way he's going, he won't even be able to do that before long. Maybe even by opening night."

O'Manion didn't say anything. Didn't nod or shake his head. Just sat, looking at me, braced as if expecting me to whack him with a two-by-four.

"We don't want him to fail," I went on. "Neither do you. This was supposed to be the start of his big comeback, right?"

O'Manion gave a barely perceptible nod.

"So work with us. Help us turn this around."

He let out a long breath.

"I thought he'd be okay here," he said. "It's such a small town. I thought there wouldn't be very many temptations."

"There aren't that many," I said. "But he's awfully good at finding the ones there are."

"Yeah." He nodded. "A pity this isn't a dry county. I was really hoping it might be."

"Unfortunately, it isn't." I refrained from pointing out that he could have learned as much from a few minutes of on-line research. "But we are doing our best to dry up whatever part of it he happens to be in at any given moment."

"What do you mean by that?" O'Manion looked puzzled.

"Mayor Shiffley has sent out the word that no one's to sell or serve him any alcohol."

"Can he do that?"

"Why not? There's no law that says they have to serve him. In fact, the Code of Virginia specifically prohibits selling alcohol to someone if you have reason to believe he's intoxicated, which lately has been pretty much Haver's normal state."

"I mean, how can you expect people to just follow this Shiffley guy's orders? He's just the mayor, not the King of Caerphilly."

"He's a Shiffley," I said. "And not just any Shiffley, but the de facto head of the Shiffley clan. That may not mean much out in Los Angeles, but here in Caerphilly it matters."

"So what happens if he figures out who's been selling booze to Malcolm? Can he toss him in jail?"

"No. But whoever did the selling will suddenly start finding life very, very trying."

O'Manion shook his head as if he wasn't very impressed with our efforts.

"Look, it's a small town," I explained. "There aren't a lot of businesses. And a lot of them are run by Shiffleys. Especially every kind of skilled blue-collar business. Your toilet breaks and you want a plumber? We've got four of them—three of them are Shiffleys and the fourth is married to one. Same with electricians or carpenters. You want gas? Need your car repaired? Want your driveway plowed? Need hardware? Most of the businesses you'd turn to for any of that are run by Shiffleys, either by birth or marriage. And it's not just the Shiffleys—most of the rest of the town is also very committed to having the play succeed. You want to eat at Muriel's Diner? Buy fodder for your livestock at the feed store? Have your Sunday suit dry-cleaned? Then don't help Haver get drunk."

"I get the picture," he said. "And people wonder why some of us flee small towns for the freedom of the big city. So if your mayor has the whole town sewed up so tight, how come my client's still managing to get soused?"

"We've made it hard for him, but we can't possibly stop every leak," I said. "We haven't yet found the bootlegger."

"Bootlegger?" O'Manion sounded startled. "You mean he's drinking some kind of hillbilly moonshine? Is that even safe?"

"We've started using the term 'bootlegger' because it's a lot quicker to say than 'the low-down, sneaky, underhanded son-of-a-gun who's helping Haver get drunk,'" I explained. "Caerphilly isn't quite that backward." Of course, neighboring Clay County certainly was, but I was optimistic that their moonshiners would be far too suspicious to sell to outsiders. "We confiscate any liquor he gets as soon as we find it—"

"Confiscate it? He lets you do that?"

"He can't very well stop us," I said. "Hotel staff members search his room while he's out and confiscate whatever alcohol they find, and here at the theater the crew do the same with any that turns up in his dressing room. And when he takes a shower—"

O'Manion suddenly slumped in Michael's guest chair, put his hands over his eyes, and started laughing. I waited until he pulled himself together.

"I'm sorry," he said. "You people really have gone above and beyond. I don't know what I can do that you haven't already."

"Get him to agree to a minder," I said. "Someone to stay

with him twenty-four hours a day from now until the end of the run. He can start drinking himself into a coma five minutes after the last curtain call on closing night for all we care. But until then, he'll have someone with him day and night to keep him sober."

O'Manion looked as if he was giving it serious consideration.

"I'm not sure even I could get him to agree to that," he said. "And even if I did, it might not work. You have no idea how . . . how . . ."

"How sneaky he is? How determined? How abrasive and combative? Yeah, we have a good idea. But this is the best plan we've come up with. Do you have any better ideas?"

He shook his head.

"So talk him into it. Because if you don't, we'll stop all our own efforts to keep him sober and let the chips fall where they may."

"You can't do that." His voice had a note of panic in it.

"We can and will," I said. "He'd have crashed and burned long ago if we hadn't been doing everything we could to keep him going. But if he won't accept a minder, it stops now."

He sat there looking at me for several long minutes. Did he need quite this much time to think about it? Or was he trying to play that game of making the other person break and speak first? If that was his angle, he was going to lose. I stared coolly back at him while contemplating the contents of my notebook-that-tells-me-when-to-breathe, mentally crossing off a few completed items, adding a few others, and deciding what to tackle next, an occupation that always calmed me and improved my mood. And would help me win a staring contest, if that's what we were doing. I was in the middle of a mental inventory of what the boys' Christmas stockings would contain when O'Manion finally spoke.

"I'll try," he said at last. "But it's up to you people to find the minder."

"I can take care of that." Actually, I was sure Mother could, which for practical purposes amounted to the same thing.

"I need some time to work myself up to this," he said.

"We don't have a lot of time to spare," I pointed out.

"Maybe I could collect him at the end of rehearsal tonight and tackle him then. That will give me a few hours to figure out how I'm going to position it."

I was tempted to suggest positioning it as "do this, or find another agent."

"It would help if you gave him a little encouragement now," I suggested. "Do whatever you can do to keep him on his best behavior for rehearsal."

"Yeah, I guess." He didn't look happy. "Show me the way back through this maze to his dressing room, will you?"

I followed him out of Michael's office, locking the door behind me, and we walked in silence back to the elevator. From the look on his face, O'Manion was bracing himself for the promised talk with his client. I was busy strategizing our next step. When Mother came back from her meeting at the church, I'd task her with finding someone to serve as minder. Some burly but good-natured cousin who owed her a favor, perhaps.

And even if O'Manion couldn't talk Haver into the minder, we could pretend he'd said yes and sic one on him anyway.

The thought made me smile. O'Manion seemed to find my smile unnerving.

When the elevator reached the lobby level, we parted without speaking. Haver was no longer crooning verse to the birds. O'Manion trudged toward his dressing room with an expression of stoic determination on his face.

I counted the finches. Still thirty-three, so neither Grandfather nor Haver had pulled a fast one while I'd been talking to O'Manion. I took out my notebook, crossed off "talk to O'Manion," and glanced at the other theater-related tasks. The prop shop was probably the most urgent.

But when I turned into the hallway that would take me to the prop shop, I spotted Haver sneaking away.

Chapter 6

"What the Dickens is he up to?" I murmured as I stepped back behind a rolling costume rack so Haver wouldn't see me. He scanned up and down the hallway one more time before disappearing into the back stairwell—the one that led down to the loading dock and the parking lot beyond.

"Not again," I muttered. I could think of no good reason why Haver might be sneaking out of the theater less than an hour before rehearsal began. No good reason, only a lot of bad ones.

And yes, he was sneaking. Very obviously sneaking. He might not be Olivier, but I had to admit he was a decent actor. So you'd think he'd have figured out how to sneak around without looking quite so obvious. He could amble down the hall, staring at his script and pretending to run lines under his breath. Or saunter, looking around as if interested to see what progress had been made on the set. Or hurry as if he'd left something important behind.

But no. He'd been creeping along, almost tiptoeing, looking furtively around him every step or two. He couldn't have been more obvious if he'd held up a sign saying "Watch me! I'm up to something!"

I could never have held my own with him onstage, but I could definitely best him at sneaking. In spite of all his paranoid peering around, I reached the loading dock practically on his heels and yet apparently undetected.

He spent a while lurking behind a Dumpster and peering out to see if anyone was on to him before slinking across the asphalt to where he'd parked his shiny little silver rental Honda.

Luckily my own car was parked nearby. I made my unobtrusive way to it, watching Haver's car out of the corner of my eye and noting which way he turned when he finally stopped scanning the street in both directions and pulled out of the parking lot. I let him have a decent lead. He was heading toward town, where I was reasonably sure the tourist traffic would both slow him down and provide me with enough cover to catch up with him unobserved.

"I don't have time for this," I muttered as I went. "We should have Stanley doing it." And perhaps by tomorrow, or even this afternoon, we would have him doing it. But I didn't want to waste what could be the perfect opportunity to find Haver's bootlegger.

Still, it was annoying, so I deliberately tried to lift my own spirits by appreciating the holiday bustle around me.

The town Christmas tree looked fabulous. I didn't know offhand whether Randall had followed his usual tactful policy of getting one ever-so-slightly shorter than the National Christmas Tree or whether he'd decided to go for broke and aim for the record. Either way, its impressive size made it a favorite background for selfies and group photos. And the multicolored lights and ornaments were definitely more appropriate than last year's rather severe blue-and-silver color scheme.

The streets and sidewalks were teeming, in spite of the threatening weather forecast. Or maybe because of it—people might be trying to squeeze in a last hour or two of shopping and sightseeing before retreating to their hotels or bed-and-breakfasts, or maybe just climbing into their cars for the drive home. I lost count of the number of red, green, and gold CHRISTMAS IN CAERPHILLY shopping bags I was seeing— nearly every tourist had one, and most had half a dozen or more.

Clearly Haver wasn't in a holiday mood. Within a few

blocks, I'd caught up enough to have only one car between us. Close enough for me to see him pounding the wheel when other drivers dawdled and shaking his fist at pedestrians who impeded his progress.

During a moment when traffic completely ground to a halt. I pulled out my phone and texted Michael. "Haver left theater. Tailing him."

Then I dialed Mother.

"Where is that man?" she said. "I'm sorry—hello, dear. What can I do for you, and do you have any idea where that wretched actor can possibly be?"

"At the moment, two cars ahead of me on Church Street, near the town square, having a conniption fit and shouting obscenities through his rolled-down window at the poor FedEx driver who's double parked and blocking the street to deliver a large shipment of boxes to the toy store."

A pause

"Is there some special reason why he's driving through town instead of being here to try on the new waistcoat I made for him?"

"You made the waistcoat? I'm sure he will be sorry to miss that." Mother's talents were many, but actual sewing wasn't among them.

"The new waistcoat the costume crew made last night, under my direction." Mother's tone had become ever-so-slightly testy.

"I look forward to seeing it," I said. "I'll do what I can to bring Haver back as soon as possible to try it on, but right now I'm tailing him to see if he'll lead me to his bootlegger."

"His bootlegger? Is that how he's been getting his . . . er . . . supply?"

"By bootlegger I meant whoever's sabotaging the show by selling or giving booze to Haver."

"I hope you catch the bootlegger then, dear. Let me know if there's anything I can do to help."

"Actually, there is," I said. "Can you find someone we can hire to shadow Haver twenty-four hours a day and do whatever it takes to keep him from drinking?"

"I'm sure I can," she said. "Starting immediately, I assume. Your cousin Maximilian has some experience along that line. Or if he's not available, there's always Elspeth's youngest. Let me make a few calls. One way or another, I'll have someone here tomorrow."

"Thanks," I said, and signed off.

The FedEx man finally returned to his vehicle and drove off, and Haver jerkily put his car into motion again. Only slow motion, of course, given how crowded the streets were. And the pending snow had begun sifting gently down.

Obviously wherever he was going must be near the heart of downtown—why else would someone brave the tourist hordes this way?

"Because he doesn't know any better," I muttered to myself when Haver, after saluting a party of jaywalking tourists with a flourish of impatient horn-blowing and an extended middle finger, eased away from the crowded downtown area and headed toward the opposite edge of town from the theater. I'd have taken a couple of side streets and made the trip in two minutes.

"Of course, it makes sense that his bootlegger wouldn't be downtown," I told myself as we put more and more distance between us and the town square. Downtown was teeming not only with tourists but also with locals who would know about our Haverwatch. He might be savvy enough to avoid the citizens dressed for the duration in Victorian garb—the shopkeepers, the roving bands of carolers, and the ten-piece brass ensemble from the high school marching band. But we also had locals roaming the crowds dressed like tourists, to keep an eye out for pickpockets and troublemakers, not to mention locals going about their normal errands to and from nearby stores, restaurants, offices, churches, and friends' houses.

Away from the center of town, the decorations became a little less over the top, but still, you had to work to spot an undecorated house. I thought I'd found one on Hawthorne Street, but a closer look revealed a small but tasteful wreath on the front door, reminding me that perhaps it was time for my annual rereading of Charlotte MacLeod's *Rest You Merry*, one of my favorite Christmas books of all time.

"Where the blazes is he going?" I muttered as Haver passed the town limits and headed out into the countryside. The snow was falling in earnest now, light but steady, and a quick glance at the weather forecast on my phone confirmed that they still didn't expect it to stop anytime soon.

Should I turn back? I had no desire to spend the night stuck in a snowdrift, with or without Haver nearby.

"If the going starts to get bad, I'm turning back," I announced to no one in particular, with a baleful glance at the clouds overhead.

But the road continued to be easy going, and at least the snow gave me some cover. It also helped that I knew this particular road reasonably well, so I could drop back and give Haver plenty of space except when he approached the two or three places where he'd be coming to a possible turnoff.

We were nearly at the county line. I was just deciding that if he left the county, I should use that as an excuse to give up my pursuit, when Haver slowed, and then turned—not into a road, but a private lane.

I gave him a minute or so before following.

Chapter 7

I drove down the lane very slowly—not only to avoid over-taking Haver, but also because I quickly realized that the inch or two of unplowed snow covering it camouflaged quite a lot of nasty bumps and ruts. Only a dirt lane, I suspected, and probably one that followed an old game trail as it wound gently through the woods. Then I saw that the trees ended a little way ahead.

I slowed my car and crept ahead even more slowly until I reached the point where the lane emerged from the woods. I spotted a small, rundown farmhouse with a thin thread of smoke emerging from the chimney. To the right of the house was a disheveled barn. The dirt lane split in two as it neared the buildings, with the right fork dead-ending at the barn while the left fork petered out a little beyond the front door of the farmhouse. Haver's silver rental Honda was parked on the left side.

Just for a moment I contemplated how satisfying it would be to drive up to the farmhouse, march inside, and confront Haver and his bootlegger.

Then I put the car into reverse and backed up until I was out of sight. I was about to make a three-point turn when it occurred to me that Haver might spot my tracks and realize someone had followed him partway down the lane.

Of course, there was always the question of whether he'd even care. If I were sneaking around—and he definitely had been sneaking when he left the theater—I'd have noticed the tracks. But I'd also have been keeping a close eye on my rearview mirror. Haver hadn't seemed particularly wary during our drive—hadn't made any evasive maneuvers. But still.

I carefully backed out, so the only tracks visible were straight down the center of the lane, the way he'd expect to see them. The snow wasn't falling all that heavily, but a few more minutes of it would erase all traces of my passage. Well, not all traces—I willing to bet that almost any Shiffley in the county would have known that two cars had gone in and one had backed out—and probably even determined the make and model of both vehicles. But a city slicker like Haver probably wouldn't be able to tell my tracks from the tracks he'd made going in.

The road was deserted, so it was easy to back out onto it, point my car away from town and drive a few hundred yards until I was out of sight of the lane. Then I parked my car along the side of the road and prepared to hike back to the lane.

But first I rummaged in the back seat. Yes, my binoculars were still there. Last week I'd taken Dad and Grandmother Cordelia out to some remote location in the middle of the Blue Ridge Mountains so they could participate in their beloved Christmas bird count. It had been snowing that day, too.

It occurred to me that if someone came along and spotted my car, they might wonder why I was parked in the middle of nowhere. So I opened my copy of the Audubon guide to a plausible species—pages 638–639, the red-tailed hawk (*Buteo jamaicensis*)—and left it lying open on the passenger seat. The idea was to suggest that I'd spotted a large bird soaring overhead, looked it up in my guide, and then impulsively leaped out of the car, binoculars in hand, to stalk the wily raptor to its nest. That would also be my cover story if anyone accosted me as I hiked in to spy on Haver. "Do you know if you have red-tailed hawks nesting in your woods?" I could exclaim. "I think I saw one flying across the road just now!"

As I trudged down the road and turned into the lane, it occurred to me to wonder if Dad's obsession with mysteries and his love of dramatizing things were beginning to rub off on me just a little too much.

I traveled down the lane as quickly as possible, though I kept a wary eye—and ear—open for anyone coming or going. As I neared the point where the lane emerged from the woods, I left it and slipped through the trees on the right side until I reached a point at the edge of the woods, around a hundred yards from the lane.

I found a spot where two dead trees had fallen, one across the other, making a slight shelter—the trunks and branches overhead kept off the worst of the snow, and the overlapping trunks cast a shadow that should make me less visible if anyone from the farmhouse looked my way. I sat on a stump, pulled out my binoculars, and focused in on the house.

A very ordinary farmhouse, with an even more ordinary barn beside it. Both a little rundown, but not in danger of falling down anytime soon. Neither had been painted recently, so the house was a graying white and the barn a graying red. No farm animals in the field—which was a relief, because if there had been in this weather, I'd have had to make a quick call to animal welfare.

An enormous woodpile flanked the house, and smoke rose from the chimney. I also spotted a propane tank near the back door. An old but serviceable-looking pickup truck was parked under a rough plank carport between the barn and the back door. Apart from Haver's silver Accord, still parked in front of the farmhouse, there didn't seem to be any other vehicles. And no rusted hulks or bits of obsolete farm equipment lying about, so either the occupant was an unusually tidy farmer by local standards or he hadn't been here long.

And just who was Haver visiting? I pulled out my phone and opened my GPS app. It took a while to find a signal, thanks to the cloud cover, but eventually the app showed the little arrow representing me blinking in the middle of a big blank area. I could just barely see the line representing the road I'd parked on off to one side of the screen.

I clicked around until I found the place where the app showed me my latitude and longitude. I copied it down, then texted it off to Randall Shiffley, asking him if he could figure out who lived there.

"I can," he replied. "Why?"

"Could be Haver's bootlegger," I texted back.

"Grr. I'm on it."

I shoved my phone back into my pocket and returned to surveying the house with the binoculars. Haver's visit seemed to be taking rather a long time. I'd more than half expected to have to dive into the woods on my way down the lane— why would Haver stay here much longer than it took to hand over money and receive a bottle?

Unless—we'd jokingly referred to the unknown miscreant who'd been supplying Haver as his bootlegger. What if whoever lived here really was a bootlegger? And what if Haver had to wait until his latest batch of moonshine was ready? Or—

The front door of the farmhouse opened, and Haver stepped out. He was cradling something in his left arm. Something wrapped in brown paper, but the shape was unmistakable. A bottle.

He was followed by a tall, angular man carrying a box covered with a quilted blanket, the kind movers used to wrap furniture.

"Blast," I muttered. "Is that a whole case of booze?"

Haver opened the rear door of his rented Honda and the man carefully deposited the blanket-covered box inside. Then they turned to face each other. They stood for a few moments, looking uncomfortable, as if not sure whether a handshake was required. Then the unknown man nodded, turned on his heel, and went back inside.

Haver stowed the brown-paper-wrapped bottle in his passenger seat with meticulous care before getting into the driver's seat and starting the car. He turned around slowly in the snowy farmyard and headed back down the lane.

No way to get back to my car in time to follow him, but I was pretty sure I knew where he was going. I pulled out my phone again and texted Ekaterina, my contact at the Caerphilly Inn.

"Haver has found another bottle," I said. "Possibly headed your way. See if you can intercept."

"Affirmative," she texted back. "Over and out."

Apparently I'd managed to approximate the CIA-approved way for one operative to talk to another.

I glanced at my phone. It was one forty-five. Haver had fifteen minutes to get to the afternoon rehearsal. Clearly he wasn't going to make it. I couldn't make it, and I knew every possible shortcut.

So I called Michael.

"Do you want the good news or the bad news?" I asked.

"There's good news? That'll be a first for the day. Start with that."

"I think I just managed to tail Haver to his bootlegger's house."

"If that's the good news, I'm not sure I want to hear the bad. Although I bet I can guess—he's getting smashed."

"He wasn't the last time I saw him, but who knows what he'll get up to on the way back to town. The bad news is that he's definitely acquired a bottle, and may even have a case, and even if he has decided to save it for tonight, he's going to be at least fifteen minutes late for rehearsal."

"Blast. Well, I'll alert the chief that his officers might have a crack at that long-awaited DUI arrest and then see what we can get done without the one actor who's in every damned scene in the play. Are you coming back now?"

"Not till I get as much info as possible on the bootlegger," I said.

"Good idea."

"Oh, and I convinced O'Manion that it's to his advantage as well as ours to force Haver to accept a minder."

"I'm not sure we have the budget for a minder."

"Mother's finding someone," I said. "So whoever it is will work free or cheap."

"Free or cheap is good."

"Also, since I've found the bootlegger, we won't need to hire Stanley to do it," I added. "And maybe we can sell all the booze Ekaterina has confiscated and use the proceeds to pay the minder."

"I like the way you think."

We said our good-byes, and it wasn't till after we hung up that I realized I hadn't asked how his meeting with the Dean of Finance had gone. But given his mood when I'd called, perhaps I didn't need to ask.

I continued to study the farmhouse for a few more minutes to give Haver plenty of time to get clear before I headed for my car. But just as I was about to stow my binoculars in their case, the door opened again and the tall man strode out.

Tall and gaunt. He ambled across the farmyard and disappeared into the barn. I studied his face as he did. From a distance, when all you could see was his general build, he could easily be mistaken for Randall Shiffley, or any of his enormous extended family. But the more I watched, the more the resemblance vanished. He didn't move like a Shiffley—he had an awkward, abrupt pace instead of a Shiffley's loose-limbed grace. And with the binoculars I could see that his thin, almost skeletal face didn't look a bit like a Shiffley. I breathed a sigh of relief. If Randall caught one of his cousins undermining the festival by getting Haver drunk, there would be hell to pay. Of course, out in the more rural parts of the counties, it seemed as if every fourth mailbox was a Shiffley. The bootlegger could still be a Shiffley by marriage. Or one who had gotten shortchanged in the genetic pool.

I wondered if it was safe to leave now.

The gaunt man emerged from the barn, pulling keys out of his pocket, and got into the truck. I hunkered down again. I pulled out my phone again, texted Randall the pickup's license plate number, and asked, "Also, who is this?"

The pickup roared into life and rattled across the farmyard and down the lane to disappear into the woods.

I checked my phone. I figured I'd give Mr. Bootlegger another ten minutes before I hit the lane.

But there was no reason not to start picking my way through the woods. I eased myself out of my shelter—

Just then a loud roaring echoed over the fields. I froze. It sounded just like—

"Caligula," I murmured. Caligula had been the largest and nastiest of the tigers at Grandfather's zoo, until common sense had prevailed and Grandfather had given him to the Doorley Zoo in Omaha, where there were plenty of keepers to handle him and his disposition wouldn't prevent him from playing a valuable role in the zoo's breeding program for endangered species. Tiberius, the remaining male tiger, was too old to cause much trouble, and the tigresses, Livia and Vipsania, were sly and sneaky rather than overtly violent. But Caligula had given me nightmares.

And what I'd heard sounded incredibly like the sullen, angry way Caligula would roar when he was profoundly not in a good mood.

Chapter 8

The tiger roared again. Definitely a tiger.

Could there be a tiger loose in the woods? Not impossible. Only last year, Grandfather had helped rescue a tiger that someone had turned loose in the woods outside Waynesboro when it grew too large for its backyard cage.

If a tiger was loose, I should definitely head back to my car immediately. Or should I forget about stealth and seek refuge in the farmhouse?

Perhaps it wasn't a tiger. Were there any native big cats that could be roaming the woods? Something the cold weather had driven out of the Blue Ridge Mountains in search of food? Bobcats possibly. I seemed to recall hearing about a mountain lion attack along the Appalachian Trail, but hadn't that turned out to be only a bobcat? But there was no way a bobcat could have made that deep, primeval roar. Bobcats were closer in size to a house cat than a tiger. Not that I'd want to meet one in the middle of the woods, of course.

I found myself wishing Grandfather were here, just for a moment. He would know exactly what kind of animal had emitted that roar. Or if he didn't, he could make an educated guess. He'd know what kinds of native big cats might be wandering around the woods of Caerphilly. He'd probably even have some helpful thoughts on how to avoid getting eaten by them. And—

The roar came again, and I realized it wasn't coming from the woods around me.

It was coming from the farmstead. Probably from the barn.

I waited for yet another roar. It took a while—maybe whatever had riled the tiger was over with. But the noise was definitely coming from either the house or the barn.

On the one hand, a relief. On the other hand, I needed to get a peek into that barn.

I eyed the layout. Probably not a good idea to make tracks directly from here to the barn, across a long stretch of snowy open field, where I'd be as obvious as a crow in a flock of swans. But if I went along the edge of the woods until I had the barn between me and the house, I could probably cross the open fields unseen. I even could follow the line of the fence that divided two sections of pasture, which would give me a little bit of cover. The side of the barn I could see had several windows that were high, but not entirely out of reach. Odds were the back would have a window or two.

I began picking my way through the underbrush.

The tiger roared only once more before I reached a point where I couldn't see the house for the barn. Keeping my fingers crossed that either the bootlegger was the farm's only occupant or that any other members of the household were holed up in the house rather than the barn, I began trudging through the field, keeping as close to the fence as possible without stumbling into the drifts that had piled up against it.

As I walked, I kept scanning the barn ahead and the fields on either side of me as I rehearsed the story I'd tell if anyone challenged me: "Thank goodness I've found you! Where am I? I followed a red-tailed hawk into the woods, and got completely turned around. Can you show me the way back to the highway?"

But no one popped up to bar my way. The barn windows remained blank and staring. Over the top of the barn roof I could see the thin thread of smoke coming from the house beyond.

I reached the barn and flattened myself against its weath-ered boards. This side of the barn had three windows. The ground sloped sharply, so there was one window I could eas-ily peer into, one that I might be able to manage, and one would be out of reach unless I stumbled over a stepladder. I was panting slightly, less from exertion than tension, so I breathed for a few moments.

The tiger—or whatever—uttered a throaty growl so low I almost felt rather than heard it. This close to the barn, I could also hear other noises. A small chorus of whining and whimpering, like small dogs. Or maybe not-so-small dogs trying to sound small and inedible. A chorus of barks burst out, and then the tiger roared again, and I heard a sound like a truck hitting a chain-link fence and the dogs shut up.

No one had come to nab me or accost me, so I got up, ap-proached the lowest of the windows, and stood on my tip-toes so I could peer in.

And I saw the tiger. Only half grown, at a guess, since it was smaller than either Livia or Vipsania at the zoo. And a lot skinnier than either of them, for that matter. Though it still looked cramped and uncomfortable in the chain-link cage that filled that section of the barn. It was lying on its stomach in the cage with all four paws under it, tucked but ready for action, head close to the ground—almost precisely the pose a cat might adopt while guarding a likely mouse-hole. It appeared to be staring at something on the other side of the barn.

I shifted my position so I could follow the tiger's line of sight. Another chain-link cage, this one containing half a dozen lean reddish-brown dogs. Hunting dogs by the look of them. They were lying in a loose bunch. One or two of them were watching the tiger with expressions that seemed to express wariness and dislike more than fear. The rest were watching me through the window with the sort of focused attention that made me hope both the chain-link pen and the barn door were securely locked. One of the ones watching me curled his lip and began a low, menacing snarl, only to be silenced by a brusque growl from the tiger.

Then the tiger glanced over at my window, twitched his tail, and put his head down on his front paws, as if announcing his intention to fall fast asleep.

I didn't buy it.

The faint whimpering noises began again, and I moved to the second window. The ground sloped slightly downward, so I couldn't quite see through this window, even on tiptoes. I reached up, grabbed the windowsill, hoisted myself up, and peered in to see—

Puppies. Beautiful, silky, golden-furred puppies. About a million of them. Well, maybe only a hundred or so I realized, after a moment, but even that was a large number of puppies. And all of them the same. Golden retrievers, I deduced from the appearance of the half-dozen adult dogs almost buried beneath the squirming mass of puppies that filled this chain-link cage. The puppies were cute, but the mother dogs had a lean, anxious look that made me wonder how well fed and treated they were. The bootlegger was also running a puppy mill.

And beyond the puppies—

Suddenly a horrible grinning face appeared in the window and shrieked at me. I choked back a scream of my own and lost my grip on the windowsill.

I landed on the ground with a thud and crouched there for a few moments. The ghastly shrieking continued, and I realized it wasn't human.

It was a chimpanzee.

I hoisted myself up to the window again, ignoring the chimp, which continued to caper and grimace just inside the window, making faces at me and chittering until the tiger uttered another of his curt snarls. I also saw several smaller primates in the background—at a guess, some species of capuchin monkey. Grandfather could figure exactly which one when he saw them—and that was when, not if, because when I got back to town I was definitely going to report this outfit to animal welfare, who would undoubtedly enlist Grandfather to help them figure out if the bootlegger should be allowed to keep any of these poor animals.

Animals and birds, I amended. In between the chimp's antics—he was alternately making faces at me and pressing his bubblegum-pink backside against the window—I spotted yet another cage, this one containing a small cluster of brightly colored birds. I recognized them: more Gouldian finches. Had Haver filched some of them before I'd begun counting them and locking them up? Or had these come from the same source as the ones Grandfather's Fish and Wildlife friend had dumped on him? I even wondered if this could be the headquarters of the smuggling ring, but with only four or five finches, that seemed unlikely, thank goodness. From the way they were huddled together, I suspected the barn was none too warm. I didn't see any signs of a heating system, only a portable space heater that wasn't even plugged in.

Time to head back to town and sic Animal Welfare on this place. Animal Welfare, and maybe Grandfather's friend from the Fish and Wildlife Service. I let go of the windowsill and dropped back to the ground.

But before I went back, I wanted to check out the house.

I slid around the edge of the barn. The snow was falling more briskly now, which gave me at least a little cover. A little cover and a lot of reasons for getting back to town before the roads got too bad. I crept up to one of the lighted windows—near the front of the house, so I suspected it would be the living room—and peered in.

Cats.

The world couldn't possibly contain so many cats. Well, maybe the world could, but a room this small shouldn't.

It was a tiny room, and the well-worn, old-fashioned furniture filled it just a little too tightly. Or maybe it only seemed that way because of the overabundance of cats. There were cats sitting on the chairs and the sofa. Cats on the end tables. Cats on the coffee table. Cats on the mantel. Cats basking in front of the fireplace. Cats atop the old-fashioned tube television. There were even half a dozen cats draped over the white-haired little old lady sitting in her wheelchair in the middle of the room. Luckily, her back was to me. She held the TV remote with one hand and absentmindedly patted a cat with the other.

In one corner of the room stood a lopsided Christmas tree, largely devoid of ornaments, swaying gently under the weight of the dozen or so cats that were perching in its limbs or using its trunk as a scratching post. A small plastic nativity scene stood on a sideboard, surrounded by cats. At least half of the figures were missing or askew. The two surviving wise men shared a lone camel, not a single shepherd watched over the miniscule flock, and Joseph appeared to have been bowled over with astonishment and was lying flat on his back behind the stable with a tiny bit of its sphagnum moss roof draped over his eyes like a cold compress. Perhaps the missing cast members were on the floor, being batted back and forth along with what I hoped were unbreakable plastic ornaments from the tree. But the stable wasn't unattended. Half a dozen cats sat solemnly in a circle around it, creating the eerie impression that a delegation of Easter Island heads had come along to join the adoration of the magi. Although the effect was rather spoiled by the fact that one of the cats was scrabbling at the manger with his paw, attempting to extract baby Jesus.

I backed away from the window and took a couple of deep breaths. Not because I could smell anything—the window was tightly shut against the outside cold, thank goodness—but because I could imagine all too well what it was like inside.

"It's the trifecta of animal welfare issues," I murmured. "Cat hoarding, a puppy mill, and private ownership of wild animals."

I realized that I might need some proof to show Chief Burke and Animal Welfare. So I slunk back to the window, pulled out my phone, and took half a dozen shots. I circumnavigated the house, peering in all the windows, spotting more legions of cats and snapping more pictures, but the old lady seemed to be the only human occupant.

I stopped at the barn to take a dozen or so shots of the menagerie there—the parts of it I could see, anyway. At least a third of the barn wasn't visible from the windows I could reach. Who knew what other creatures were hidden there?

That would be a job for Animal Welfare. And possibly also for Chief Burke. I tucked my phone back in my pocket and began slipping along the fence again. As I disappeared into the woods, I heard the tiger roar one last time and had to talk myself out of breaking into a run.

Chapter 9

I was glad to see my car still there, and obviously unmolested since it was evenly coated with about an inch and a half of new snow. Definitely time for me to be getting back to town. I checked my phone—no signal now. So I cleaned off the snow and climbed inside, wishing I had a pair of dry socks to change into. Then I carefully eased my car back onto the road and headed for town.

After a couple of miles, I heard the ping of an incoming text. I pulled over to check it out.

"Farm belongs to a Venable Pruitt," Randall had texted. "But he's not living there now. Probably renters. I have some cousins over that end of the county—I'll see what I can find out. Want to meet me at the courthouse to discuss?"

"Meet me at the police station," I texted back. "We have a lot to discuss, and for some of it we'll need Chief Burke. If you get there first, let him know I'm on my way."

"Roger."

But since I was pulled over anyway, I opened up my email program and sent off half a dozen of the most interesting animal pictures to Chief Burke. Then I called the non-emergency police number.

I got Debbie Ann, the dispatcher, anyway.

"What's wrong, Meg?" she asked.

"Any chance I can speak to the chief?" I asked. "If he's not sure he wants to talk to me, ask him to check the email I just sent him."

"Will do."

I knew she was dying of curiosity, but she didn't stay to interrogate me. So while I was waiting for the chief, I forwarded my email with the photos to her.

"Meg." The chief came on the line just as I was pushing the SEND button. "What in blue blazes is this? And please tell me that cat house isn't here in my county."

"Sorry, but it is," I said. "And I'm not sure the barn the rest of the animals are in is heated, so we could have a serious animal welfare issue. I'll fill you in when I get to town."

"Blast. What is the—?"

The rest of his sentence was lost to a long blast of static, and then the call dropped completely.

Rather than call back, I texted "talk to you at the station." Then I put my phone away and started the car. Easier to bring him up to speed in person. I eased the car back onto the road, now covered with several inches of snow that was fortunately still light and fluffy, and headed for town at a suitably reduced speed.

I was relieved when, a few miles outside of town, I encountered recently plowed pavement. And then the snowplow itself. Probably with Randall's cousin Beauregard Shiffley driving—Beau's plow had an impressive set of ten-point antlers mounted on top of the cab, and this time of year he draped them with a set of battery-operated multicolored Christmas lights that twinkled merrily as he crawled down the road.

I decided to opt for safety over speed. I pulled up a safe distance behind Beau, shifted into low speed, turned on my hazard lights, and relaxed, at least a little, for the rest of the way to the police station.

When our festively lit procession reached the outskirts of town, I could see that the snow had slowed down the Christmas in Caerphilly celebrations—but only a little. Fewer people were plodding down the street carrying shopping bags, but the ones who were seemed cheerful enough. The start of the snow had triggered Randall's inclement weather plan, which meant that the various carolers and strolling bands left their usual corners and routes to take turns performing for the tourists in the lobby of the town hall. As I passed the town hall, I could see that the tourists were spilling out of the front doors onto the portico, and there were even some standing on the steps, nursing steaming cups of coffee or hot chocolate.

Good. The show must go on, even if Mother Nature wasn't cooperating.

When I got to the police station, I had to wait for a moment while a small snowplow, driven by Chief Burke's oldest grandson, cleared the entrance. As I waited, I studied the cars. Randall's wasn't there, but he'd almost certainly walked over from the town hall. I spotted Dad's blue sedan, which probably meant both he and Grandfather were here. And Clarence Rutledge, the local veterinarian who was also Caerphilly's animal welfare officer, was just parking his white van at the far end of the lot.

"Looks like a quorum," I muttered to myself as I parked my car. "Let's get this rolling."

When I walked in the chief was standing in the lobby, apparently waiting for me. "You can leave your boots there," he said, pointing to a large collection of assorted snow boots lined up just inside the doorway. Right beside the boots was the bin for donations to the Caerphilly Food Bank's special Christmas drive, and I felt a pang of guilt that I hadn't brought anything. I reminded myself that this wasn't the only bin in town, and that I'd already deposited more bags of food than I could count in one or another of those bins. And would be bringing more bags as the season progressed. Not today's priority, though.

When I'd shed my boots and hung up my heavy coat, I followed him down the hallway.

"Meg's here," he announced as he opened the door to his office. He then stepped aside to allow me to enter. He'd arranged a semicircle of four chairs on the guest side of his desk. Dad, Grandfather, and Clarence Rutledge were already seated in three of them. Dad and Grandfather were wearing what Grandfather referred to as expedition clothes—cargo pants and a khaki fisherman's vest, with all the pockets of both garments bulging with objects they thought might be useful while hiking or birdwatching or whatever they'd been doing when the chief called them. Clarence was still wearing his white doctor's coat, though as usual it looked incongruous with his denim and leather biker clothes beneath. Randall Shiffley, dressed for the weather in jeans and a flannel shirt rather than the suit in which he usually did what he called his mayoring, was perched in the windowsill. And my friend Aida Butler, who was one of the chief's deputies, was standing beside the desk in her sharply pressed uniform with a notebook in her hand. And all of them except Aida in stocking feet, which probably accounted for the surplus of boots in the entrance.

I could see that the chief had printed and handed out to everyone the photos I'd sent.

"Shall I fetch another chair?" Aida asked as the chief followed me in.

"I'm too restless to need one," Randall said, waving his hand in dismissal.

"If you'd like one yourself." The chief took a seat and opened his own notebook.

"I'll be dashing back and forth," Aida said.

"Very well. Meg," he went on, looking at me. "I took the liberty of contacting Dr. Blake, Dr. Langslow, and Dr. Rutledge. I suggested—"

"Where the blazes did you find this tiger?" Grandfather demanded, as if the chief's mention of his name had been a starter's gun. "And those finches?"

"Did you get a chance to examine any of the animals?" Clarence asked at the same time. "What was their condition?"

"Did you speak to that poor woman in the wheelchair?" Dad asked. "Does she need anything?"

"What about—"

"How can we—"

"Quiet!" the chief shouted. He so seldom raised his voice that we were all startled into silence.

"Let Meg tell her story," the chief said. "Where she was, how she happened to be there, and what she saw. Then we can decide what we need to do about it."

I related my afternoon, from the moment I spotted Haver trying to sneak out of the theater to my own furtive departure from the farm.

"So I did not check on the little old lady," I said as I drew my story to a close. "Partly because I didn't want to alert Haver's bootlegger that we're on to him and partly because technically I was trespassing, and some people get rather touchy about it, and that far out in the country a lot of them keep shotguns around. I didn't find out much more about the animals, for much the same reasons."

"Based on what Meg has told us, plus the evidence of her photographs, it seems to me that we may have need of an intervention," the chief began.

"A raid!" Grandfather's tone sounded both belligerent and cheerful. "How soon can we start?"

"Let's take this one step at a time," the chief said. "So what do we know about the human occupants of this farm?" The chief looked up at Randall as he spoke.

"Man by the name of John Willimer," Randall said. "Not from around here. Moved in about ten months ago, him and the old lady, his mother. And they're renting the farm—it actually belongs to Venable Pruitt."

"It would be a Pruitt," the chief muttered.

"Yeah, there's no love lost between the Pruitts and all the people here in town that they used to boss around." Randall was looking at Grandfather as he said this, since he knew the rest of us were well aware of the longstanding enmity. "And the farm isn't really much of a farm—only five acres. Not anything you could easily live off of unless you were doing some kind of pretty specialized farming, like raising fancy organic herbs or something. And there's been no sign of that."

"And we know this how?" the chief asked.

"My cousin Threepwood, who has a farm a couple of miles away. Venable's place was vacant for two or three years until Willimer and his mother moved in. Threepwood made a few neighborly visits but didn't feel his efforts were much appreciated, so he gave up and left them alone, which seemed to be what they wanted."

"Did you ask him if he noticed any animals about the place?" the chief asked.

"I did." Randall leaned back against the wall and folded his arms. "He said Willimer had a couple of half-grown dogs that you might mistake for redbone coonhounds if you hadn't seen the real thing for a good long while."

"Did the dogs look as if they were mistreated?"

"No. Not well trained and not all that friendly, but they were healthy enough. He'd have said something to Clarence here if he'd thought otherwise. Threepwood's right partial to dogs, especially hunting dogs. And those were the only animals he saw."

"That actually corresponds with what little information we have about Mr. Willimer," the chief said. "This spring—which would have been shortly after he arrived—we received several complaints from Mort Gormley, whose farm is also nearby. He claimed Mr. Willimer's dogs were attacking his sheep."

"I remember that," Randall said. "You sent Vern out, and

he followed the tracks from the latest dead sheep to a coyote den."

"A remarkable animal, the coyote," Grandfather exclaimed. "Since the regrettable extermination of the wolf in many parts of North America, the coyote's range has expanded considerably, and it has showed an admirable ability to adapt to changing circumstances and coexist with human beings."

"This pair didn't manage to coexist too well with Vern," Randall said. "And after that the sheep attacks stopped, but I'm not sure Vern ever convinced Mort it had been coyotes and not some kind of big, shaggy, grayish-brown dog coming over from Willimer's place."

"We'll keep our eyes open in case he's acquired some shaggy, grayish-brown dogs in the meantime," the chief said. "If his farm's too small to live off of, do we have any idea what Mr. Willimer does for a living?"

"Not really." Randall shook his head. "Threepwood had a notion maybe Willimer was doing a little business in the used car line—buying old beaters, fixing them up just enough so they'd run, and selling them to people who didn't know any better. You'd usually see an old car or two around the place."

"No sign of any when I was out there today," I put in.

"They'd be under the snow by now," Randall pointed out.

"Making large used-car-sized lumps that I would have spotted," I said. "There weren't any."

"Could be he gave up on it, then," Randall said. "Didn't look to Threepwood as if he was getting rich on it anyway. And Willimer was hardly ever there in the daytime, so maybe he was commuting to a job somewhere. Just not here in Caerphilly."

"Maybe he's making a living selling puppies and exotic animals," I suggested.

The chief looked up at Aida.

"Can you go get Debbie Ann started seeing what we can find out about this Mr. Willimer?"

Aida nodded and bustled out.

The chief turned back to the rest of us.

"Seems to me we have valid concerns about the welfare of these animals. I think we need to go in there."

Chapter 10

Everyone sat up straighter, as if the chief's few quiet words had been a bugle call.

"We also need to think about the welfare of that poor woman in the wheelchair," Dad said. "You can see from Meg's pictures what a completely unhygienic condition the house is in. I think we need to involve Adult Protective Services."

"Oh, Lord, do we have to?" Randall muttered. "That woman could give St. Peter homicidal urges."

"Meredith Flugleman, the county social worker," the chief explained for Grandfather's benefit. "She can be a little overwhelming, but she means well. I'll do the liaising with her if you'd like, Randall."

"I'll owe you one," Randall said.

"We don't have any county ordinances regulating the number of domestic animals a household can have," Clarence said. "Might be something we should consider for the future. But we do have the state animal cruelty statutes. From what I see in those pictures of the cats, it'd be a miracle if we went in and didn't find violations. So we're completely justified in conducting a search as long as Meg is willing to make a sworn complaint—"

"Absolutely," I said.

"Another thing—our records don't show any validly licensed dogs at that address, or under the name of Willimer at any other address," Clarence said. "At a minimum, we need to ensure that all those poor animals are disease-free and have been properly vaccinated."

"And Willimer doesn't have a business license on file," Randall put in. "He'd need one if he's operating a kennel. And I can't imagine any other reason why someone would have a whole blasted barn full of puppies."

"And just in time for Christmas," the chief said. "I'm sure if we look hard enough we'll find somewhere that he's advertising puppies for sale."

"We'll also need to check with the state to see if Willimer has a permit to own that tiger," Grandfather said.

"And the monkeys, I assume," the chief said.

"No, Virginia's laws on private ownership of wild animals are pretty lax," Grandfather said. "You need a permit for bears, wolves, and big cats, but there's no regulation at all on primates. But we should probably notify Fish and Wildlife about all the wild animals—including the finches. In fact, especially the finches. They've been battling an epidemic of Gouldian finch-smuggling lately. Maybe this Willimer acquired his finches and his tiger and all the rest of them perfectly legally, but you never know. Could have some connection to that big smuggling ring Fish and Wildlife has been investigating."

"I think we've established that we need to intervene out there on humane grounds, and that we have ample legal justification for doing so," the chief said. "We can sort out the legal issues when we have more information. But this is going to take a bit of organizing. Dr. Blake, can you get me the contact information for the appropriate person I should notify at Fish and Wildlife?"

"I can take care of it myself if you'd like." Grandfather squared his shoulders as if he'd just offered to carry the flag up San Juan Hill.

"If you have good contacts there, that would be excellent," the chief said. "I confess, I'm feeling rather annoyed with them at the moment. Someone identifying himself as a Fish and Wildlife agent was snooping around town about a week or so ago, asking a lot of peculiar questions."

"What kind of questions?" Grandfather asked.

"Asking the pet store if they could procure a three-toed sloth for him," the chief said. "Asking Mr. Wu at the House of Mandarin if they served shark-fin soup."

"Two staples of the wildlife trafficking racket," Grandfather said, nodding.

I found it hard to believe that three-toed sloths were a staple of anything, but I kept my mouth shut.

"That is exactly the sort of thing Fish and Wildlife is trying to get a handle on," Grandfather went on.

"Yes, but I gather this particular agent was unnecessarily persistent," the chief said. "Became verbally abusive when they told him they couldn't help him. Told Mr. Wu he'd look into having him deported."

"Well, that's a crock," Randall said. "Not only was Danny Wu born here in Caerphilly, I think three of his four grandparents were. And one of them a Shiffley."

"A baseless threat, but still alarming to Mr. Wu," the chief said. "And I am not pleased with the fact that the agent in question didn't even have the courtesy to notify me that he was investigating something in my jurisdiction. In fact, I wouldn't even have known he was from Fish and Wildlife if he hadn't lost his temper when the Caerphilly Inn couldn't accommodate him with a room. According to Ms. Voro—Ms. Voro—Miss Ekaterina, he slammed his fist down on the registration desk and told her she couldn't treat Fish and Wildlife this way." He surprised us all by chuckling at this. "She told him that she was sorry, she did not have a room, even for Fish and Wildlife, but perhaps he could find accommodations at the local zoo. When she started giving him directions there, he stormed out, and that was the last anyone saw of him."

"Typical bureaucratic behavior," Grandfather said. "Especially from some of the new lot that have been coming in lately. I hope you complained to his management."

"I called both the state and national offices of Fish and Wildlife, got transferred a dozen times, left messages, and haven't heard a thing. And if they're so all-fired busy investigating a giant smuggling ring, they'd probably consider our problem here pretty small potatoes. So if you have good contacts there, have at it. Just keep me in the loop."

Grandfather nodded.

"Clarence," the chief went on. "Can you organize the logistics of our raid? Keeping in mind that we won't know exactly what we're facing till we get in there. Meg's photos are helpful, but they don't show the whole interior of the barn."

"They only show about two-thirds of it," I said. "If that much. There could be a lot more animals."

"But however many animals we find, we need to be prepared to seize any or all of them if their welfare requires it." The chief's voice was solemn.

Clarence was looking anxious, but at the chief's last words he lifted his chin and nodded.

"And I'm sure those of us here represent only a small portion of the local citizens who will be willing to help," the chief added.

"Of course!" Dad wiggled his sock-clad toes vigorously as if to underscore his own readiness.

"I'll bring as many zoo personnel as possible," Grandfather said. "And I'll put the word out to the Brigade."

"We probably do need them," the chief said with a slight sigh. Clearly he had mixed feelings about Blake's Brigade, the loosely organized cadre of volunteers Grandfather called on whenever he was organizing an animal rescue or a protest. I could understand the chief's misgivings. The Brigade members were almost universally good-hearted and well-meaning, but they often displayed more enthusiasm than common sense. For my part, I always wanted to breathe a sigh of relief and take a long nap when the Brigade left town.

"So I'll leave it to you to organize the crates and cages and the transport," the chief said. "Dr. Blake, can we safely house the exotic animals at your zoo, at least for the short term?"

"No problem. Depending on how many we find, we might need to transfer some to the Willner Wildlife Sanctuary in the longer term. But we can talk that over with Caroline when she gets back from that silly cruise of hers."

Did Grandfather actually miss Caroline, his usual co-conspirator, or was he only annoyed that she wasn't on hand to help?

"And Clarence," the chief continued. "I assume you can tap your network of foster families to handle the rest."

"There are an awful lot of animals," Clarence said. "But with a little help from the Brigade, we'll manage."

"I'll strong-arm a few cousins if you fall short," Randall said.

"Mother could probably do the same with our family," I suggested. Dad beamed at the idea.

"So how soon can we make this raid?" the chief asked.

"Immediately!" Grandfather roared, leaping out of his chair. "While we sit here talking, animals are suffering!"

"And if we rush in without proper preparation, we could add to their suffering rather than alleviating it." The chief extended both hands, palms down, and gently patted the air in front of him. Grandfather took the hint and sat down.

"But quickly," Grandfather said. "Today."

"It will take us a few hours to round up the necessary supplies, transport, and personnel," Clarence said. "And the statute prohibits a search after sunset unless specifically authorized for cause by the proper authority."

"Well, either I'm the proper authority or I'm sure Judge Jane Shiffley would do," the chief said. "But is there cause?"

Clarence considered.

"Cold is the biggest thing to worry about in the short term," he said. "Assuming Meg's right about the barn being unheated. Still, snow's a pretty good insulator, and the temperatures aren't going to get more than a degree or two below freezing tonight. The animals should be okay for that long. But I hear there's an arctic air mass headed our way by to-morrow night. Record cold temperatures. I wouldn't want to leave them out there for that. So I think we should go in tomorrow."

"But in the meantime, the animals could be suffering!" Grandfather exclaimed. "Why not go now?"

"Call me a worrywart," I said. "But we're talking about going into an unfamiliar place, looking for an unknown number of animals, some of them potentially quite danger-ous, and with no idea whether or not the human occupants are armed. Do we really want to be dealing with all those unknowns in the dark?"

"And in the middle of a snowstorm." The chief nodded. "My thinking exactly. Can we all be ready by dawn tomorrow?"

One by one they all nodded.

"Dawn's at seven fifteen," the chief said. "Rendezvous here at six thirty. I'll work out all the legal issues—Randall, I hope you didn't have anything else for the county attorney to work on today."

"Nothing that can't wait."

The chief looked at me.

"Meg, I know it's an imposition, but I'd like you to go along if possible. You're the only one who's had eyes on the place—we may need your knowledge. If we had more lead time I'd find a way to get one of my officers to scout the place, but I don't want to risk spooking the occupants this close to our search."

"Count me in," I said.

Chapter 11

"Till tomorrow, then, everyone," the chief said. "Meg, if you could stay behind for a few minutes we'll take care of that formal complaint."

"Absolutely," I said. "Oh, just one more thing before everyone runs off."

But Dad and Grandfather already had. Still, Randall and Clarence paused in the doorway and the chief froze in place at his desk, all of them with tense, earnest expressions on their faces, as if expecting me to unleash some final bit of news that would complicate our project even more.

"Completely unrelated and probably not urgent," I said. "But I did promise the Reverend Robyn I'd ask: Do any of you know what Weaseltide is?"

They all blinked and looked at each other as if they thought it was a trick question.

"Someone wants to hold a Weaseltide celebration at Trinity Episcopal," I explained. "And Robyn was too polite to ask what the heck that was."

"Nothing I've ever heard of," Clarence said. "And I have a keener interest in weasels than most folks."

He pulled up his sleeves to display the long, slender, furry creatures tattooed on both forearms.

"I always thought those were ferrets," I said.

"Which are a subspecies of weasel," Clarence said. "*Mustela putorius furo.* Thought to have been domesticated from the European polecat. But I've never heard of this Weaseltide thing. I could ask a few fellow Mustelid fanciers if you like."

"That would be great. Unless either of you know anything?" I turned to Randall and the chief. "Some local thing, perhaps?"

"Not that I know of," Randall said. "Though I admit, from the name it does sound like the kind of peculiar thing some of my family would get up to. I'll ask some of the old-timers."

"Not familiar to me, either," the chief said. "Did Robyn get the impression that it was some kind of sinister or illicit gathering?"

"A pretty tame one if they wanted to hold it in a church," I pointed out.

"True."

"I think she's just worried that it might be something unsuitable."

"Some kind of pagan fertility festival, maybe?" Randall chuckled at the idea. "Like that time your cousin Rose Noire invited those nudists to camp out in your back pasture?"

"In her defense, she didn't know they were nudists," I protested. "They described themselves as 'nature lovers.' She was expecting tree-hugging vegetarians, not people running about in the altogether. But yes, that's exactly the sort of mix-up Robyn wants to avoid."

"I'm on a discussion list for sheriffs and chiefs of police," the chief said. "Covers most of Virginia and parts of West Virginia, North Carolina, and Maryland. I can ask if any of them have ever run into this Weaseltide thing. But you might want to check with your brother. See if it could be something from one of those computer games of his."

"A good idea." There had been a time when I'd have known whether or not something was from one of Rob's games without asking—in the early days of Mutant Wizards, Michael and I had pitched in to play-test most of the company's new games. But in the past ten years, Rob's company had grown to nearly a hundred times its original size and put out a dizzying array of game titles every year—and ten-year-old Josh and Jamie now took up most of the time I'd once spent in Rob's cyber worlds.

"Yeah, could be a game thing," Randall remarked. "Remember that time we went on high alert, thinking a big Caribbean drug kingpin was coming to town, and it turned out that a bunch of tourists had freaked out after overhearing a couple of Rob's programmers working on a scenario for *DEA: You're Busted!*"

"I will definitely ask Rob," I said. "In fact, I'm going to text him now."

"Good," the chief said. "You can do that while I get the paperwork going for your complaint."

"Oh, by the way," Randall said, pausing in the doorway. "The bicycles arrived."

"Is the town getting official bicycles?" The chief sounded puzzled.

"The boys are, for Christmas," I explained. "And since they've become expert at sniffing out presents, Randall kindly agreed to let me have them shipped to him."

"I assume you want me to keep them until closer to Christmas," Randall said.

"If they're not in your way, that would be great."

"Heck, I can drop them by whenever you want. Christmas Eve, after the boys are in bed, if you like."

"Unfortunately, the bikes will need assembly, so we'll need to take them off your hands a little earlier than that. We don't want to be up all night with wrenches."

"I could have my cousin Cephas do that if you'd like," Randall offered.

"If you think he wouldn't mind," I said.

"It'd be like giving him a present." Randall chuckled. "Only thing he likes better than putting things together is taking them apart again, and I can stop him before he gets to that point. And then I can deliver them all assembled on Christmas Eve, so all you have to do is stick a bow on them."

"That would be wonderful," I said. "And tell Cephas his next pizza is on me."

"Will do." Randall gave a mock salute and ambled out the door.

And I breathed a sigh of relief. No one had uttered the words I had been expecting to hear: "And, of course, if we don't have enough foster homes for all of them, we can always keep them in Meg's barn."

There was no way I wanted a single one of those adorable golden retriever puppies near my highly susceptible twin sons.

Or my equally susceptible brother, who sometimes appeared to be at about the same emotional age as my sons. Lately Rob had been dropping hints about the possibility of adding another dog to the household. He needed our agreement, however grudging, because he still occupied a third-floor bedroom in the huge Victorian farmhouse Michael and I called home. As I had repeatedly pointed out, not only did Rob already have a dog, but since Tinkerbell was on the large side even for an Irish wolfhound, he had several times more dog than most people considered reasonable. So far I hadn't brought Rob around to this point of view.

"Please let him be too busy to even hear about the puppies," I muttered as my fingers typed out the text to him:

"Do you know what Weaseltide is?"

I was about to put the phone away when an answer popped up.

"No, should I?"

"No idea. Can you ask around? Small but real reward to the person who can tell me what it is."

"Roger."

I was tucking my phone away when the chief came back and we dived into the legalese of my sworn complaint.

"You realize, of course, that the occupants of the farm may seek to have you charged with trespassing," the chief pointed out.

"Well, technically I was," I said.

"Not necessarily." He lifted his eyes up from the complaint document and looked at me over his reading glasses. "Under the Virginia Code your presence on someone else's property isn't enough for a trespassing conviction—you have to have had notice that you weren't allowed there. Oral or written notice—did you see any 'no trespassing' signs?"

"I don't remember any," I said. "And even if there were any, they might have been covered up by snow—it was coming down pretty steadily by that time. I brushed at least an inch and a half off my car when I got back to it."

"Good. I plan to check tomorrow on whether there are any reasonably prominent 'no trespassing' signs, but even if there are, the snow does raise the question of visibility."

"Doesn't the fact that I was trying to protect Haver count for anything? For all I knew, he could have been planning to get drunk on the spot and then head out on the already slippery roads. Isn't there something that lets you barge in when there's imminent danger?"

"Exigent circumstances." The chief was suppressing a smile. "It only covers law enforcement officers barging in without a search warrant. But don't worry—in the unlikely event that the occupants mount a credible charge of trespassing, we can ask them to drop it in return for a reduction in some of the charges against them."

"Not if it lets them get off scot-free," I said.

"Not a chance." He turned his attention back to the paper. "We won't need to bargain away more than a few, and there will be plenty of charges."

In the middle of our work on the complaint, Horace stuck his head in the open door.

"Chief? Your copy of the report on that body in Clay County."

He laid a folder on the chief's desk and turned to leave.

"Horace?" the chief said. "Don't let it get you down."

"Don't let what get him down?" I asked.

"Those idiots over in Clay County." Horace turned back, and I saw his fists were clenched in anger. "I was only able to get a couple of partials. It may not be enough to identify the guy. Maybe if they'd called me in sooner I could have gotten more."

"It may still be enough," the chief said.

"If they ever send them in to AFIS," Horace said. "Apparently they weren't too impressed with a couple of partials. And besides, Floyd Dingle's the only person over there who has the slightest idea how to use the AFIS system, and he broke his leg and a couple of ribs bungee jumping over the weekend and there's no telling how long he'll be out on medical leave."

The chief pondered for a few moments.

"Then I'll send them," he said.

"But it's their case."

"If they give us any difficulties, I'll say I thought that given Floyd's illness we were supposed to send them. That's why you gave me the file, isn't it? So I could send them to AFIS?"

The chief smiled, and Horace gradually did, too.

"Thanks, Chief."

"And I know you've been working long hours lately, but I could really use you for the animal welfare operation tomorrow," the chief went on. "So take a couple of hours off this afternoon, get to bed early, and I'll see you here at six thirty."

Horace smiled and left.

"I feel as if I should apologize for uncovering this animal welfare thing just now," I said. "In the middle of the festival, this close to Christmas, when you're already swamped."

"What better time than Christmas to do a good deed for some of God's creatures?" the chief said. "And frankly, I'm glad to have something to distract Horace and your father from their frustrating experience over in Clay County. I'd give Sheriff Whicker a piece of my mind, but it would do about as much good as yelling at my boots. It's officers like him who give rural law enforcement a bad name. Well, at least here in Caerphilly we don't have a John Doe hanging over our heads this Christmas."

"No—we have an undisclosed number of puppies," I said. "I like our side of the bargain."

The chief chuckled, and we went back to working on the complaint document. I was relieved when the chief was finally satisfied with it and I could go back out to my car. Which had accumulated another inch of snow.

When I started the car, I realized that while tailing Haver I'd gone into stealth mode and turned off the radio. I turned it on again and let "O Holy Night" coax me into a holiday mood.

I drove back to the theater through the increasingly empty streets of downtown Caerphilly. Most of the tourists' cars were gone, and most of the locals had had the good sense to go home or stay home. Everything still looked festive because of all the lights, and a couple of restaurants were doing a lively business—I suspected the diners were tourists staying in the various bed-and-breakfasts within walking distance of the town square. Beau's antler-decked snowplow was working on the town square, and closer to the theater I waved at Osgood Shiffley, who had painted his snowplow black and customized it into an uncanny replica of Darth Vader. It was quite startling to see the Sith lord emerging from the darkness, appearing to glide facedown and headfirst over the road, sucking up the snow with the metal grill of his helmet and spewing it to either side.

I wondered what they had planned for the new snowplow, assuming the distributor ever delivered it.

As I drove by the front of the drama building, I could see that Grandfather's name was now framed—but not obscured—by evergreen garlands and red bows. I spotted a sign on the door—almost certainly a CLOSED DUE TO INCLEMENT WEATHER sign. I nodded with approval.

I was also relieved to see, as I drove past the stage door, that the Rabid Fan was not keeping vigil in the snow. And equally relieved to remember that she was staying in a bed-and-breakfast not too far away.

But when I reached the parking lot, I was dismayed to see only three cars there. One of them was Michael's. Neither of the others was a silver Honda Accord. It was only four thirty. Rehearsal should be in full swing. Snow or not, we didn't have that many rehearsals left before opening night. Surely they could have gotten in an hour or two of work before the roads became too bad.

I let myself in through the loading dock door and raced up the stairs to the stage.

The completely and utterly empty stage.

Chapter 12

The stage might have been empty but the building wasn't. I heard voices coming from somewhere down the hall. I followed the sounds to the scenery shop.

"It'll be fine," Michael was saying. "I bet you're the only one who even notices."

"You noticed." Jake the set designer.

"Only because you kept asking me if I noticed anything wrong. And remember, it did take me four guesses to figure out exactly what was off."

I entered to find Michael and Jake studying a flat—a piece of painted vertical scenery that would form part of the back wall of the Cratchits' poor-but-cozy parlor.

"What happened to rehearsal?" I asked.

"I sent everyone home," Michael said

"On account of the snow?"

"Well, that and the fact that Haver never showed up."

"Oh, no!" I exclaimed. "I'm sorry. I was supposed to watch him, and first I let his agent distract me while he made his escape and then I let him go back to town without me."

"Not your fault," Michael said. "And besides, you found his bootlegger, right?"

"Yes, and Chief Burke is about to make the bootlegger's life very interesting," I said. "He might not be free to scamper over to the Clay County ABC store for a while."

"I like the sound of that."

"I'll give you the whole story at home," I said. "And speaking of home—"

"Probably a good idea for us to head there," Michael said. "By the way, Jake lives halfway to Richmond, and he doesn't have snow tires—"

"So if you haven't already offered him one of our guest rooms, you should do it now," I said.

"I'll get my knapsack." Jake grinned and dashed out.

"Did you check to see if Haver made it back to the Inn?" I asked.

"Not lately," he said. "Haver's agent did, around two thirty before going out to roam the streets, searching for him."

"Then I'll check with the Inn to see if either of them has come back. Why don't you and Jake head out? I have a couple of things to do and then I'll follow you."

"Roger."

I pulled out my phone and called Ekaterina.

"Haver is not here," she said, instead of hello. "I am becoming somewhat anxious. He comes from Los Angeles, you know. California. They do not have snow in California. I suspect he knows even less about driving in the snow than Virginians do."

"I'll call the chief and ask him to have his deputies keep an eye out for Haver's car."

"Good. He is not the most pleasant of guests we have ever had, but he is a guest. I feel responsible. And what should I do about the bird?"

"The bird?"

"At some point this afternoon, he smuggled in a caged bird. Some sort of parrot, I think."

A parrot? I remembered the object Willimer had placed in the back seat of Haver's car. And the Gouldian finches in Willimer's barn.

"Can you describe this parrot?"

"Let me take a picture of it."

"Even better."

Ekaterina must have been very near Haver's room if not

actually in it—the picture popped up on my phone screen in mere seconds.

"It's not exactly a parrot," I said. "It's a Gouldian finch."

"Do they talk?"

"I don't think so. Grandfather would know for sure."

"I would be grateful if you would ask him for me. I do not want to waste time if this is not a talking bird."

I was puzzled.

"Have you been trying to teach him to talk?" I asked.

"No, I have been listening to him. Waiting for him to talk. I thought perhaps he might say something that would turn out to be a clue."

Okay, that explained why she happened to be in Haver's room. And I spotted something in the corner of the picture.

"Can you take a picture from a little farther off?" I asked. "Showing the cage and that blue object that's on the sofa?"

"That filthy blanket?"

"Yes. Humor me."

Another picture appeared. The cage was square, and looked to be about the size of the object I'd seen Willimer place in Haver's car. And the object I'd spotted in the corner of the previous picture was the same kind of bright blue quilted moving blanket the object had been wrapped in.

"Thank you," I said. "This is helpful. I now know where Haver got the bird."

"About the bird: Should I be feeding him? His cage has a food dish, but there is nothing in it. I refreshed his water, but I do not know what birds of this kind are permitted to eat."

"I'll check with Grandfather," I said.

"Excellent. And I will inform you immediately if we determine Mr. Haver's whereabouts."

"And what about Mr. O'Manion?"

"Also not here. Should I also notify you if he returns?"

"Please. By the way, I thought the Inn had a no pets policy."

"Our policy discourages pets," she said. "But I have the

discretion to authorize pets, on a case-by-case basis. If the bird proves troublesome, we will inform Mr. Haver that he will need to make arrangements elsewhere."

"Let me know if that happens," I said. "Or if you see any signs that the bird's not being treated properly. I'm not sure Haver's someone I'd want to trust with the welfare of a helpless animal."

"Will do. Over and out."

So where was Haver? Obviously he'd made it back to the hotel—the bird hadn't been there when Ekaterina made her morning inspection. And then he'd gone out again.

With his agent, perhaps?

And they were both from Los Angeles. I thought Ekaterina had an overly jaundiced view of Virginians' snow-driving skills, but perhaps she did have a point about Californians.

I called the chief.

"Haver's not in his hotel room," I said. "And neither is his agent. Is there any way you could put out a lookout for them? Just to make sure if they're safe? Because they're both driving rental cars, and they're both strangers to our roads, not to mention coming from California, so they probably have no clue how to drive in snow and—"

"Relax. I'll send out a BOLO on silver Honda Accords. In fact, I can call Van and find out the license numbers of the ones they're driving. Then I can put out a BOLO asking anyone who spots either of them to perform a welfare check and encourage them to return to the safety of the Inn."

"Perfect. Thanks!"

I hung up, closed my eyes, and took a few deep breaths. I sometimes made fun of my cousin Rose Noire's fascination with all things New Age and metaphysical, but some of her notions did work. I focused on breathing out stress and breathing in calm and felt noticeably better after a couple of breaths.

Better enough that I decided I had the energy to search

Haver's dressing room before heading home. He hadn't spent much time in it today, of course, but you never knew. And I'd make it a nice, thorough, leisurely search. The first few times I'd searched, I'd done so hastily and furtively, almost paranoid about the possibility of being caught. I'd grown less worried about getting caught—after all, by now he must have figured out someone was stealing his booze. But the sheer volume of things I always had to get done at the theater had kept me from doing more than a quick check of the most obvious places to hide a bottle.

Not today. With the rehearsal called off, I suddenly had a block of time to devote to whatever I wanted. And right now, I wanted to snoop.

I left the set workshop and made my way to Haver's dressing room—boldly and blatantly. I unlocked the door with my master key—assistant directorhood hath its privileges—and stepped inside.

"What a dump."

If I'd said that within earshot of Michael's fellow thespians, they'd race to be the first to mention that Bette Davis had uttered those immortal words in *Beyond the Forest*. And they'd probably try to top it with a Shakespearean quote. Possibly "something is rotten in the state of Denmark." Better still, "a foul and pestilent congregation of vapors."

Both very apt, I thought, as I sniffed the air. No trace of alcohol, but there was definitely a smell of rotting food on top of the typical dressing room smell, which was a mixture of sweat, aftershave, and the peculiar half-sweet, half-chemical smell of theatrical makeup.

I set my tote down just inside the door and fished out the baggie containing the plastic gloves I kept handy for my searches.

"I think your dad is rubbing off on you," Michael had said, laughing, when he first spotted me gloving up for a search.

"Or maybe it's Horace. Do you really need to worry about leaving fingerprints?"

"Laugh all you want," I'd answered while snapping my gloves in place. "It's not fingerprints I'm worried about. I'm going to be pawing through his dirty underwear and possibly finding more decomposing week-old sandwiches in the drawers. Would you want to do that bare-handed?"

Today the dressing room was noticeably tidier than it had been when I'd first begun searching, mostly thanks to Mother, who couldn't resist tidying whenever she came in. There were now far fewer empty soda cans, half-empty potato chip bags, used coffee cups, aging newspapers, and stained tissues and napkins.

It was still a pigsty.

I turned on Haver's radio and fiddled with it until I found the college station. I figured a little Christmas music would lighten my search, and if I kept the volume low I could hear anyone approaching. "While Shepherds Watched Their Flocks" made nice music to search by.

I started to the left of the door and began to work my way clockwise around the room. And this time I wasn't just checking for bottles. I was examining every object in the room, no matter how small. I wasn't entirely sure what I hoped to find. Since yesterday's search a nasty thought had occurred to me: What if we did succeed in cutting off Haver's alcohol supply, only to have him fall back on pills of some kind?

And it had also occurred to me that Haver didn't have a brilliant memory. Even considering that he had the largest part, he'd taken much longer than anyone else to learn his lines. If he had more than one contact who was supplying him with booze, mightn't he have their names or addresses or phone numbers written down somewhere?

So I checked every pill I came across: Excedrin, Advil, Tums, Alka-Seltzer, Imodium, Colace, Pepto-Bismol, NyQuil, Ambien, and Tic Tacs. No unidentified pills or powders.

I threw away a rotting apple and a half-eaten ham sandwich that was well past its prime.

I sifted through the mail he'd had forwarded from California. Both Southern California Edison and SoCalGas were threatening to cut off his service. His bank balance was anemic. He still owed the November portion of his Actors' Equity dues.

I checked the pockets of all the clothes. And the linings. I straightened a paper clip and used it to probe the various pots of makeup on his dressing table. I checked behind and under drawers. I held my breath and delved into the dirty clothes hamper Mother had installed.

I did find a couple of pieces of paper with phone numbers on them—a few had initials, mostly only the numbers. I took pictures of them with my phone and put them back where I'd found them.

I finished my search with the piles in the center of the room—mostly more dirty laundry that hadn't yet joined the collection in the hamper. I decided Haver probably wouldn't care or even notice if I took care of that housekeeping detail, so after I finished searching the laundry I hampered it.

"I give up," I said, sitting down in his dressing table chair. The fact that I hadn't found any alcohol failed to cheer me because it only meant the bottle he'd bought was still with him. And the glimpses I'd gotten of what seemed like a sad, lonely, and impoverished life depressed me. I was feeling sorry for Haver.

"What are we going to do with you?" I muttered, leaning back in the chair and raising my eyes to heaven—or at least to the dressing room's utilitarian acoustical-tile ceiling.

One of the tiles was askew.

Curious.

I stood up and climbed up on the chair so I could reach the offending tile. It had probably just been knocked askew by accident. Then again, the space between the tiles and the concrete ceiling wouldn't be such a bad hiding place. So just in case, before settling the tile back into place, I shoved it a little farther aside and felt around the periphery of the open area.

My gloved hands encountered something. Not a bottle. Smaller than a bottle. And metal rather than glass.

I grabbed the object and pulled it into the light.

A gun.

Chapter 13

In my initial shock I almost dropped the gun. Then I took a better grip on it, being careful to point it away from me, and stepped cautiously down from the chair.

Haver had a gun. The noisy, belligerent drunk who lost his temper when crossed and had no qualms about kicking a hole in the scenery had a gun. In the theater where he acted with my sons and had pointless, violent arguments with my husband.

My first impulse was to confiscate it. Put it in the attic room where we were storing all the booze, so we could prove, if needed, that we hadn't stolen it—we were only holding it for him until the end of the show's run.

But what if he kicked up a fuss? A gun was, after all, slightly more valuable than a few bottles of alcohol. Well, not more valuable than all the alcohol we'd confiscated. I'd toyed with the idea of selling the attic bottle collection at the end of the run and making a donation to the local food bank in Haver's name. At the rate he was going, it would be a generous donation. Although I was also considering the notion of using the proceeds to pay for his minder if the college wouldn't. But still, the booze was something to be consumed—rather rapidly in Haver's case. The gun was a very permanent object. He'd probably make a big fuss.

Or worse, what if he got another gun, just as he'd gotten countless other bottles of liquor?

My next thought was that I should report the gun to Chief Burke.

But what could he do? Owning a firearm was legal in Virginia. And taking it away, even from someone who shouldn't be trusted with a slingshot, was almost certainly illegal.

Still, I should tell the chief. I had a sudden vision of the chief stopping Haver for the DUI that we all knew was in his future, only to find himself looking down the barrel of this gun. The chief, or Horace, or Aida, or Vern Shiffley or—

Inspiration struck me. I could unload the gun. If Haver went to grab it in a drunken rage, he wouldn't be able to do any immediate damage with it. In fact, with any luck, he might not be a particularly meticulous or observant gun owner. Maybe he wouldn't ever notice his ammo was missing.

Of course, first, I had to figure out how to unload it.

A few years back, after having a gun pointed at me by someone who did not have my best interests in mind, I took a gun safety course Vern Shiffley was teaching, with the general idea that if I ever found myself in such a situation again, I might be better off knowing how the things worked. Vern had spent a considerable amount of class time making sure we knew how to load and unload a gun without killing ourselves.

Armed with what I'd learned in class, I determined that Haver's gun was a semi-automatic, rather than a revolver. Which meant that it had a little metal thingie that slid into the grip—a magazine, that was the term. If I could slide out the magazine, I could remove the bullets. Which I should probably remember to call cartridges if I explained what I'd done to anyone who actually knew something about guns.

I looked around to see what direction to point the gun. Not toward the door, where someone could be passing. Or at the mirror over the dressing table. And Mother would kill me if I shot a hole in any of Haver's elaborate Victorian costumes, so the wall with the clothes rod was out. Did I really want to shoot the blank concrete-block fourth wall and have the bullet ricochet back at me?

I pointed the gun up toward the acoustic tile ceiling. Then I began figuring out which of the little protuberances was the lever that would release the magazine. I got lucky on my third attempt, and the magazine popped out. I grabbed a crumpled McDonald's bag from the floor and used it to hold the cartridges as I popped them out one by one.

Then I put the magazine back in. The gun felt appreciably lighter. Would Haver notice? I had the advantage of holding it immediately before and after unloading it. I found it hard to believe that he was such a seasoned and savvy shooter that he'd notice it. Especially if he was loaded himself.

At least, even if he realized the gun was unloaded, it would slow him down. I got up on the chair again and felt carefully around in the space above the tiles. Aha! I found a small box that proved to contain more cartridges. The ones I'd taken from the gun looked identical, so I fished them out of the McDonald's bag and laid them carefully in the box. They all fit in with none left over. Did this have any significance? Could it perhaps mean that the gun was a recent acquisition, and he hadn't yet put it to any use?

Or it could just as easily mean that he'd used up all his ammo in his last drunken shooting spree and had to stock up recently.

I'd leave that to people who knew more about guns. I took a few pictures of the gun with my phone, from various angles. Then I put it back where I'd found it and replaced the ceiling tile. I snapped off the radio, and looked around to make sure everything else was as I'd found it. I tucked the full box of ammunition into my purse.

Then I hurried down to my car and from its safety—or at least relative privacy—I called the police station's non-emergency number.

"Chief Burke's not in," Debbie Ann said. "Can anyone else help you? Or can I take a message?"

I hesitated. I had been planning to break the news to the

chief gently, glossing over how I happened to have found the gun. I still could.

But that would mean waiting to warn his officers.

"Haver has a gun," I said.

"Haver that we have the BOLO out on?"

"And Haver that the whole force has been trying to catch in the act of committing a DUI, yes. He doesn't have it on him at the moment—I found it while searching his dressing room. And I took the ammo out and confiscated that. But I didn't think I should just confiscate the gun. And I thought the chief should know."

"Thanks," she said. "I'll let him know and we can get out a notification. You home?"

"Heading there in just a minute," I said.

"Be careful," she said. "It's piling up out there."

Great.

But before starting my car, I made a quick call to Ekaterina.

"No sign of the subject," she said.

"Rats," I said. "Tell me—have you ever seen a gun in his room?"

"A gun? No, never. I would have reported that." She didn't sound as anxious as I felt. In fact, she sounded rather pleased at the news. Searching for and confiscating liquor was probably getting rather tedious.

I explained about finding the gun and unloading it.

"So you have disarmed him! Well done!"

"Not permanently," I said. "He may have more ammo. But then, if I'd taken the gun, he could have replaced that. So keep your eye open for any sign of weaponry, and remember that we're dealing with a potentially armed subject."

"He begins to show his true colors," she exclaimed. "And do not fret! I will be circumspect."

I wished her a Merry Christmas again, and after she gargled back the Russian equivalent at me, we hung up.

I was dreading the drive home. I don't mind driving after dark, and I don't really mind driving in the snow—not when I knew the Shiffleys, with their festively decorated snow-plows, were diligently clearing the roads. But I hated driving in the snow after dark. And even more I hated that I wouldn't get the little hit of Christmas cheer I got from checking out the decorations along my route. All the nativity scenes and Santas with sleighs would have turned into featureless snowmen. Most people would have turned off their outdoor lights by now, or even if they hadn't, you'd barely see them for the falling snow.

And while most residents either dreaded the snow-induced inconveniences—the shoveling, the dripping boots, the possibility of a power outage—or cheered at the thought of sledding and maybe even a white Christmas, I had another perspective. Since one of the responsibilities I juggled was my theoretically part-time job as executive assistant to Randall, I couldn't look at the snow without seeing dollar signs. We were already well over our snow removal budget for the year. But we couldn't just ignore the stuff. Especially given how dependent we were on the revenues the tourists brought in—tourists who couldn't get to the shops and restaurants to spend their money if they were snowbound.

Clearly I needed to get home to my family and let the boys' enthusiasm for the snow and the upcoming holiday overwhelm my bad mood. I started my car and pulled carefully onto the road.

My trip home was uneventful. And once I got home, I settled in for a quiet night. Rose Noire had overcome her vegetarian scruples far enough to produce a pot of chili with ground beef along with her standard vegetarian version, and we all stuffed ourselves silly. In lieu of rehearsal, Michael drilled the boys on their lines, and then he and they disappeared upstairs for a bout of present-wrapping. From the size and shape of the boxes that appeared under the tree later in the evening, they'd made a very productive raid on the board game section of the local toy store, the better to feed our new family hobby.

Spike, our eight-and-a-half pound furball, dozed in his usual spot, sprawled expansively right in front of the fireplace, leaving Tinkerbell, Rob's wolfhound, to squeeze into the minimal space left on his left or right. When I offered them the chance to go outside, they both looked at me as if I'd lost my mind.

I called Grandfather to confirm that Gouldian finches didn't talk and to find out what they should be eating and texted the results to Ekaterina.

I found a moment, when the boys were watching *A Charlie Brown Christmas* to tell Michael about my day—including my discovery of the gun.

"This is scary," he said. "I'm glad you stole his bullets, but I almost wish you'd just stolen the gun."

"Confiscated, not stolen," I said. "I was afraid taking it might set him off. It's not as if he's doing anything illegal."

"Well, drinking himself to death isn't illegal, either. I tell you what we can do—I'll get in touch with Abe Sass tomorrow."

"And ruin the first real vacation he's taken since he became department chairman?"

"And get him to let me issue a rule that no firearms are allowed in the drama building."

"What about the dozen or so in the prop collection?"

"Drat," he said. "You have a point. Although we keep those locked up, for obvious reasons."

"So make the rule that no firearms are allowed in the building unless under lock and key in the prop shop or under the direct control of the prop crew for a performance or rehearsal," I suggested. "And no live ammunition under any circumstances."

"That should work," he said. "And if Haver protests, we tell him to appeal to Abe, who won't be back until two days before the end of the run. So don't worry about the gun. By this time tomorrow, it will be officially confiscated and safely locked up."

That thought improved my mood considerably.

"I'm glad you've got that animal welfare raid tomorrow," Michael said.

"Let's not call it a raid," I said. "I think the chief prefers 'search' or 'mission.' And it's easy for you to be glad—you don't have to get up before dawn to help with it."

"Well, that's no fun—but at least it will distract your dad from moping over Clay County's failure to appreciate his detective skills."

"Oh, dear," I groaned. "He wasn't going on in front of the boys about their John Doe being a murder victim, was he?"

"Don't worry. He mentioned it this morning in passing, but he was obviously a lot more interested in the idea that if they gave him more of a chance to examine the body he could glean enough clues to let them identify the poor guy. And when we saw him this afternoon he was completely focused on getting ready to help Clarence and your grandfather with whatever veterinary challenges the rescue mission might bring."

"Good," I said. "And maybe by the time the mission is over the Clay County police will have gotten around to checking the missing persons reports and solved the mystery of John Doe's identity."

"Amen. By the way, Stanley dropped by the theater today and gave us this."

He dug something out of his pocket and handed it to me—a black metal and plastic object about the size of an old-fashioned matchbox.

"Is this the thing for tracking Haver's car?"

"Yes. And I figure you're a lot more likely to get a chance to install it than I am."

I studied the elegant little device for a moment. Then I tucked it into one of the pockets in my purse, where I could grab it quickly when I saw my chance.

And then we both went back to having a quiet night with the boys. Charlie Brown gave way to Settlers of Catan, a favorite family board game, accompanied by steaming hot chocolate and a playlist of medieval and Renaissance Christmas carols on Michael's iPod.

Rob was working late at Mutant Wizards and would probably crash on the couch in his office, but he did break away from testing his latest top-secret game to text me a question.

"Is that one word or two?"

I'd have been baffled if it hadn't occurred to me to scroll up to see that the last text conversation we'd had, several hours ago, had been about Weaseltide. Or was it Weasel Tide?

"No idea," I texted back.

Without my having to ask, Rose Noire volunteered to take care of the boys the next day and take them in to rehearsal when needed, so I could focus on the rescue, and Michael on all the other things that needed to get done for the play.

A quiet night. It should also have been a peaceful one. But I'd been fretting all night, though trying not to let the boys see it.

Fretting about Haver. Where was he? What was he getting up to? Ekaterina called in to report every hour on the hour, like clockwork, but all she could report was that Haver hadn't returned to the Inn.

Neither had O'Manion.

I considered calling Dad, to see if he'd heard anything on the police band radio he was so fond of listening to. But that would only encourage him to stay up all night with the radio, and he needed his sleep for the raid.

The search, I corrected himself. Or the investigation.

Jake, our last-minute guest, who had been working long hours on the set, pleaded exhaustion and went to bed at nine. Michael suggested, since I had to get up so early, that he let me put the boys to bed so I could follow Jake's example.

"You have a busy day ahead of you, too," I pointed out.

"Yeah, but my day will start a lot later than yours. Rehearsal's not till noon."

"Does Haver know that?" I kept my voice down, so the boys wouldn't hear, just as I'd been doing every time I reported to Michael on the latest call from the Inn. Though after the first couple of calls, all it took was a head shake. "What if he doesn't show up?"

"Then I fill in as Scrooge until he does show up again," Michael said. "Including opening night, if he's picked right now to disappear off the face of the earth."

It wouldn't be entirely a bad thing if Haver disappeared, I found myself thinking as I trudged upstairs. Not off the face of the earth, of course, and not forever. I didn't wish him ill. But it would be so much easier if he'd just put himself out of commission for a few weeks. If, for example, we got the news that he'd checked himself into the nearest residential rehab treatment center.

Even after I got into my nightgown and turned out the light, I kept picking up my cell phone from its bedside charging station to check the time and my email.

"It becomes late," Ekaterina said in her ten o'clock call. "I will, of course, continue to monitor the subjects' rooms. But do you wish to continue receiving my reports?"

"Why don't you text me instead of calling?" I suggested. "I'll turn the sound off on my phone, so if I'm asleep, you won't wake me."

I did manage to drop off after that, though I woke when Michael came to bed, and again at random intervals throughout the night.

Chapter 14

Why does your body always know when you have to get up early and do its best to make sure you can't take advantage of what few hours you have for sleeping?

At a little before 3:00 A.M., I woke to find a text from Ekaterina. "02:37. Subject O'Manion has returned. No sign of primary subject."

And when my alarm went off at 6:00 A.M., I groped for the phone to find Ekaterina's identical 3:00 A.M., 4:00 A.M., 5:00 A.M., and 6:00 A.M. reports. "No sign of subject Haver."

"I hope the wretch isn't lying dead in a ditch somewhere," I muttered, as I hurriedly threw on my clothes. Most of my clothes. I was completely out of clean shirts, so I raced down to the basement to raid the load of clean laundry I hadn't gotten around to putting away.

Incompletely hidden behind the dryer was a shoe box. No, a boot box. This close to Christmas I knew I should ignore all unexplained bags and packages but I couldn't resist taking a quick look—and yes! Boots. The boots I'd been drooling over when the boys and I realized they'd outgrown theirs and we'd gone online to order new ones. The boots Michael had discouraged me from getting by saying that the long-range forecast was for a mild winter. I gazed at them fondly, and a little longingly, and then shoved the box far enough behind the dryer to give me plausible deniability if anyone noticed I'd been in the basement. Clearly I needed to get a little more involved in doing the laundry, if this was the boys'—and Michael's—idea of a secure hiding place.

And then I shoved the boots out of my mind so I could prepare to act surprised on Christmas morning. I ran upstairs, grabbed my keys, and put on my old boots. Which were still serviceable enough to last a few more snows.

The snow had stopped, though not before depositing another five inches of snow on the Twinmobile, which I decided would be more useful for today's purposes than my car. But Beau and Osgood had been busy overnight—or possibly other Shiffley cousins who took over when they reached the end of their ropes. The road into town was passable. And I'd parked near enough that I only had to do a modest amount of shoveling to clear a path to the road.

The college radio was playing soft, instrumental carols. Very nice ones, but they were definitely carols to drift back to sleep with, not carols to wake you up and get your blood stirring on a cold winter morning.

The parking lot at the police station had also been beautifully plowed sometime in the middle of the night, before the members of our expedition had begun to gather. The vehicles spilled out of the parking lot and into the street. Four police cruisers. One police transport van. Clarence's white Caerphilly Veterinary van. Half a dozen minivans and SUVs. A huge RV. Half a dozen trucks from either the Shiffley Construction Company or the Shiffley Moving Company. I was a little startled to see a hearse among the gathered vehicles, but then I remembered that Maudie Morton, owner of the local funeral home, was a big animal lover. And the cats and dogs weren't apt to be squeamish about what kind of vehicle took them to their new homes.

I had to park half a block away from the station, but at least the sidewalk was snow-free all the way, thanks to two of the chief's grandsons. They had moved on to shoveling a path along the side of the building toward the side entrance— the one officers used when they were taking someone directly to jail rather than bringing them in through the police station to be interviewed or interrogated. Were they just being thorough, or had the chief suggested it might be needed?

Inside the station, Muriel, owner of the local diner, was passing out coffee and doughnuts to the assembled rescuers.

"Here," she said, thrusting a cup into my hands. "You look like you need this."

"Thanks." I wasn't sure which was more welcome, the caffeine or the heat from the cup. "I owe you one."

"Then do me a favor—if any of those cats shows signs of being a decent mouser, snag it for me. I could use a good mouser."

"Er—sure."

She handed me a doughnut and bustled off with her coffeepot and pastry plate to greet another new arrival, leaving me puzzled. How did one tell if a cat was a good mouser? Short of capturing one with a furry tail hanging out of its mouth, I had no idea. Maybe one of our experts would know. Clarence. Or Dad. Or better yet—Grandfather! I strolled over to where he was standing, sipping his coffee.

"Are you good at telling whether one animal's a superior predator?" I asked. "Superior to other nearby examples of the same species, I mean."

"Hmm." He took another bite of his chocolate-covered, jelly-filled doughnut and looked thoughtful. "Not at first glance, of course. But if I had the opportunity to observe their behavior, I could figure it out with no difficulty. Why?"

"Muriel wants a mouser," I said. "So use your eagle eye on the cats today."

"Muriel?"

"Lady who makes the doughnuts."

"She made these?" Grandfather looked at his doughnut, and then at Muriel, with new respect. "She also the one who makes the pies?"

I nodded. Muriel's pies perennially won first prizes at the county fair.

"Impressive," he said. "Yes, I think we can find her a good mouser."

I left him to enjoy the rest of his breakfast and went in search of the chief, all the while congratulating myself. I was learning to delegate almost as well as Mother.

The chief looked tired and even slightly disheveled, as if he'd been up much of the night.

"Thank you for the information about your find over at the theater," he said. "Unfortunately, however disquieting I find the news, I'm afraid there may not be much I can do about it."

"Because he isn't doing anything illegal." I nodded as I spoke. "That's why I didn't confiscate it along with the liquor. Michael's going to issue a department rule against firearms in the building and then confiscate it under that."

"Good plan," the chief said. "Though that would not prevent him from acquiring another gun and making use of it elsewhere. I've left a message for the county attorney, to see if she has any ideas on the subject. And at least, thanks to your warning, my officers will be forewarned if they attempt to apprehend him."

"He's still missing, then?"

The chief nodded.

"Maybe he's left the county?" I suggested.

"Or maybe his car is buried under half a foot of snow," the chief said, waving at all the car-shaped snow lumps parked across the street from the station. "I can't ask my officers to go around brushing the snow off every license plate in town. They've had a busy night."

I nodded. I found myself thinking of the little GPS tracking device, sitting uselessly in my purse when it could have been helping us locate Haver's car if only we'd thought of it a day earlier.

"I'd have postponed this animal welfare mission if the temperature wasn't about to drop so dramatically," the chief went on. "We'll have to worry about Mr. Haver later today. Here comes Osgood with the snowplow to lead us in. In case Mr. Willimer hasn't yet plowed his lane," he added, seeing my surprise.

So led by Osgood's Darth Vader snowplow, the caravan set out for the far end of the county. I wasn't sure whether to be relieved or disappointed that the tourists wouldn't get to see our unusual procession. Well, except for one pair, so bundled up that I couldn't tell if they were men or women, who were trying to dig out their car with a whisk broom and a plastic coffee cup. In spite of their tedious task, they waved cheerfully and wished us a Merry Christmas, and one of the Shiffley trucks dropped behind to help them out and then caught up with us a few miles down the road.

When we reached the end of the Willimers' lane, the caravan ground to a halt and the chief and the three deputies who had come along—Vern, Horace, and Aida—got out of their vehicles.

"We're going in to secure the premises," the chief said. "Deputy Hollingsworth is in charge until I get back. Horace, I'll radio when we're all clear."

We all watched as Vern, Aida, and the chief trudged down the lane. It hadn't been plowed, but clearly at least one reasonably large vehicle had lumbered over the snow sometime in the night, creating two big ruts that made for easier going than the rest of the road.

After about ten minutes, Grandfather hopped out of Dad's SUV and began pacing up and down the road.

"We should go in there," he said. "Who knows what's happening?"

"The chief said to stay here until he radioed," Horace said.

"What if they've been ambushed by bloodthirsty finch smugglers with semi-automatic weapons?"

"We'd have heard the semi-automatic weapons," Horace pointed out.

"Bloodthirsty finch smugglers with machetes."

Horace looked stumped.

"We'd have heard the screams," I said. "Look if you want to go in, go ahead."

Grandfather looked triumphant. Horace gave me a look of exasperation.

"Just remember—you're about the same height as Willimer. Don't blame us if they mistake you for him and shoot you."

"They wouldn't shoot me."

"They're probably really on edge right now—looking over their shoulders every second for those bloodthirsty finch smugglers."

Grandfather frowned for a few moments.

"Well, if you're going to get all upset about it, I'll wait in the damned vehicle." He hopped back into Dad's SUV, slamming the door behind him.

Horace let out a sigh of relief. I winked at him.

I didn't envy Clarence—Grandfather had been riding in his van, and was probably giving him an earful of complaints.

And I had to admit that I was relieved when Horace's radio crackled.

"Get Osgood cracking with that snowplow," I heard the chief say. Osgood, who was also within earshot, started his engine, and I almost missed the chief's second sentence. "And can you send Meg and the social worker in on his heels?"

Everyone tapped their feet while Meredith Flugleman, the social worker, leaped out of the chief's patrol car and scampered over to the Twinmobile.

"Isn't it a wonderful morning?" she exclaimed as she jumped into my passenger seat.

"Morning," I said, with as cheerful a smile as I could muster.

"Are we wearing our seat belts?" She was, and she reached

over to test mine, in much the same way I usually checked my sons' seat belts. "Good! Tally-ho!"

I was remembering why Randall found Meredith so tiring. She was unfailingly perky. I had a hard time with perky in general, and found it particularly trying this soon after dawn.

"My goodness! This van has seen some hard use, hasn't it?" If she thought that was a polite way of calling attention to the Twinmobile's less-than-pristine condition, she was wrong. "Did you know the high school marching band does car detailing every month or two to raise money for their trips?"

I decided not to tell her that yes, I took advantage of the detailing every time the high school did it, and that afterward it generally took Josh and Jamie a good two or three days to restore the Twinmobile to its usual condition.

Luckily, even with Osgood and Darth Vader plowing the lane ahead of us, the road was treacherous enough that I could pretend it took most of my attention. She didn't seem to mind that our conversation was one-sided. As we left the woods and the farmhouse came into view, she exclaimed over how isolated it was, and treated me to statistics about the prevalence of child, spousal, and elder abuse in rural communities. Her unfailingly cheerful voice contrasted oddly with the grim data.

The chief was standing on the front stoop of the farmhouse, frowning.

"Thank goodness," he said. "Apparently Mr. Willimer did not come home last night, and his mother is distraught."

"The poor dear!" Meredith hopped out of the Twinmobile, frowned slightly at the faint trail of boot prints that led through the unshoveled snow between her and the door, then bravely plunged in.

The chief held the door open for her.

"Mrs. Willimer?" Meredith trilled as she skipped into the room.

I stopped at the threshold, when the smell hit me. I turned back to the chief.

"Where do you need me?" I asked him.

"Well, you could start by—"

Just then Meredith burst out of the door, rushed down the steps, and bent over to retch in the snow.

Chapter 15

The chief rushed over to check inside the house. I stood back, hoping Meredith wanted privacy rather than help but keeping an eye on her anyway.

"What's wrong?" called voice from inside the house. "Is something wrong? Has something happened to Johnny?"

The chief popped back out of the house, looked at Meredith, and then turned to me.

"Maybe you could help Aida with Mrs. Willimer?" The chief's face showed that he knew what he was asking. "Just until Ms. Flugleman recovers."

I took what I hoped wouldn't be my last breath of fresh air ever and strode into the house.

At first glance, the whole room appeared to be in violent motion and I wondered for a few moments if the smell was triggering a vertigo attack. Then I realized the room wasn't moving—it was the cats. They were all running, jumping, and leaping about in a frenzy. And at the heart of the maelstrom was Mrs. Willimer in her wheelchair, waving her arms and shrieking.

"No! Don't let them out! Close the door! There could be foxes out there! Where's Johnny? I need Johnny! Why won't you tell me what's happened?"

Aida Butler was crouched by the old woman's wheelchair, patting her arm with one hand while she fended off cats with the other. Her mouth was moving, which probably meant she was saying soothing things, but the old lady's shrieking drowned her out.

I waded through the waves of cats covering the floor until I reached the other side of the wheelchair. I thought of taking my coat off, but I realized the room was only marginally warmer than the outside. There was a fireplace with no fire—was that the only heat they had?

Time to worry about that later.

"Sssh!" I said, holding my fingers to my lips. "You're upsetting the poor kitties! They need peace and quiet and calm."

I began patting Mrs. Willimer's other arm, while continuing to make shushing noises. She gradually stopped wailing and subsided into rocking back and forth slightly and whimpering.

"What happened to the social worker?" Aida asked in an undertone.

I opened my mouth and stopped shushing long enough to point into it several times.

"No guts, no glory," Aida said.

I didn't actually blame Meredith—the stench was every bit as bad as I'd expected it to be, a toxic blend of cat pee and stale cat food, with undertones of rotting vegetables and mold.

But the sooner we dealt with Mrs. Willimer, the sooner we could get out of this hellhole.

I squatted down beside her chair.

"Can you tell us what happened?"

"Johnny didn't come home last night," she said. "And the power went out around nine o'clock, and took the phone lines with it, or I would have called the police to report him as missing."

"Don't worry," Aida said. "The chief's put the word out now. I'm sure we'll find he just holed up someplace till the snow was over."

"He could be dead in a ditch somewhere," the old lady wailed.

"Now, now," I said. "Think of your cats."

"Yes," she said. "I must be brave for their sake. Although if anything's happened to Johnny, I don't know how we can afford to live."

"I'm sure he's fine," Aida said. "We haven't had any reports of fatalities on the roads—not here, and not in any of the nearby counties. Had to rescue a few people who got stuck in snowdrifts. Lots of people stranded in town until they can dig their cars out. Some of them are sleeping on cots in the high school gym. And the roads are still pretty bad in Clay County. Lots of perfectly normal reasons why he might not have come home yet. But don't you worry. He'll probably come home before too long."

"I won't rest easy till he does." Mrs. Willimer shook her head as if she didn't put much faith in our reassurances.

"Meanwhile we need to take care of you," I said.

"Might help if someone built a fire." Mrs. Willimer's voice was suddenly calm and practical. "The furnace went out with the power. I can manage to put a log on the fire, but I ran out of firewood in the middle of the night, and I can't get out to the woodpile to haul it in."

"I'll take care of the firewood." Aida beat me to the punch on that one.

As she went out to raid the woodpile, Meredith appeared in the doorway, wearing a feeble imitation of her usual perky face.

"My goodness," she said in a shaky voice. "She can't possibly stay here."

"What do you mean I can't stay here," Mrs. Willimer wailed. "We don't know for sure that anything's happened to Johnny. You can't kick me out yet."

"No one's kicking you out," I said. "But you have no power. Are you on the county water?"

"No." The old lady frowned. "We have our own well."

"With an electric pump, no doubt—which means you have no water. No phone to call for help till the lines are repaired. And no one here to haul in firewood if we leave. So we have to take you someplace where you'll be safe until things get back to normal."

"I suppose that makes sense." She still didn't look happy about the idea.

"We have a slight problem," Meredith said in a stage whisper, beckoning to me. I joined her at the doorway. "While I was outside I called to see if I could get a temporary placement at the Caerphilly Assisted Living. But they're full up. They only had a few vacant beds to begin with and those are all occupied right now. Holiday respite care. I might be able to get her a bed over in Tappahannock. Or we might have to take her as far as Richmond."

"She won't much like that."

Meredith shrugged as if to say "what can I do?"

"Let me try something," I said.

I stepped past her into the fresh air and just breathed for a few moments. Then I walked a few paces, until I was sure I was out of earshot, pulled out my cell phone, and dialed a familiar number.

"Caerphilly Inn, Ekaterina Vorobyaninova speaking."

"It's Meg," I said.

"Primary subject still not here," she said. "I have observers covering all possible means of ingress and egress."

"Good," I said. "But actually for once I'm not calling about Haver. Could I talk you into making a room available at a rate the county can afford to pay? It can be your smallest, cheapest room—we just need a place to put up someone for a night or two."

I explained as succinctly as I could about the raid and the need to find a temporary haven for Mrs. Willimer.

"Michael and I would take her in ourselves," I added. "She's a sweet little old lady. But she's wheelchair bound, and our house just isn't accessible."

"Of course," she said. "I will find something nice for her.

And if it's only for a day or two, there should be no need to bill the county. I have a small discretionary fund that I can use for community outreach and goodwill."

"We will owe you," I said.

"Tell me—how is she tied to this business of the finches? Is it possible that she is actually not a sweet little old lady in a wheelchair but a dangerous international bird smuggler?"

No wonder Ekaterina was so ready to help out.

"We don't know yet," I said. "But even if she isn't involved in the smuggling, her son is, so she's bound to be called as a witness. She could be in danger. You'll need to keep a close eye on her."

"Naturally," she said with audible satisfaction. "We will keep her under observation. And we will keep her safe."

I strolled back to the house and stuck my head in the door.

"There is room at the Inn," I said.

"Is that a Biblical reference?" Meredith said.

"Biblical?"

"And she brought forth her firstborn son," she intoned. "And wrapped him in swaddling clothes, and laid him in a manger; because there was no room for them in the inn."

"Nicely quoted," I said. "But no. I meant that the Caerphilly Inn is willing to give Mrs. Willimer a room for a night or two. As a gesture of goodwill, in honor of the season, and all that."

"Oh, lovely!" She turned to her charge. "Did you hear that, Mrs. Willimer? You're going to get to stay in the Caerphilly Inn! Won't that be lovely?"

"Frost," Mrs. Willimer said.

"Well, yes, I know it's still very cold in here," Meredith said. "Aida only just started the fire, and I'm not sure how well that's going to heat this chilly room without any help from your furnace. That's why we need to find a place for you to stay until things are back to normal around here."

"No," the old lady said. "I mean my name is Frost. Not Willimer. Frost. Jane Frost. Sorry—I know it's confusing."

"Oh, I'm so sorry!" Meredith exclaimed. "I should have asked. Now let's see about getting you packed."

I decided I could safely leave them to it. Meredith hadn't quite regained her usual perkiness, but she was working on it, and besides, looking after little old ladies in smelly rooms was part of her job description.

"Give me a heads-up before you bring her outside," I said in an undertone to Meredith. "Because it might be a good idea to get Maudie to move the hearse out of sight, just in case."

I went outside to see how the animal rescue was going. Osgood and Darth Vader had plowed a wide area in front of the house and barn, and the vehicles were parked in neat rows on either side. A couple of Shiffleys were shoveling a path from the ad hoc parking lot to the barn. As I watched, an empty dog crate landed on the ground behind one of the trucks, followed by a Brigade volunteer, who then picked it up and carried it toward the barn.

And between the house and the barn—wait a minute. Willimer's pickup truck was still parked under the plywood carport.

Chapter 16

Chief Burke and Aida also appeared to have noticed that even though Willimer was missing his truck wasn't. They were standing in front of it. The chief was talking on his phone.

I hiked over to them.

"No other vehicles registered under his name," he was saying to Aida. "And that truck's clearly been there since well before the snow stopped."

I followed the direction his finger was pointing. Yes, the back foot or so of the truck stuck out from under the roof, and five or six inches of snow had piled up in it. The same amount of snow blurred the tracks the truck had made driving in.

"I gather he's not hiding in the house or the barn," I said.

"We checked pretty thoroughly before we gave the all clear," the chief said. "And no fresh tracks leading to the woods in any direction. If he left here on foot, it was well before the storm let up."

"We saw one place on the far side of the barn where someone made a path while it was still snowing," Aida said. "Right along one of the fences. From what you told the chief, we figured it was probably where you came in to make your inspection."

I nodded.

"Vern's doing another close search of the barn," the chief said. "He's heard tell of a case where a moonshiner set up one of those prefabricated underground tornado shelters under his shed, so he'd have a place to hide himself and his contraband when the Feds came raiding."

"Be sure and have him look under where the tiger is after they've hauled him away," I said. "If I were a smuggler, that's where I'd put my secret hideaway."

The chief looked at me for few moments, then nodded. He headed toward the barn.

"I never cease to marvel at the deviousness of your mind," Aida said. "How soon do you think you and the social worker can have Mrs. Willimer out of there?"

"Soon, I hope, and actually she's Mrs. Frost."

"Understandable," Aida said. "Wouldn't you trade Willimer for Frost if you had a chance?"

"Or if I started out Frost, I'd refuse to take on Willimer to begin with."

"Yeah—look how fast I dumped my married name when I got rid of the jerk who owned it."

"Anyway, Meredith's helping the old lady pack."

"Good. The chief thinks it could upset her to see her cats being chased down and hauled away, so he wants her gone before we start in the house."

I nodded. We both gazed at the truck for a few more minutes.

"Haver's missing too," I said. "Him and his rental car."

"Maybe he came back and picked up Willimer," Aida said. "Anyway, someone must have. Want to bet he was over getting wasted at the Clay Pigeon and got stranded there by the snow?"

The Clay Pigeon was a disreputable bar in our neighboring county, and hands down the largest single source of 911 calls in either jurisdiction.

"Are we talking Willimer or Haver carousing at the Clay Pigeon?" I asked.

"Either." Aida laughed. "Both."

"The Clay Pigeon's about their style," I said. "I'll check on how Meredith and Mrs. Frost are doing."

I went back to the front door, braced myself, and let myself in.

"Noooooooo!" Mrs. Wi—Mrs. Frost wailed.

"Now, now," Meredith was saying. "Calm yourself. The cats are becoming unsettled."

Becoming unsettled? The cats were already in full-bore panic mode, howling and caterwauling and leaping wildly around the room. And most unnerving, a dozen or so were gathered in a circle around Meredith's feet, heads lowered, ears laid back, hissing and spitting and giving the impression they were waiting for the strategic moment to pounce on her en masse.

"The packing doesn't seem to be going very smoothly," I observed.

"We have a problem," Meredith said through gritted teeth.

"Noooo," Mrs. Frost whined. She was blinking fast to keep her pale-blue eyes from overflowing with tears. "I can't possibly go without all my kitties."

"You can't possibly go *with* all your kitties." Meredith was starting to sound a lot less like an unnaturally patient kindergarten teacher and a lot more like a woman who'd already spent far too long breathing in toxic cat pee fumes. I could sympathize.

"Just a few kitties, then," Mrs. Frost said. "Just my special favorites."

Meredith looked at me. I stifled a sigh.

"Let me talk to the Inn," I said.

I went outside, both for privacy and to get a few breaths of fresh air.

"Are you making any progress?" Clarence asked. He and one of the Shiffleys were loading several dog crates into a Shiffley Moving Company panel truck. "It will be a lot easier to round up all those cats without her present."

I liked that he didn't say "underfoot," even though that was probably what he meant.

"Working on it," I said, as I strolled to the far end of the farmyard.

I pulled out my cell phone and called Ekaterina again.

"The room awaits," she said. "Do we have an ETA for the handoff?"

"Not yet. Any chance I can talk you into making another exception to your no pets policy?"

"Is Mr. Haver acquiring another finch?"

"No, Mrs. Frost, the little old lady I'm bringing over, is refusing to go without her favorite cat. She's in a wheelchair, so technically we could just haul her out still pleading for her darlings, but—"

"But what's one little pussycat?" Ekaterina said. "Of course."

"I can't promise it will be a particularly well-behaved little pussycat," I warned as I watched a fat gray and white cat who was sitting just inside one of the front windows, sharpening his claws on the sill.

"We will cope," she said. "I always assume the possibility of higher-than-usual maintenance costs when we receive a guest who is perhaps not accustomed to staying in an establishment of the caliber of the Caerphilly Inn."

Well, she couldn't say I hadn't warned her.

"Thanks," I said aloud.

I hung up and strolled back to the door, relishing the fresh air while I could. Then I braced myself and plunged back into the cat-infested chaos.

"One cat." I held up my forefinger by way of emphasis. "And try to make it a reasonably sedate and well-behaved one."

"Ronnie, then." Mrs. Frost said. "He's a perfect lamb. Now where has he gotten to?" She craned her head and began scanning the room. "There he is!" she exclaimed, pointing to something behind me. "That's Ronnie—the big yellow tomcat sitting on top of my sewing machine."

Ronnie only stayed on the sewing machine for a few seconds before leaping via a bookcase to the mantel. Her favorite would have to be one of the livelier ones. And definitely not fond of strange humans. I went outside and drafted a couple of Brigade members to bring in a cat carrier and help me catch Ronnie the lamb. It took a good twenty minutes before we finally cornered him. And then the three of us had to fight a pitched battle to stuff the brute into the carrier.

When we finally had him safely latched in, I brought the carrier over to Mrs. Frost.

"Are you sure we have the right one?" I asked. At least 20 percent of the cats swarming through the house were yellow striped cats of various sizes. I had visions of arriving at the Inn only to have her declare we'd brought the wrong kitty and had to go back to find the right one.

"Oh, yes. That's Ronnie. Such a handsome, high-spirited boy."

I took a closer look at Ronnie. High-spirited maybe, but handsome? He was missing most of one ear, and rather a lot of clumps of fur. Perhaps I should suggest to Meredith that she take Mrs. Frost to have her eyes examined while she was in town.

Still, he did have a fine, powerful voice, which he was using vigorously to protest his imprisonment. My fellow cat nabbers, who had been standing by to make sure we had the right suspect, breathed a sigh of relief.

"Let's get patched up," one of them said. "I have a first aid kit in my car."

"I have plenty of Band-Aids in the bathroom," Mrs. Frost said. "Just help yourself."

From the look that passed over my helpers' faces, I suspected they were having the same thought I was: no way was I going to put anything from this house on my bare skin, much less an open wound.

"Oh, we couldn't think of imposing," one of them said.

"Brigade rules," the other added.

With that they fled.

"My dad would have my head if I didn't let him take care of my little scratches." I tucked my hand behind my back so she wouldn't see quite how many not-so-little scratches I had. "You know how parents are."

"Of course," she said. "If you're going outside, then, you can take Ronnie's litter box out to the car. It's under the sewing machine—the bright blue one," she added, as if suddenly noticing that there were four mismatched litter boxes there. "You know how territorial cats can get about their litter boxes."

I grimaced, but obediently picked up the litter box in question, held it up for Mrs. Frost's nod of approval, and carried it out to the Twinmobile. Luckily for me, the litter box showed few signs of use. Although most of the several dozen litter boxes tucked into nooks and crannies didn't appear to have been very recently used. Which made sense to me—cats are realists. Why bother with litter boxes when clearly there was no penalty for ignoring them and no effort on the part of the humans to keep them tidy.

Outside, I took deep breaths. My fellow cat wranglers were clustered around the rear of one of the SUVs, fishing things out of an open first aid kit and wincing as they dabbed their scratches with alcohol wipes.

"And to think we've got to go in and do it all over again a hundred more times," one of them muttered.

"It'll be easier," the other said. "Catching one particular cat in a swarm like that's hard. When we go in again, all we have to do is grab the first cat we can reach, stuff it in a carrier, and repeat until the place is empty."

"When we go in again, we use the masks," the first one said. "And gloves, the padded ones. I don't care how insulting the old lady finds it."

"With luck, the little old lady will be gone by the time you have to go in again," I said as I joined them at the SUV and helped myself to the alcohol wipes and bandages.

Just then Clarence and another of the Brigade emerged from the barn, carrying a large plastic dog crate. From the amount of yipping and squealing emerging from the crate, I deduced it had more than one occupant.

"Meg!" Clarence called out. "Just the person I was looking for. I wanted to ask you something."

"The answer is no," I said.

Chapter 17

Clarence blinked with surprise.

"I haven't even asked my question yet," he said.

"I know what your question is. You want to know if you can keep all these animals in our barn. And the answer is no. Michael and I are both incredibly busy with the play and the festival and all the other seasonal events, on top of which we have a houseful of two-legged guests arriving today and tomorrow. We don't have time to babysit dozens of four-legged ones."

"I can get volunteers to do that. But there are so many more animals than I was expecting—we just don't have the sheer physical space to put them in."

"Other people have barns."

"How about if we just use your barn as a staging area?" he said. "Since everybody does already know where it is. We can do all the vaccinating and chipping there, and it will give us a closer-in place where people can come to pick up the animals."

Actually, that didn't sound too unreasonable.

"And I promise we'll have them out within, say, three days."

"No," I said. "If you can have them out by nightfall, you can stage them in our barn. But not for three days. Twelve hours."

After a bit more haggling as we hauled another crate full of puppies from the barn to Clarence's van, we settled on twenty-four hours.

"And don't worry," he said. "When people see how cute these golden retriever puppies are, we won't have enough to go around. I expect a record number of foster fails on this mission."

"Foster fails?" I echoed. "How is that a good thing?"

"A foster fail is when the foster family falls in love with the animal and doesn't want to give it back," he said. "And since they've already been screened and approved as foster families, the adoption's a breeze."

"Let's hope we have a lot of them, then," I said. "I'll go and see how Meredith's coming with Mrs. Frost."

"Look out," Clarence called to a pair of volunteers who were lifting up a very large dog crate. "That latch on that one doesn't look too secure. It could—"

Suddenly the door of the crate flew open and a small river of golden fur poured out onto the snow. Then the puppies, undeterred by their fall—which was only about a foot anyway—took off in all directions yipping with excitement.

"Catch them!" Clarence shouted.

The volunteers and I all took off after puppies while Clarence ran to the barn to call for more help. People poured out of the barn and joined in the chase. The puppies seemed to think this was the best game they'd ever played. And they might have been small, but they were fast, energetic, and agile. They could turn on a dime and dart between the legs of a human who thought he had them cornered. They could duck under parked cars and trucks and tease their pursuers with mock fierce barks and growls

In addition to the puppies, an adult dog had also landed on the snow. She didn't take off—just sat there on the snow for a few moments, glancing around before putting her head on her front paws with a sigh. Maybe she was wiser than we were, and knew her puppies would come back eventually. Maybe she was just too tired and dispirited to care. I remembered days when I'd felt like that, especially the first year of the twins' life.

"You take it easy," I told her. "We'll round them up."

And then I took off after a puppy who ran in an ever widening circle, yipping with delight, until he caught sight of something in the direction of the woods and made a bee-line for it. He was heading for roughly the same patch of woods I'd hidden in the day before—to my left, I could see a faint indented line where the snow had covered over the path I'd made.

I redoubled my speed—if he got into the woods, we might never find him again. And he might think himself very fierce, but he'd be easy prey for foxes. Hawks. Owls.

To my relief, he stopped just short of the woods and began barking furiously at something. Whatever he was barking at was right along the path I'd taken to the barn from my hiding place. Was someone there now? I could worry about that later. I managed to get near him, and though he dodged my first several pounces, I finally managed to grab him and clutch him to me.

"You don't know how lucky you are," I told him.

He responded by wriggling in an effort to get down again, and finally gave up and began licking my face.

I stood there for a few moments to get my breath back, and watched the end of the puppy roundup. When Clarence, looking like a mother hen, began shouting "We're still missing one! There should be nine!" I held up my wayward ball of fur and everyone cheered with relief.

The puppy settled down in my arms and appeared to be going to sleep.

"Let's get you back with the rest of your litter before I start getting the crazy idea that Spike and Tinkerbell need a little brother."

I glanced back at the woods the puppy had come so close to disappearing in and spotted something. Possibly the something the puppy had been barking at.

A boot.

No, not just a boot. A boot-clad human foot, sticking out from under the snow.

Chapter 18

I took a few steps backward, staring at the foot. Then I turned and hurried back toward the house and barn.

"Where's the chief?" I called out as I drew near. "I think we have a problem here."

I handed my puppy to a volunteer. Chief Burke appeared from behind one of the trucks.

"What's the problem?"

"Let me show you," I said. I led the way to the much-trampled area by the woods where I'd finally caught the puppy and pointed to the foot.

"Oh, dear." He pushed up his glasses and studied the foot. "Do you recognize it?"

"A snow boot," I said. "From this angle, it looks a lot like the North Face boots Michael and I are giving Rob for Christmas."

He glanced at me with a look of mild exasperation on his face.

"I know, I know," I said. "No, I have no idea who's wearing the boot."

"We should get your father over here to see if— Let me check." He inched close enough to the body to reach out and touch the leg, just above the boot. He shook his head. "Freezing cold. Pretty sure he's dead. But if you'd be so kind, go send your father and Horace over here. And tell Vern and Aida to have everyone stop where they are till further notice. This farmyard may just have become a crime scene."

I nodded. I noticed that he'd told me to send Horace and

Dad, not bring them. I might pretend not to have grasped that subtlety.

"And have them bring some snow shovels," the chief called after me.

Dad and Horace were among the crowd waiting by the vehicles. Horace, together with Vern and Aida, were discouraging people from going any closer to where the chief was standing.

"The chief says for everyone to keep back and stay where you are," I said.

"What's wrong?" One of the volunteers.

"I found a body in the snow," I explained. A murmur ran through the group.

"Dead?" Dad asked.

"The chief wants you to make sure," I said.

Dad grabbed his old-fashioned black doctor's bag, which had been sitting near his feet, and trotted out to the body. He'd probably customized his bag today with a few extras that might prove useful in dealing with any ailments the rescued creatures might be afflicted with—along with any injuries they might inflict. But it would always hold the basics—both for saving lives, as he'd done for decades, and for fulfilling the duties of his recently acquired role as the local medical examiner.

"He wants you, too," I said to Horace. "He's probably hoping you brought your crime scene kit."

"He knows I'm never without it." Horace ran toward his car.

"Can I have a pair of those?" I asked, pointing to the snow shovels several of the Shiffleys carried.

"Who is it?" one of the Shiffleys asked, as he handed me his shovel.

"It's Willimer, isn't it?" Randall had grabbed the second offered shovel.

"No idea," I said. "The body's buried under the snow. And remember, he's not the only person missing at the moment."

"I'm exercising mayoral privilege and going out to supervise the crime scene." Randall shouldered the shovel as if he were a soldier about to carry his rifle in a parade and headed toward where the chief was squatting in the snow, scribbling in his notebook.

"Out here it's county manager privilege," I reminded him as I tagged along at his side. Ever since the departure of the unloved Pruitts, the century-old enmity between town and county had disappeared, and Randall now held both jobs—just as the chief, here on the Willimer farm, was actually functioning in his dual role as sheriff.

"Let's just hope the chief doesn't say it's baloney and to get away from his crime scene," Randall said in an undertone as we approached where Dad and the chief were standing. "Because I need to know what's going on and how it's going to affect our festival."

Horace came running up behind us.

"Horace, take a few pictures, quick," the chief said. "Then we're going to dig him out. Dr. Langslow thinks it unlikely this poor soul is alive, but we're going to mess up your crime scene, just in case."

Horace's camera was already clicking.

"Ready," he said, after a few seconds, and held out his hand for a shovel.

We watched as Randall and Horace quickly but carefully uncovered the foot's owner. It soon became obvious why his boot was sticking up out of the show—he'd sprawled back over a small fallen tree whose trunk held the foot up just enough to make it stick out of the snow—and at just the right angle for the snow to slide off. If the tree hadn't been there, or if we'd had a few more inches of snow, we might not have found him for days.

I noticed we were saying *he*, but at first there wasn't anything to indicate whether our victim was a man or a woman. The boots could have belonged to either. The same with the jeans-clad legs. Though they were such long legs that I was betting on a man. The quilted jacket, partly unzipped, and the plaid flannel shirt beneath weren't too different from what I sometimes wore on snowy days.

But the next shovel full of snow left bare an Adam's apple. And the one after that revealed a face.

My first reaction was a sigh of relief. It wasn't Haver. I saw a thin, sunken-cheeked face with several days' growth of beard and a receding chin. His eyes were open and staring. And there were two bullet holes in his forehead.

"Meg?"

I looked up and realized everyone was staring at me.

"Is it Willimer?" the chief asked.

"I don't know," I said. "Pretty sure it's the guy I saw coming out of Willimer's house and putting the box in Haver's car. Of course, keep in mind that I only saw him briefly through binoculars and people look different when they're . . . um . . ."

"Dead," the chief said, nodding.

"Actually, I was going to say frozen—but yeah, that too. So if the guy I saw coming out of the house was Willimer, that's him."

The chief took out something from between the pages of his notebook and handed it to me. A DMV document with a copy of Willimer's driver's license photo.

"Yeah," I said. "That's the guy I saw."

"And it seems to be the gentleman we have here," the chief said, after we'd looked back and forth between the corpse and the photo. "Although we should probably still get an ID from Mrs. Frost." The chief didn't sound happy about the idea.

"Okay for me to do my thing?" Horace said.

"Yes," the chief said. "Meg, could I have a word with you?"

We walked halfway back toward the watching crowd before he stopped.

"That gun you found in Mr. Haver's dressing room has just become a great deal more interesting to me," he said.

"You think Haver could be the killer?" It seemed a leap, unless he knew something I didn't know.

"It's far too early to speculate on that," he said. "But it's a gun that was in possession of someone who may be one of the last people to have spoken to the deceased."

"Not to mention someone who appears to have vanished during the night when the murder occurred," I said.

"Precisely," the chief said. "Could you describe the gun's hiding place to Aida with sufficient accuracy that she could find it? And arrange for her to enter the drama building to secure it?"

"Absolutely."

"I'm trying not to be superstitious," he said. "But I can't help feeling chastened. Only yesterday I was feeling so smug about the fact that, unlike Clay County, we didn't have any dead bodies on our hands."

"But not a John Doe," I pointed out. "You've already identified him."

"And God willing, we'll find out who killed him. But in future, I will take this as a lesson to be more charitable in my thoughts."

He turned and began trudging back toward the body.

"Chief," I called. "What about the animal rescue? Should that continue?"

He turned and winced as his gaze traveled over the assembled rescuers, who were all standing and staring, with or without puppies in their arms.

"Good lord," he said. "This won't be the first time I'd had half a hundred well-meaning civilians contaminating my crime scene before I even knew it *was* a crime scene. But it will be the first time I brought them along myself." He looked up at the sky and shivered. "That arctic air mass is definitely rolling in. Temperature's dropping already. We should get the animals out of here, pronto. Yes, we should get everybody moving." Although he didn't do anything right away—he just stood staring glumly at the rescuers.

"The power's out," I said. "So we should probably transport Mrs. Frost before too long."

"I should break the news to her soon. I need to ask Horace and your father a few things, then I'll take care of it. Randall!" he called, a little louder. "Get the rescue moving again!"

He then took out his phone and punched a few buttons.

"Debbie Ann?" I heard him say. "We have a homicide at the Willimer farm. I want all hands out here, on the double. . . . yes, the tourists will have to mill about on their own for a while. And another thing . . ."

I realized that I was shamelessly eavesdropping. I strolled away before the chief could notice, pulled out my own phone, and glanced at the time. Eight thirty. Unless Rose Noire had been unusually persuasive in begging the boys to let their daddy sleep in, Michael was probably up. I hopped into the Twinmobile, as much for protection against the wind as for privacy, and dialed him.

I was relieved when he answered on the first ring, sounding post-coffee coherent.

"Good morning! You're missing some excellent pancakes. How's the roundup going?"

"It just turned into a murder investigation."

"Oh, God. Hang on."

I heard quick footsteps and could imagine him hurrying out of the pancake-filled kitchen into the hall.

"Is it Haver?"

"No, it's the bootlegger." I gave him the high points of my morning so far. "And Haver's still AWOL, which means he's a suspect, or maybe the chief is just using his absence as a reason to confiscate the gun I found in his dressing room. Any chance you could arrange for someone to meet Aida at the theater, let her in, and show her which dressing room is his?"

"I'll do it myself," he said. "I can be there in twenty minutes or so. I don't want to sound lugubrious, but how certain are they that our bootlegger is the only victim?"

"Not certain at all," I said. "He was buried in the snow, all but one foot. If one of the puppies we're rescuing hadn't gotten loose and started barking at the foot, we probably wouldn't have found him till the snow melted. So yeah, there could be another body out there. I don't have to tell the chief that."

"Let me know if Haver turns up," he said. "Dead or alive."

"And you do the same," I said.

I told Aida that Michael was on his way to the drama building, and she took off—no doubt happy to escape being enlisted to help extract Mrs. Frost from her lair.

I studied the little knot of activity around the body. Dad seemed to be dividing his attention between watching what Horace was doing and scanning the nearby landscape with binoculars. The chief was nowhere in sight.

Randall came to stand beside me.

"The chief inside breaking the news?" I asked.

Randall nodded.

"Please tell me Dad's not birdwatching at the crime scene."

"He's probably watching the volunteers the chief sent in to search the woods."

"In case Willimer's not the only body?"

"Yup." He nodded slowly. "And the chief also had me track down my cousin Dagmar to bring her dog. Lot of woods and pasture out there. We were lucky to find Willimer—if he hadn't fallen the way he did, with one leg sticking up, he'd have been just another lump under the snow. We might not have found him till spring. It's not like the old lady could roll herself out here and look for him."

"Is Dagmar's dog a search-and-rescue dog or a cadaver dog?" I asked.

"Trained for both, so we're covered either way."

We stood there watching for a few moments. The wind was definitely getting fierce and the temperature seemed to be dropping precipitously. Randall shivered, in spite of his heavy coat.

"The chief sent Vern over to talk to Mort Gormley," Randall said. "The sheep farmer who thought Willimer's dogs were killing his flock."

"Does he think Mr. Gormley might have done this?" I asked.

"He can be a hothead."

I found myself fervently hoping that the hotheaded sheep farmer would turn out to be the culprit. Caerphilly could get along with one less sheep farmer, but if Haver turned out to be the killer—I shoved the thought aside. I'd worry about that later.

"Let's hope the dog gets here soon," I said. "Or the search-and-rescue part of its training will be pretty useless."

"Gets here soon and comes up empty-handed," Randall muttered as he took off toward the crime scene.

Chapter 19

I went inside the barn to help with the puppies. The volunteers were nearly finished with the task of sorting out which puppies belonged to which of the eight adult female golden retrievers so they could be transported and then fostered in family groups.

"Most of these puppies look a little young to be separated from their mothers," Clarence was explaining. "So initially we really need eight families willing to take in a mother and her whole litter."

"Is it really that much of a disaster to separate the puppies earlier?" one of the volunteers asked.

Those of us who knew how strongly Clarence felt about this subject groaned inwardly. For the next fifteen minutes or so, as we sorted puppies and loaded them into the crates with their mothers, Clarence gave us chapter and verse on the behavioral issues that could arise from too-early separation from the mother dog, and I amused myself by trying to figure out whether this could account for the behavioral problems of some of my less-than-favorite humans.

At the other end of the barn, Grandfather and two Brigade volunteers were sitting in folding camp chairs watching the tiger. The chimps—two of them—and the four smaller monkeys were sulking in large nearby cages. The finches and the hunting dogs were long gone. But the tiger was still pacing restlessly up and down its tiny cage.

"He'll be a lot happier with all the space he'll have out at the zoo," one of the volunteers said.

"Are you planning on packing him up and taking him there anytime soon?" I asked as I strolled over to join them.

"We're waiting for the tranquilizer darts to take effect," Grandfather replied.

I looked more closely. Yes, protruding from the tiger's hip was a little glass and metal projectile with a festive pink and yellow tip. Another dart lay on the floor of the chain-link cage.

"I still think we should have fed him the tranquilizers," one of the Brigade volunteers said. "Knead it into a couple of pounds of ground sirloin—he wouldn't know what hit him."

"The darts are usually faster," Grandfather said. "Assuming you hit your target properly."

The other volunteer winced. I deduced that he had been the dart shooter.

"I don't think the first one even broke the skin," the first volunteer said.

"We can't be sure," the second volunteer said. "It's a pity he chose that moment to pee all over everything, so we can't tell how much of the tranquilizer's contents went into him and how much dribbled down on the straw."

Grandfather growled in frustration. The tiger, alerted to the nearby presence of a fellow predator, narrowed his eyes and laid back his ears.

"We need to give it a little more time," Grandfather said. "In case the dart did hit him and he's just a slow reactor."

"Look, he stumbled!" The second volunteer was pointing at the tiger. "That's a good sign, right?"

"Meg?" Randall stuck his head into the barn. "Chief's looking for you."

I left Grandfather and the volunteers to their tiger watch.

I saw the chief standing on the front steps of the farm-house, taking deep breaths. Was he only recovering from the stench, or was he also counting to ten, or even twenty, as I knew he did when struggling to keep his temper.

I strolled over to him.

"Any idea how soon we can transport Mrs. Frost?" I asked. "The volunteers are nearly finished with the animals in the barn and they'd like to get started on the cats."

"Soon," he said. "Ms. Flugleman is helping her finish up her packing. I broke the news to her and got confirmation of Mr. Willimer's identity."

"That's good, I guess."

"I may ask your father to see if he can get Dr. Kelleher in to see her," the chief added.

"The shrink? You think she took it that badly?"

"No." He shook his head slowly. "Well, yes and no. One minute she's weeping and wailing over her dear Johnny, and the next minute she's cooing over a cat, and then the cat knocks over a vase and she tells Ms. Flugleman not to worry, Johnny will clean up the pieces. So we break the news to her again and she's inconsolable again. She could have cognitive issues."

"Could have?" I echoed. "One look at that house—or one whiff—and you know she has cognitive issues."

"Good point." He glanced back at the house and shuddered slightly. "I hope we can find some other family members— she certainly isn't capable of taking care of herself out here. She couldn't even get out of the house in an emergency— there are steps at both the front and back doors. They've been here nearly a year—you'd think Willimer could have found the time to build her a ramp."

"Maybe there wasn't anything she wanted to come outside for," I said.

The chief nodded as his eyes swept the landscape. The snow made the weathered buildings prettier, but it did nothing to hide how isolated the run-down farmstead was.

"I'll ask her about family later," the chief said. "I'll have to come by the Inn to interview her again. Every time I tried to ask her what, if anything, she remembers about last night, the waterworks started up. So are you the one taking her and Ms. Flugleman back to town?"

"I want to be there to ease her arrival at the Inn," I said. "Aha—they're backing the big truck up to the barn. They must be ready to move the tiger."

The biggest Shiffley moving truck was carefully backing up to the barn door, with the largest of the cages in its huge freight compartment.

"Move the tiger?" The chief sounded alarmed. "Just how are they going to do that?"

"They shot him with a couple of tranquilizer darts a while back," I explained. "Grandfather must have decided he was finally completely unconscious."

The chief didn't seem to find that entirely reassuring. He set off toward the barn at a quick pace. I trailed along after him.

We reached the barn door and peered in. The door to the tiger's chain-link pen was open. Clarence was sitting by the tiger, listening to its chest with a stethoscope. Grandfather was directing the seven or eight volunteers who were laying out a giant canvas stretcher beside the tiger. The stretcher arranging wasn't going all that smoothly, in part because most of the volunteers couldn't tear their eyes off the tiger and kept tripping over the stretcher and each other.

I could understand. I didn't want to take my eyes off him, and I wasn't in the cage with him.

"That's got it," Grandfather said at last. "Now line up on the other side and put your backs into it."

The volunteers obediently lined up and began trying to roll the sleeping tiger onto the stretcher. At first their combined efforts seemed to do nothing. Perhaps they were afraid if they pushed too hard they'd wake him. Or perhaps they didn't realize at first how hard it would be to move the dead weight of an unconscious animal. But then gradually his body began to move, little by little, until they had him on the stretcher.

"Okay—grab that stretcher!" Grandfather called. All eight of them grabbed one or another of the stretcher poles and heaved the sleeping beast into the air. Then they made their slow way to the truck. As he rolled, the dart stuck in his flank came into view, and Clarence carefully plucked it out.

"Just slide the stretcher in," Grandfather said. "No need to take him off the stretcher. If he's still unconscious when we reach the zoo, we can carry him off on it, and if he wakes up, he'll bounce out under his own steam once we open the door."

The volunteers set down the stretcher and scampered very briskly out of the cage. Clarence and Grandfather swung the cage door closed, and they both double-checked to make sure the locks were closed tight.

When they finished, Grandfather pulled out his cell phone, looked at it, and frowned.

"Damn," he said. "Still no word from Ruiz."

"Your Fish and Wildlife contact?" I asked.

"Yes. Well, he does spend a lot of time undercover. He'll call when he can. Let's get this big boy out to the zoo." He went to climb into Clarence's van.

"Can you take charge of the rescue while I'm gone?" Clarence asked Randall.

"No problem." Randall grinned. "It's only the cats left now, and ever since they elected me mayor I've become an expert cat herder."

"When we get the tiger settled, I'll call to see if you're still rounding up all his smaller cousins or if I should just meet them over at Meg and Michael's barn."

Randall nodded, and waved as first the van and then the truck carrying the tiger rumbled slowly across the farmyard and headed for the lane.

"Meg!"

I turned to find Meredith standing in the doorway.

Chapter 20

I braced myself for some new complication, then relaxed again when I saw that Meredith was smiling broadly.

"I think Mrs. Frost is ready now," she called. "But we need to carry her down."

"As long as he's been here, you'd think Willmer could be bothered building a ramp," Randall said. "Duane! Come help me carry the little old lady and her wheelchair."

Duane seemed to be one of Randall's larger cousins—not that any of them were small, but Duane was not only tall but uncharacteristically bulky. As they were going inside, another pickup truck arrived. A woman was driving, and from the two lab heads, one yellow and one black, peering out the windshield from the passenger seat, I deduced she was Dagmar with the search-and-rescue dogs.

Dagmar jumped out, immediately followed by the black dog. The yellow lab, whose muzzle was actually more silver than golden, took Dagmar's place in the driver's seat and watched with a wistful expression as the younger dog threw herself into the snow and joyfully rolled in it.

"That's my old girl, Peaches," Dagmar said, seeing me looking at the yellow lab. She reached out to scratch the dog's head through the open door. Peaches thumped her tail happily on the seat. "She's retired now, but she pines if I leave her at home when Piper and I go out."

"But she doesn't get to have any of the fun," I pointed out.

"Yeah, she will." She smiled. "I always bring along some training materials, so I'll have something for the dogs to find and be rewarded for if the search comes up empty. She'll get her share." She scanned the horizon. "Kind of hope we do come up empty on this one. We already have one dead body too many, and anyone who's still alive out there under all that snow could be in a very bad way by now."

I was hoping to stay and watch the search, but just then Meredith emerged from the house carrying two small, battered suitcases. She took them over and put them in the Twinmobile. Then she stepped a few paces away, pulled out her cell phone, and made a call. Randall's cousin Duane emerged from the house carrying Mrs. Frost, while Randall followed with the wheelchair. I wished Dagmar good luck and went inside to collect Ronnie's cat carrier.

"Oh, thank you," Mrs. Frost said, as we helped her get settled in the front passenger seat. "This is very nice. Do you have many children?"

Did the van look that bad?

"Only two," I said. "Twin ten-year-old boys."

"Oh, how nice. Twins run in my family, too. I was always hoping that Johnny and Becky would have twins when they got around to having kids, but they never did. Get around to it, that is. And now that I've lost them both . . ." Her voice trailed off and she applied a damp tissue to her nose.

"All buckled up?" Meredith chirped, as she tested my seat belt and Mrs. Frost's before buckling up her own. "Rather tight quarters in this row," she said, giving Ronnie's carrier a shove. He responded with an irritable hiss.

"Sorry," I said. "The suitcases and the wheelchair take up most of the cargo area."

"I'll manage." She assumed a look of noble martyrdom.

"Is this going to take long?" Mrs. Frost asked.

By the time I started the Twinmobile I was already looking forward to depositing them both at the Inn.

"So," Meredith began. "Did you have snow like this where you were living before you came to Caerphilly?"

"Snow's snow." Mrs. Frost frowned out the side window at it. "What's so special about this snow?"

"I think what she meant was 'where were you and your son living before you came here—was it someplace that gets as much snow as Caerphilly?'"

Meredith glared at me but Mrs. Frost didn't appear to take offense.

"Son-in-law, actually," she said. "I'm sorry—didn't I explain that? I forget sometimes that people don't know. And I've been talking to so many different people today."

"So Mr. Willimer—Johnny—is your son-in-law?" Meredith asked.

"Yes." Mrs. Frost settled back with a nostalgic look in her eye. "Only my son-in-law, but like a son to me—I practically raised him. He's also—well, before he and Becky got married, I used to call him my nephew, but once they got together that sounded so hillbilly, so I gave him the proper term—first cousin once removed. Which meant he and Becky were only second cousins—nothing wrong with that, is there? And my cousin Deedee—his mother—lived just down the street, and we were close, so he was in and out of my house all the time growing up. Why I remember . . ."

Mrs. Frost rattled on, wandering from stories about Johnny's boyhood to the details of their intertwined family tree. And then on to fond memories of bygone church potluck suppers. I didn't quite tune her out entirely—I had to follow along enough to make the right kind of noises to punctuate her monologue. The sad "oh, dear" when commiseration seemed in order. The encouraging "oh, yes," when agreement was called for. The mildly astonished "really?" when she revealed something she thought would astonish us. It was a familiar feeling. I had aunts like her. And first cousins once or twice removed that I referred to as aunts because that's what you called everyone in your mother's generation. The accent was slightly different—a mountain twang instead of a soft Tidewater drawl—but the rhythm was the same. I could play my part quite well and still have plenty of brain cells left over to do some thinking.

Although I tried to pay enough attention to pick up on any place-names she might mention. The fact that they attended the First Baptist Church didn't help much, because I knew there were at least a dozen of those in Virginia alone. The fact that she mentioned going "up" to Blacksburg for her granddaddy's cataract surgery probably meant that their previous home was south of Blacksburg, and in the western part of the state—but I could have guessed that from her accent.

Meredith, meanwhile, appeared to have decided that being in the back seat meant she was off duty as far as interacting with Mrs. Frost was concerned. She sat silently with a pinched look on her face and her eyes closed, except for her frequent glances down at her phone. Was she expecting an important text or email? Or just checking to see how much time had passed. I had already decided that if she uttered the fateful words "Are we nearly there yet?" I would offer her the opportunity to stretch her legs.

But she managed to hold her tongue until we pulled up at the entrance to the Caerphilly Inn. Before I even shut the engine off, Ekaterina's tall, model-thin form appeared, as if by magic—although I knew there was actually nothing supernatural about her ability to greet guests. She'd had sensors and a security camera installed just inside the entrance to the Inn's mile-long driveway. She was accompanied by two bellmen and an elegant brass luggage cart.

"Welcome to the Caerphilly Inn," she said, opening Mrs. Frost's car door.

I introduced Mrs. Frost, and then let Ekaterina take over. While the bellman whisked the two well-worn suitcases upstairs, along with Ronnie and his litter box, Ekaterina helped settle Mrs. Frost in her wheelchair and took her on a short tour of the ground floor. Mrs. Frost didn't seem very impressed—you'd think she'd been staying in five-star hotels all her life.

I marveled, as I always did, at how the Inn had managed to create such a festive holiday atmosphere without being too heavy handed. Hints of cinnamon and evergreen potpourri teased the senses rather than bludgeoning them. The omnipresent Christmas carols were soft, lush, and definitely relegated to the background. I spotted candles, red velvet, metallic gold, and fragrant greenery, but they accented the existing décor rather than completely obscuring it. And were most of the decorations antique, imported, or just plain expensive—or did I only assume they were because they were in the Inn?

The only thing that seemed to impress Mrs. Frost was the hotel restaurant. More specifically, its bar.

"Do they make those frozen drinks with the little paper parasols?" she asked.

"Of course," Ekaterina said. "And you can even order one from room service if you don't feel up to coming downstairs."

I wondered if room service normally did this, or if Ekaterina would be arranging it to keep Mrs. Frost from appearing in the bar. She didn't look all that bad, but she did waft a slight but noticeable odor of cat pee. Or maybe it only seemed slight to me because I'd been in her house.

In due course we delivered her to her room, where her two shabby little suitcases were laid out on matching brass luggage stands. Ronnie's cat carrier and his litter box were neatly aligned along the other wall, and a home health care aide was awaiting our arrival. I mentally gave Meredith points for efficiency.

"I'm not sure I want someone underfoot all the time." Mrs. Frost frowned at the aide.

"Oh, she's just here to help you get settled," Meredith said. "And if you get along, we can arrange for her to come in the morning and the evening, for an hour or so, to help you with dressing and grooming."

"Well, that would be a comfort."

"Would you like a nice hot bath to warm you up after being out in the cold?" the aide asked. "Or do you prefer showers?"

We left Mrs. Frost in the hands of the aide. I breathed a sigh of relief when we finally stepped out into the hallway and watched her room door close behind us.

"I'm not quite ready for that frozen drink with the pink parasol," Meredith said. "But I would kill for a cup of coffee before we go."

"There is a complimentary pot in the lobby," Ekaterina said. "I wanted to show Meg something before you leave—"

"I'll meet you in the lobby, then."

Meredith hurried down the hallway and punched the elevator button with such force that I could easily believe that caffeine deprivation was turning her homicidal.

"Anything important?" I asked Ekaterina when Meredith was out of earshot.

"I just wanted to point out to you that I have placed our new guest in the same corridor as the existing two subjects," she said. "She is in 310, Mr. Haver is in 314, and Mr. O'Manion in 317. I cannot promise to keep any of them under constant observation—the members of my staff do have other responsibilities—but by keeping them in close proximity, we can make our efforts as effective as possible."

"I appreciate it. By the way, Chief Burke will be coming by sometime later today to interview her."

"We will be pleased to see him. Has there been any word of Mr. Haver?"

"No. And since you're asking, I gather you haven't seen him."

"No, but I do have some interesting news about Mr. O'Manion. Who appears to be still sleeping." She glanced at the door of 317 before moving farther down the corridor, gesturing to me to follow her. We stopped near the elevator—I suspected to make sure O'Manion could not eavesdrop on what she was about to say.

"One of my staff members is dating one of the chief's deputies," she said. "Do not ask me which, because I do not wish to get the young man in trouble."

I nodded, and didn't ask which, since I already knew that Sammy Wendell had at least temporarily given up on his long and unrequited infatuation with my cousin Rose Noire and become smitten with the Inn's night desk clerk. Caerphilly was a very small town.

"When Mr. O'Manion returned here at two thirty this morning, he claimed to have gotten stuck in a snowbank while searching for Mr. Haver."

"Sounds plausible," I said.

"Yes, but he said it in front of the deputy," Ekaterina said. "Who happened to be dropping in for coffee—we encourage local law enforcement to partake of our complimentary coffee, especially during the night shift."

Thereby ensuring that the Inn got extra patrols. I didn't begrudge them that, especially since I knew they often threw in complimentary pastries or sandwiches with the coffee, and sometimes even a hot meal on nights like last night.

"When he heard Mr. O'Manion's words, the deputy had difficulty repressing his laughter. Apparently he had observed Mr. O'Manion's car several times during his patrols. It was not stuck in a snowbank. It was parked in front of a certain house in Westlake."

Westlake was the ritzy section of town, full of houses that I'd have called tasteless McMansions if they hadn't been on two- to five-acre lots. Though the size of the lots didn't eliminate the tasteless part.

"Okay, I give up," I said. "What's so funny about him being parked in Westlake instead of a snowbank?"

"The chief has instructed his deputies to keep a close watch on this particular house," Ekaterina said. "They suspect the woman who lives there of being a lady of the evening."

It took me a second to get it.

"You mean a prostitute?" I asked.

"I think nowadays they prefer the term 'sex worker.'"

"Does this mean there's a bordello in Westlake?" At least half of Mother's garden club members were from Westlake. The annoying half.

"Only one young woman," Ekaterina said. "I do not think that amounts to a bordello. And she is very discreet. Sa—the deputy says they have not yet been able to acquire sufficient evidence to take any action."

"Well, I'll be," I said.

"So depending on the time of the murder, Mr. O'Manion may have an alibi," she said. "But I wonder if it is an alibi he will want to make public."

"And there's also the possibility that the alibi may want to disavow any knowledge of him if she's trying to fly under the police radar. Interesting."

"Yes." Ekaterina's smile looked very catlike. "We will continue to observe the situation, and I will keep you posted if I learn anything else."

I thought of suggesting that she keep the chief posted. But then Sammy would do that. And for all I knew, information could well flow not only from Sammy to the Inn, but also the other way round.

"Thanks," I said, and she punched the button to call the elevator.

We had just reached the lobby when my phone rang.

"Meg?" It was Aida. "Where are you? Can you come over to Haver's dressing room? We may have a problem."

Chapter 21

Another problem. I wasn't sure I wanted to hear about another problem. I glanced at the clock over the checkout desk. Only ten thirty, and already I'd been up dealing with one problem after another for four and a half hours.

But that wasn't Aida's fault.

"I'm over at the Inn, just finishing up getting Mrs. Frost settled," I said aloud. "You want to tell me what the problem is, or are you just going to tantalize me?"

"Haver's gun has disappeared. It would be helpful if you could come over and show me if I'm looking in the right place."

"Damn! I'll be right over."

I hung up and turned to Ekaterina. "Could you—" I began.

"Do not worry about Ms. Flugleman," she said. "I will arrange to have her dropped off in town."

I shouted my thanks over my shoulder as I dashed for my car.

I tried to stay within the speed limit on my way to the theater. Just because I was on my way to meet a cop didn't mean her colleagues would cut me any slack if I earned a speeding ticket.

Aida's police cruiser was parked in the ticket pickup zone in front of the theater, and around back there were already a dozen vehicles in the parking lot, even though rehearsal wasn't till noon. I had mixed feelings about that—I very much approved of people showing up early to get in a little more rehearsal time. But we didn't really want a whole lot of witnesses if Aida and I were going to be turning the building inside out, looking for Haver's gun.

When I let myself in the stage door, the lively strains of "Sir Roger de Coverley," greeted me. I could also hear the brisk, rhythmic pounding of sixteen pairs of feet and over all the voice of Gemma, the stage manager, shouting orders.

"Frank, you're lagging behind. Clockwise, Darcy! Ryan, don't swing her that hard; she's a lady, not a sack of meal. Ladies, clap more delicately. Frank, watch it; you're stepping on her feet again."

I paused to watch, just for a moment, as the dancers skipped and twirled through the measures of the old English country dance. I wasn't generally stagestruck, and had declined all of Michael's previous offers to give me nonspeaking bit parts in the plays he directed. But for some reason I passionately envied the actors who got to be part of Fezziwig's ball. I'd filled in often enough, during rehearsals when one or another of the performers was out, that I knew the steps, and if cold or flu felled anyone during the play's run and Michael was looking around for a substitute, I just might volunteer.

The tune came to an end, and the dancers all collapsed in small panting heaps.

"That wasn't bad," Gemma said. "But it wasn't good, either. Grab some water, everyone, and then let's take it from the top."

I left them to it and made my way to the other side of the stage, and then down the shadowy hallway down to the dressing rooms.

The door of Haver's dressing room was open and light spilled out into the corridor.

I found Aida sitting in Haver's dressing table chair, talking on her cell phone. The chair was out of its usual place—a small stepladder stood where it would normally have been, right beneath the hole where Aida had pushed the tile aside.

"Here she is now," she said into the phone. "I'll let you know what we figure out."

"That's where the gun was," I said, pointing to the space in the ceiling. "I suppose you already looked to see if it got pushed back too far from the edge."

"Michael got me the stepladder and we both peered around. With my flashlight. You want to take a look, and see if you notice anything not the same?"

I decided not to point out that since I'd only had the chair, not the ladder, I hadn't actually seen the space above the tiles. I got up, took the flashlight when she handed it to me, and peered uselessly in all directions, seeing nothing but dust bunnies and wiring.

"We also looked in all the other dressing rooms along the hall," Aida said while I was peering. "Just in case you were so tired you got confused about which room you were in when you found it. Which isn't something I can ever imagine you doing, but it's important to dot all your i's, in case whoever we arrest for this gets a sneaky defense attorney who tries to cast aspersions on our police work."

"No offense taken." I climbed down from the ladder. "And no insights to offer. So now what?"

"Can you describe the gun?" She had taken out her notebook and had her pen poised over it.

"It was a semi-automatic." I pulled out my phone and turned it on, figuring it would be more efficient to show her. "I learned that much in Vern's class."

"Anything else?" She sounded impatient.

"It was black. About this long." I held out my hands to indicate the size.

"Do you remember the make or model? Or what caliber it was?"

Was there just a faint trace of irritation in her voice?

"Sorry—I don't remember the make and model," I admitted. "And I couldn't necessarily tell you the caliber if I had it here in front of me." And my phone, dammit, was taking forever to turn on.

She sighed and wrote something in her notebook.

"I confiscated the bullets, if that would help," I said. "I mean the cartridges. They're still in my car."

She looked up and glared at me.

"Why, yes." She sounded slightly annoyed. "The cartridges will definitely help us determine the caliber. Let's go and get them, shall we?"

"And here's the picture I took of the gun before I put it back." I held out my phone, which had finally decided to cooperate. "Will this help?"

"Show me."

When I held up the picture, Aida grabbed my phone out of my hands, whipped out her own phone, and pressed a couple of keys.

"More info about the missing gun. It's a Smith & Wesson M&P twenty-two . . . No, but she took a picture of it with her phone before she put it back. I'll tell her."

She hung up.

"The chief says, 'good job on the picture,' and right now he's wishing you weren't quite so honest and had just taken the gun. Let's go down to your car and get that ammo."

In the hallway, we ran into Michael.

"You want the bad news?" he asked.

"Isn't it customary to offer us the option of hearing the good news first?" I replied.

"I'd have offered the good news if I had any. I'm almost certain the back door was propped open last night."

"Damn those kids," I muttered.

"Show me this door," Aida said. "And what do you mean about the kids?"

"The building's tobacco-free." Michael led the way down the hallway. "Inside, and within five hundred feet of the building. So all the smokers and vapers go out the back door, near the loading dock. And because most of them don't have keys, they're always propping it open so they can get back in without going all the way around to the front. And yeah, as Meg said, mostly kids, because at least around the theater, most of the smokers seem to be kids who haven't yet realized they're not immortal."

"Is Haver a smoker?" Aida asked.

"No, but odds are he's figured out the back door," I said. "If you'd noticed that someone was searching your dressing room and confiscating your booze while you were onstage, you'd probably start keeping it in the trunk of your rental car and sneaking out to the parking lot when you needed a pick-me-up. At least that's what I suspect he's doing."

"Everyone knew about the back door," Michael said. "I must have read them the riot act about it at rehearsal at least once a week. Heck, I did it yesterday."

"Any idea when it was left open?"

"No." Michael shook his head. "I usually check it before I leave the building, but at this stage of the rehearsal period, I usually leave more like ten or eleven than four. There weren't many people still around, thanks to the snow, and I just didn't follow my usual routine."

"Don't blame yourself," I said. "I think I was the last out of the building and it slipped my mind, too."

"So Haver could have snuck in here at any time and retrieved his gun," Aida said.

"Any time after I left the dressing room." I pulled out my phone and checked the time of the call I'd made to tell the police about the gun. "Which would mean any time after four thirty-six."

"It's also possible that someone who saw Haver hide it could have come back and stolen it," Michael pointed out.

"Very possible," Aida said. "Or someone who saw Meg finding it."

"You're giving me the creeps," I said.

"Sorry, but maybe we all should have the creeps. If Haver shows up here, call us." She studied us for a few moments. "So how bad will it be for your play if it turns out Haver is the killer?"

Michael and I looked at each other.

"The show will go on," Michael said. "I can step into Haver's role. But . . ." He shrugged.

"What we don't know is how much Haver's name is helping the box office," I said. "Ticket sales are very good, and it's my theory that his reputation is making only a minor contribution. But I could be wrong. If Haver has to drop out and a whole bunch of people decide to return their tickets, it could be bad."

"Look on the bright side," she said. "If he gets arrested for murder, don't you get a lot of free publicity? Maybe not the best kind of publicity but— Hang on."

Her phone had started ringing. From the all-business expression on her face, I suspected it was the chief on the other end.

"Butler. . . . Roger. Yes, sir—on my way."

She hung up and turned back to us.

"Meg, I have to go. Could you drop those cartridges by the police station? And forward that photo of the gun to the chief? And could someone show me the way back to the door I came in by?"

"My car's right outside this door," I said. "So I'll leave Michael to show you the way out."

I waited until I got into the car to unleash a few words that still lingered in my vocabulary, even though I'd tried to delete them to make sure the boys wouldn't pick them up. Had my stupid qualms about confiscating Haver's gun cost someone his life?

Chapter 22

"It might not even be the murder weapon," I muttered, as I took out my phone and emailed my photos of the wretched gun to the chief. "It's not like there's a shortage of guns in Virginia."

But I was still kicking myself when I arrived at the station. The sight of Kayla decorating the departmental holiday tree cheered me, but only a little.

"I brought the bullets." I set my tote down on the desk and fished in it for the cartridge box.

"Oooh, goodie! I can put them on the tree right now."

"On the tree?" I clutched the box protectively. "I thought the chief wanted them for evidence."

"Are we talking about the silver bullets?"

"No, we're talking about the very utilitarian brass cartridges that might have some connection to the murder weapon." I put the case down on the front desk. "What's this about silver bullets? Are we having a werewolf-themed Christmas tree? Wolfsbane and the mistletoe?"

"We're doing this little tree all in blue and silver." Kayla pointed to a tiny living tree in a sparkly silver pot on the desk. It was festooned with blue lights and silver-colored ornaments with a crime and detection theme—tiny guns, knives, handcuffs, magnifying glasses, and sheriff's badges. "Mom said she thought she could find someone who could spray paint some cartridges silver for us."

"That would be a nice addition," I said. "Be sure and get

Fred to take a picture of it for the *Clarion*'s article on themed Christmas trees."

"That's the plan," Kayla said. "Meanwhile I should fill out the paperwork on this box of cartridges. It'll only take a minute."

The chief walked out, holding a sheet of paper. And his notebook, of course. I sometimes wondered how the police ever found time to patrol, given all the paperwork their jobs seemed to involve.

"Kayla, we need to put out an update to the BOLO for Mr. Gormley," he began. "Sorry—finish what you're doing first." He set down his sheet of paper on her desk.

I tried to look blasé, as if I wasn't excited by the news that he'd put out a BOLO for Mort Gormley. A suspect who wasn't Haver.

The chief strolled over to me.

"Meg, thanks for the pictures of the pistol. Did you happen to glean any information from Mrs. Frost while chauffeuring her to the Inn?"

"She's a fountain of information," I said. "Almost none of it useful. Willimer was both her son-in-law and her first cousin once removed. His wife—which would be her daughter—was named Becky, his mother's name was Deedee, and they attended the First Baptist Church. But I'm not sure any of that is useful. After all, there are dozens if not hundreds of First Baptist Churches in Virginia, and I never did get her to reveal the name of the town they lived in."

"Bear Paw Junction." The chief had been making notes as I spoke. "I did get that much. It's supposed to be in Virginia, although I haven't yet found it on the map."

"Judging by the old lady's accent, I'd be looking in the far southwest tip of the state," I said. "The bit that could just as easily have ended up part of Kentucky or Tennessee."

"I wouldn't know about the accent." Although the chief

had been in Caerphilly longer than I had, he was a Marylander by birth. I suspected he could place any native of Baltimore, city or county, within a few miles or even blocks of his birthplace, but he tended to rely on his deputies and other locals for the subtleties of Virginia history and culture. "But Aida Butler told me she thinks she's gone through this Bear Paw Junction place on her way to visiting relatives down in Knoxville, Tennessee."

"Passed through it?" I echoed. "It's on the Interstate?"

"No, and neither was she. She was taking her great-aunt Venetia, who doesn't ever want to go over thirty-five miles an hour. You pass through some pretty strange little places when Venetia's riding shotgun."

I nodded. I'd been stuck with taking Venetia home from a couple of meetings in Richmond of the Ladies Interfaith Social Services Council, so I could imagine what Aida had gone through hauling her all the way to Knoxville.

"Anyway, a fair piece away from Caerphilly, and not much bigger than a mosquito bite, according to Aida. She only remembered the name because it sent Venetia into such a panic that she saw bears behind every bush for the next hundred miles. I've sent inquiries to a couple of the sheriffs down that way. As soon as we locate the blasted town, we can start figuring out why our victim and Mrs. Frost left it and came here to enrich our lives."

"And whether there's anyone down there who might dislike Mr. Willimer enough to pay him a visit last night?" I suggested.

"That too," the chief agreed. "So, he's her son-in-law rather than her son. I didn't get that much. Of course, come to think of it, she never referred to him as anything but Johnny. I assumed the son part. I don't suppose she mentioned anyone who might have had it in for him? Anyone he'd quarreled with?"

I shook my head.

"How are Dagmar and her dogs getting along?" I asked.

"Meg," Kayla said. "I've finished logging in your box of cartridges. Can you sign this?"

As I was doing so, the front door opened and a middle-aged woman walked in. She was wearing a long, elegant cream-colored down coat and a crocheted hat, glove, and scarf set in off-white with sparkly threads. I decided it was unfair that some people could actually manage to look chic while still dressing appropriately for the weather. Seeing that Kayla was busy with me, the lady nodded and stood politely back, yet near enough to make it obvious that she wasn't just ducking in out of the cold.

"We'll let you know if we have any other questions," the chief said.

"Roger." I stepped aside to let the new arrival take my place at the desk. She nodded pleasantly at me, as if to say thanks. She looked vaguely familiar, and I racked my brain to remember where I knew her from.

"I'm Doris Hammerschmidt," the lady said. "The new owner of the Bluebird House Bed and Breakfast."

Of course. I'd seen her at some of the Christmas in Caerphilly merchant meetings. And I was pretty sure she'd attended a couple of Mother's Garden Society festivities.

"What can I do for you, Mrs. Hammerschmidt?" Kayla asked.

"I'd like to report . . . an intruder?" She sounded as if she wasn't sure of the term.

"A burglar?" The chief stepped forward and took over.

"No, I don't think you could call him a burglar," Mrs. Hammerschmidt said. "A trespasser—that might be the right term. Yes. A trespasser."

She smiled triumphantly, as if by defining her problem she had more than halfway solved it.

"Did this happen last night?" the chief asked.

"No," she said. "Well, it started last night—technically very early this morning. But it's still going on."

The chief blinked.

"The intruder's still there?"

"Yes. He's been there all morning. It was bad enough when he was fast asleep—well, passed out—on my sofa and snoring like a freight train. But then he woke up and began yelling for breakfast as if he were in some kind of tacky diner. I want him gone."

"Kayla, have Debbie Ann see who's available to go over to Mrs. Hammerschmidt's," the chief said. "How did this person get into your bed-and-breakfast in the first place?"

"Two of my guests brought him in," she said. "They found him by the side of the road—his car had broken down—and they brought him back to the bed-and-breakfast so he could— I don't know. Call his friends or family to pick him up, I suppose. Or call a taxi. They left him in my hands. I showed him into the living room and pointed out the phone, and then I had to leave for a moment to get some hot chocolate for a guest who was suffering from insomnia, and when I came back he had passed out on my Hepplewhite couch."

"I see," the chief said, although his expression suggested he wasn't entirely sure he did.

"I tried to wake him, but with no success," Mrs. Hammerschmidt went on. "I assumed he was worn out from his ordeal and . . . well, I thought there was a possibility that he might be a little bit the worse for drink. So I covered him up with an afghan and went to bed."

"That was very kind of you," the chief said. "Although you could have called us to deal with the situation. In fact, you probably should, if something like this ever happens again."

"I will if—but I can't imagine this ever happening again," Mrs. Hammerschmidt said, drawing herself up to her full height and glaring indignantly at him. "Not in *my* bed-and-breakfast. I can't imagine how it happened this time."

"So he went to sleep on your couch," the chief said. "And he's still there."

"Not only is he still there, he woke up at some point in the middle of the night and forced the lock on my liquor cabinet." Mrs. Hammerschmidt quivered with indignation. "He finished off half a bottle of gin and spilled most of a bottle of amontillado on the couch. And then this morning he became unwell."

"Unwell?" the chief repeated. "We can send an ambulance if you think he needs medical assistance."

"He doesn't need medical assistance," Mrs. Hammerschmidt said. "He needs assisting out of my kitchen, where he's eating the breakfast intended for my guests. Becoming unwell all over my antique Aubusson carpet seems to have given him an appetite."

"Did you tell him to leave?"

"Several times."

"And what did he say?"

"That he likes his eggs over easy, and wants real cream for his coffee."

A thought had been growing in my mind.

"Chief," I said. "May I ask Mrs. Hammerschmidt something?"

"Please do," he said. "And Kayla, see if Debbie Ann's found someone who can take the call ASAP."

I reached over to where Kayla had a couple of the pictures of Malcolm Haver the chief had been using to brief his officers. I picked up the top picture and held it out for Mrs. Hammerschmidt's inspection.

"Is this your intruder?"

Chapter 23

"Yes! That's him!" Her voice trembled slightly. "You already know about him? Is he a wanted criminal?"

"No," the chief said.

"Not yet, anyway," I added,

"Merely a missing person," the chief clarified. "For the moment."

"Vern can be there in two minutes," Kayla said.

"Mrs. Hammerschmidt, why don't I accompany you back to your bed-and-breakfast?" The chief offered her his arm. "I can inspect any damages and take a statement from you."

"I don't want to go back until he's gone."

"One of my officers should have him in custody in a few minutes," the chief said. "By the time we get there, he should be on his way back here. Or if he's not, you can wait safely in the car until he's off the premises."

"Well, if he's coming here, I suppose I should leave." Re-assured, Mrs. Hammerschmidt took the chief's arm

"Kayla," the chief said over his shoulder. "Let Vern know exactly who he'll be taking into custody. And make sure he's aware of Aida's latest discovery."

In other words, that the gun I'd found was missing and Haver might be armed. Kayla nodded, and she and I watched as he led Mrs. Hammerschmidt out to her car.

"Good thinking, Meg," Kayla said. "No wonder we couldn't find him anywhere. Do you suppose this will give him an alibi for the murder?"

"Maybe," I said. "We don't yet know the time of the murder. What if he killed Willimer and ran out of gas on his way back to the Caerphilly Inn?"

"Yes," Kayla said. "And it doesn't sound as if anyone was keeping an eye on him after he got to the Bluebird House. What if he was only pretending to be drunk and snuck out to commit the murder?"

"He'd also have to be pretending to have had car trouble," I said. "But yeah, also possible. I like the way you think."

"Just for the record, I am not going to change my major," Kayla said. "No matter how much everyone tells me how good I would be at police work and how wonderful it would be for me to follow in my mother's footsteps and be a third-generation law enforcement officer. I am a music major!"

"Right on," I said.

"Although criminal justice would make a fascinating minor," she added. "Oh! Here's Vern calling. I need to brief him."

I glanced at my phone. Almost noon. Rehearsal was technically due to start any minute, but obviously Haver wasn't going to make it on time. Whether he made it at all would depend on what he had to say when the chief got him back here to the station.

I waited for Kayla to get off the phone.

"Could you do me a favor?" I asked.

"Sure—what?"

"When the chief finishes with Mr. Haver, could you give me a call? I'll need to know whether to pick him up for rehearsal or find him a defense attorney and deliver his jammies to the jail."

"Can do. Good grief."

"What?"

"The update to the BOLO on Mort Gormley." She held up the paper the chief had put on her desk. "Says he may be driving a 1956 Ford F-100 pickup truck. Would something that old even run?"

"Probably not very fast," I said. "And it would certainly stand out on the highway."

"Well, that's good, I suppose. Not much chance of a high-speed chase. The chief hates those."

I laughed, and waved good-bye, since she had already turned to the microphone to send out the updated BOLO. I strolled out to the parking lot. When I got to my car, I called Michael.

"I *do* have both good news and bad news to offer," I announced when he answered the call.

"Go ahead—rub it in."

"The good news is that we've located Haver."

"I'm waiting for the other shoe to drop."

"The bad news is that he probably won't be there in time for rehearsal, and may or may not have an alibi for the murder."

"Damn."

"But all is not lost," I added. "There's at least one other suspect—a neighbor who thinks Willimer's dogs were killing his sheep."

"I'm not sure I like that any better," Michael said. "Especially at this festive time of year, aren't the shepherds supposed to be out abiding in their fields, keeping watch over their flocks by night?"

"Maybe that's what he thought he was doing," I said. "If something attacked one of his sheep again couldn't he have gone in search of the neighbor he suspected of owning a sheep-killing dog?"

"It's possible." He sounded dubious.

"You don't like my theory of the crime?"

"I like any theory of the crime that doesn't end up with one of my cast locked up for it," he said. "Just feeling a little pessimistic. What are you up to next?"

"I'm going home to take a shower, throw the filthy clothes I wore into the House of a Million Cats into the washer, and see how crowded our barn is getting before I head back to the theater. Unless you really need me for anything at rehearsal. Will you be starting late?"

"No, we'll be starting on time, with me doing Haver's role. Just in case we need to do without him permanently. Or as on time as possible, given that some of the cast members might be still shoveling themselves out. But I can do without you for an hour or two. We might be going late tonight. Take a nap. I'll call if I need you."

A nap. Yeah, that sounded enticing.

I pointed the Twinmobile for home.

There were only a few cars parked outside our house, and most of them belonged to Mother's helper bees. Since so many family members were coming to see the opening of the play, she'd gone into decorating overdrive, and the downstairs floor of our house looked more like an upscale Christmas boutique than any place people really lived. The helper bees seemed to be standing around in the front yard arguing about something. I stopped to inquire what the trouble was.

"We spent hours doing the fairy lights," one male helper said. "Draping them over the hedge and the shrubs and the trees and the sheds and the fences and—"

"Yes, I know," I said. "Over everything that didn't run away when you approached it with a string of lights. It looks very nice." It was also so bright outside you could read a book with only the fairy lights on, which made it a little difficult to get the kids to go to sleep on time, but I kept reminding myself that Christmas only came once a year. And only stayed a month. Or possibly two in the years like this one, when Mother got a particularly early start.

"And now all the fairy lights are covered up with snow," the helper said.

"And this idiot wants to knock all the snow off," a woman helper said. "Which will take forever, and won't look that nice when it's done. What's wrong with just leaving the snow? It's just as beautiful as the fairy lights, and when it melts, the fairy lights will still be there."

"Leave the snow," I said. "We like the snow. The boys would be heartbroken if a single flake went away."

The male helper looked glum, but he nodded.

"But hey—the fairy lights are waterproof, right?"

He nodded again.

"Plug some of them in—let's see if you can see them glowing through the snow."

"I never thought of that!" the woman helper exclaimed. "That might look rather nice."

"And unusual," the man said. "We'll test that right away."

They all scurried away, presumably to do the testing. I headed for the barn.

Which looked as if someone was setting up a pet shop there. Someone with a profound fondness for cats and absolutely no notion of what constituted a proper assortment of dogs. Dozens of enormous cat carriers were lined up all along one wall, some of them stacked two or three high, and an undertone of mewing, hissing, growling, and purring filled the room. The golden retrievers occupied the vacant stalls, with the puppies adding their excited high-pitched yipping to the concert.

Mrs. Wiggins, our recently acquired Guernsey cow—named after a character in *Freddie the Detective,* one of the boys' favorite books—was peering over the door of her stall, watching everything that was going on with her usual calm curiosity.

I found Dad and Grandfather in a box stall that seemed to have been set up as a temporary veterinary clinic. They were working on one of the golden retriever puppies. The mother dog was lying in the straw nearby calmly watching, as if she knew her puppies were finally in trustworthy hands. The puppy's littermates—a seemingly improbable number of them, at least eight or nine—were running riot all over the rest of the stall.

"What are you doing to them anyway?" I asked, as the puppy they were holding began yipping in pain or protest.

"Chipping them," Dad said. "Giving them a thorough checkup."

"Collecting stool samples to check for worms," Grandfather added.

"And starting them on their vaccinations," Dad finished. "The chief's search of Willimer's house showed no medical records whatsoever for any of the animals."

"Disgraceful," Grandfather muttered.

"Although fortunately so far, all of the animals are basically healthy." Dad beamed as he announced this. "Some of them a little undernourished, but that will be easy to take care of. I think this little guy is the last of this litter."

We chased puppies around the stall for a few minutes, checking to see that they all had their new collars—each pup within the litter, Dad explained, had a different colored collar, so the foster families could tell them apart. And each collar carried a tag whose number corresponded with the microchip they'd just implanted in the collar's owner. As we collected them we popped them into a large dog carrier in one corner of the stall. As soon as we deposited the first puppy in it, the mother dog rose, took a leisurely stretch, and walked over to the door of the carrier, where she waited patiently for someone to let her in. Clearly she was adjusting well to her new surroundings.

"This batch is ready," Dad said.

"Where's it going?" Grandfather asked.

"Judge Jane, I think. Randall's going to pick them up as soon as we give him a call. Yes, here it is."

Dad and Grandfather were studying a list. I peered over their shoulders and saw that it was a list of people, mostly locals. Some had already been assigned one or more dogs or cats—the animals' chip information was scribbled beside the foster's name, and a few even had check marks in the column marked "Delivered." Most of the other names had notes indicating how many animals they'd agreed to take. A few had a bold "no!" written beside them, and the rest bore question marks—meaning, I assumed, that either they hadn't yet been asked or they hadn't yet made up their minds.

"Yes, that's Jane's batch," Grandfather said.

"That's six litters down and only two to go," Dad said. "Time to do some more cats, I think."

"Bloody cats," Grandfather muttered.

Chapter 24

Dad and Grandfather walked outside the stall and contemplated the wall of cats with expressions that fell far short of enthusiasm. Which was odd—neither of them disliked cats. In fact, Grandfather was fond of remarking, in approving tones, that cats were better survivors than dogs, having retained more of their original wild behavior.

I noticed that the wall of cat cages was divided into two segments, with a four-foot break between them. On the right side of the break, all the cats wore collars and the cages had tags on them. I walked closer and inspected some of the tags, which contained the animal's chip number, a list of the tests and vaccinations and general notes about the observations they'd made during their examination. And most of the cats wore the same expression of indignation and resentment that Mother's cat usually displayed when I brought him back from a visit to Clarence.

The cats to the left of the break were devoid of collars and their cages bore no informative tags, so I decided they were the patients-in-waiting. And at least two-thirds of the cats were on the left side.

No wonder Dad and Grandfather were less enthusiastic about the cats. Most of them were full grown and could do more damage with a single swipe of one paw than an entire litter of fuzzy little puppies could dream of in a lifetime.

"Where's Clarence, anyway?" I tried not to make it sound too much like "why isn't he doing some of this?"

"You just missed him," Grandfather said. "We're running

low on veterinary supplies, so he's driving over to Tappa-hannock to borrow some from a colleague."

"Meg, could you bring over the next cat in line on the left?" Dad said, pointing.

"I'll get the bait," Grandfather said.

Bait? Well, I'd find out soon enough what he meant by that. I picked up the top cat carrier on the last stack on the left, which looked fully large enough to fit Tinkerbell, Rob's Irish wolfhound. But to my relief the carrier contained only a single cat, a large gray tabby with white tuxedo and four white paws. He—or she—didn't like being singled out, and made a futile but persistent effort to get a paw through the holes in the side of the carrier and scratch me.

"Put the carrier down on the floor and we'll expose him to the bait," Grandfather said.

"What do you mean, expose him to the bait?" I asked. "What bait?"

As if to answer, Grandfather held up a small wire cage in which a white mouse was vigorously turning his running wheel. Grandfather then set the cage in front of the still-closed door of the cat carrier.

The gray tabby immediately became transfixed. He pressed his nose to the wire grille in the front of the plastic cage and stared unblinkingly at the mouse, occasionally lashing his tail and uttering soft, throaty noises.

"Reasonably strong response to the prey animal," Grand-father said, nodding with approval while Dad made notes on his clipboard. "Don't worry," he said, noting my frown. "I knew you'd fuss if we brought a mouse into your barn, even if we were planning to keep him in a cage, so I neutered him before I brought him over. They only live about two years, so even if he gets loose he can't possibly cause more than a small, temporary infestation."

"Actually, I was about to ask if that's someone's pet mouse you're traumatizing."

"No, I snagged one of the live mice we keep for the snakes we haven't been able to train to eat their food frozen," Grandfather said. "I've given him a reprieve."

"A permanent one, I hope, considering what you're doing to him."

"Yes, I think so." Grandfather studied the mouse, whose only response to the proximity of the cat was to redouble his running speed. "I did pick him because he seemed less timid than some of the other mice, but he has definitely exceeded my expectations. I'm almost sorry I neutered him. But with his help, I think we can find your friend Muriel an excellent mouser. In fact, so far at least two thirds of these cats show excellent promise as mousers. Should make them easier to place in a rural community."

"So that's what this is all about," I said. "Sorry, Mr. Mouse; I am the cause of all your suffering today."

"He'll be fine," Grandfather said. "I'll give him a really good dinner when we're finished for the day."

"Just as long as he doesn't become someone's dinner," I warned.

"Put him away for now and let's get working on the cat." Dad had donned long padded gloves and something that looked like a fencing mask, and was holding out a similar set of equipment for Grandfather. "Meg, can you get ready to hand me the cat blanket?"

"As long as I can keep my distance." I picked up the blanket Dad was pointing to, which looked as if countless cats' claws had already made a good start at turning it into confetti.

Together Dad and Grandfather extracted the gray tabby from his carrier, wrapped him so that only his head protruded from the tattered blanket and began the arduous task of examining, chipping, and vaccinating him. Even after his claws were safely swaddled he seemed remarkably adept at causing trouble and inflicting damage.

"Clearly, given the large number of cats in her possession,

Mrs. Frost was unable to do much toward socializing any of them," Grandfather said through gritted teeth.

I began to understand why they'd made more progress with the dogs than the cats. I confess, I watched the whole process with fascination. Amazing that an ordinary housecat could wreak so much havoc against two highly trained professionals. As they were finishing up, I went out into the main part of the barn and did a quick count of the cages left. Seventy-four of them.

I wasn't optimistic that we'd make that deadline of having the animals out by tomorrow morning—at this rate, they'd still be chipping and vaccinating on Christmas Day. Maybe even on Easter Sunday. But by the look of it, they were making some progress, and had enough foster prospects to take care of at least three-quarters of the animals. When my deadline arrived, we'd have a lot fewer leftover animals than I'd feared.

"I gather all the wild animals are out at the zoo," I said.

"And doing just fine," Grandfather said. "Although they compound the problem of where to put that big batch of finches if Fish and Wildlife seizes them anytime soon."

"Which reminds me," Dad said. "Has Ruiz called back? That's your grandfather's friend from Fish and Wildlife."

"No." Grandfather shook his head. "Normally he's very quick to respond—especially when I leave him a message about a possible link to a smuggling ring. Of course he does have that big bust going down."

"Or perhaps he's taking a few days off for the holiday," I suggested.

"Laurencio? Hardly." Grandfather shook his head decisively.

I turned to go, and then remembered something.

"I have a question," I announced to Dad and Grandfather. "Does the word 'Weaseltide' mean anything to either of you?"

"Not offhand." Grandfather tested the latch on the gray tabby's carrier. "Is it supposed to?"

I explained about the person who had asked Robyn for permission to hold Weaseltide at Trinity.

"That sounds rather ominous." Grandfather frowned and paused in the act of adjusting the cover on the mouse cage. "I think you need to find out what this Weaseltide is all about."

"That's why I asked you if you'd heard of it," I said.

"Maybe I'm overly suspicious," he went on. "But I would hate for Trinity to enable some kind of weasel hate group."

"Are there organized weasel hate groups?" I asked.

"Groups that have bought into all the negative press that weasels get."

"What negative press?"

"A great many cultures have very negative associations about weasels." He had settled into his lecture mode, and I realized that whether I wanted to or not, I was probably about to learn a great many fun facts about weasels. I reminded myself to be patient—after all, something he said might give me a clue to what Weaseltide was.

"The Native Americans considered the weasel a bad sign," Grandfather proclaimed. "If it crossed your path, you could look forward to a speedy death. In Greek folklore, they're bad luck around weddings, because of an unhappy bride who was transformed into a weasel and enjoys destroying wedding dresses. And in English, calling someone a weasel brands him as untrustworthy. We talk about someone weaseling out of things, or using weasel words. And of course in *The Wind in the Willows,* while Toad is in prison, Toad Hall is overrun by weasels and stoats, and Rat, Mole, and Badger have to help him drive them out."

"In other words, weasels have a gotten an undeserved bad rep," I said.

"Precisely," he said. "They're quite efficient predators, and consume such a highly useful quantity of rodents. And they're fairly intelligent for small mammals."

All very interesting, but it didn't answer my question.

"Weaseltide," Dad murmured. "Are you sure she didn't say Weasel War Dance?"

"Pretty sure," I said. "Weaseltide and Weasel War Dance don't sound at all alike."

"Because a Weasel War Dance would be rather interesting," Dad said. "It's something they do when they've just captured a toy, or stolen an object, or sometimes successfully stalked some kind of prey. Pretty much whenever they're feeling pleased with themselves. They arch their backs, fluff out their tails and hop about, backwards and sideways. Like this."

Dad bent over so his fingertips were almost but not quite touching the ground and began executing a series of rapid hops and jumps—backwards, forwards, and from side to side.

"They also do backflips," Dad said, a little breathlessly. "But I'm not sure I can manage that."

"No, no," Grandfather said. "You can't leave out the dooking." He bent over in imitation of Dad and began his own series of leaps and hops, but accompanied by a loud, high-pitched clucking noises.

"Oh, yes!" Dad exclaimed. "The dooking!" He began to make clucking noises of his own.

They both rather seemed to be enjoying themselves, leaping about, clucking, and occasionally shaking their heads as if worrying some bit of prey.

I was just reaching into my pocket to take out my phone and capture a short video when the barn door opened and Chief Burke walked in.

"Dr. Blake," he began, and then he fell silent, watching the war dance.

Chapter 25

After a few seconds, Grandfather spotted the chief and came to a halt. Dad, who hadn't yet noticed the new arrival, careened into Grandfather and ricocheted off him onto a large (and fortunately empty) dog crate.

The chief and I rushed to make sure Grandfather didn't fall, and that Dad hadn't seriously injured himself in landing on the crate.

"No problem!" Grandfather exclaimed as we steadied him. "Ferrets and weasels can be rather clumsy when they're dancing."

"Evidently," the chief said, as if it made perfect sense.

"That was invigorating," Dad said, pulling out his handkerchief and wiping the shiny top of his bald head.

"I see what you mean about the weasel war dance being interesting," I said. "But I'm afraid I don't quite understand why anyone would rent the parish hall to hold one."

"Then that's what you need to find out," Grandfather said. "Come to pick up your puppy, Chief?"

"We've got the ones that are old enough for adoption corralled in here," Dad said. "Let's bring you a couple to choose from."

They both dashed into my office.

"Weaseltide?" the chief asked.

"Yes," I said. "Still trying to figure out what the heck it is."

"So far, no one on my law enforcement list has any idea," he said. "Sorry."

"I gather by your presence here that you're finished with Mr. Haver?"

"No." He grimaced. "You may gather by my presence here that Mr. Haver's attorney has not yet arrived at the station. I decided to nip out here and snag a likely-looking puppy to foster while I was waiting. See if the grandchildren are ready for a dog." I suspected the grandchildren had been ready for a dog for a while. I was glad to see that the chief, though still mourning the recent loss of his beloved and ancient rescue dog, was considering the idea. "I also wanted to ask your father how soon he thinks he can perform the autopsy."

"You mean he hasn't yet?"

"He's eager to," the chief said with a smile. "But apparently Mr. Willimer was partially frozen, and that complicates things. They have to thaw him very slowly at a steady temperature or bad things happen. Don't ask what bad things—I made that mistake. Evidence could be lost; let's just leave it at that."

"So we don't yet know the time of death."

"We may never know it with the kind of accuracy your father usually prides himself on," the chief said. "Which could mean that all the alibis I'm trying to collect and verify could be relatively useless. About the only thing we do know with any certainty is that the murder weapon was a twenty-two caliber. Your dad did recover a bullet in pretty good shape. We should have no difficulty making a forensic comparison . . . assuming we ever find even a single twenty-two caliber gun with any connection to any of our suspects."

"Haver's gun isn't a twenty-two, then?" I asked.

"Oh, it's a twenty-two, all right. But since it's still missing, we have no way of determining if it fired the fatal bullets."

He looked so gloomy that I wished I could say something to cheer him up or distract him.

"You're making my quest for Weaseltide seem pretty silly," I said. "I'm beginning to think Weaseltide must be something Melisande invented."

"Melisande?"

"Melisande Flanders—or something like that. The person who asked Robyn about Weaseltide. You'd think sooner or later she'd drop back by the church to see if Robyn had made up her mind about hosting her event."

"Melisande Flanders. That sounds familiar."

He pulled out his notebook and began flipping through the pages.

"Here it is. Flanders. Milly Flanders rather than Melisande, but . . ."

"Could be the same person. Milly could be short for Melisande. I know better than to ask you for her contact information, but is there any chance you could contact her? Tell her we're trying to sort out this Weaseltide business? Ask her to call me?"

"You could talk to her yourself," he said. "She's the woman who's been hanging around the stage door all day ever since Haver came to town."

"You mean the Rabid Fan? Melisande Flanders is the Rabid Fan?"

The chief nodded. He couldn't quite keep his mouth from twitching, but at least he didn't burst out laughing.

"Okay, I guess I can talk to her myself," I said.

"In the unlikely event that the snow has caused her to abandon her vigil, you can find her at Niva Shiffley's," the chief said. "One of my officers has been checking all the bed-and-breakfasts in town—long story."

Looking for guests who had suddenly absconded? I'd find out in due time.

"If the Rabid Fan—Melisande—is involved, it stands to reason Weaseltide has something to do with Haver," I mused. "Although damned if I can figure out what."

"The words 'Haver' and 'weasel' do rather fit together in my mind," the chief said. "But I doubt if his fans would feel the same way."

"Nor would Grandfather," I said. "He has a very high opinion of weasels. Thanks—I'm going to talk to her."

"Don't mention it. Oh, and something else I'd appreciate your keeping to yourself—your discovery of Mr. Haver's gun. I want to see what he says when I ask him if he owns a gun."

"My lips are sealed."

Dad and Grandfather emerged from my office, each carrying a brace of adorable golden retriever puppies. They set the puppies into a small pen in the middle of the barn floor—I recognized it as the portable plastic playpen we'd used to corral the boys—or at least slow them down—when they were much smaller. The chief stepped into the pen, squatted down, and picked up the nearest puppy.

"Meg," Dad said. "Do you have time to make a few deliveries?"

"No," I said. And then a thought came to me. "Unless—didn't I see Niva Shiffley on the list to take some cats?"

"Why, yes," Dad said. "She said if we had any long-haired cats, she'd give a couple of them a try. We're optimistic that we'll have a foster fail there," Dad said.

"A foster fail?" the chief repeated.

"When the foster family ends up adopting their charge," I explained.

"Then I hope we have a great many foster fails," the chief said with a laugh. From the look on his face as he played with the puppies, I suspect he was contemplating one himself.

"So do we all," I said. "Okay, Dad. Wrap up your two most adorable long-haired cats for Niva, and I'll take them—I need to drop by there anyway. And then I have to go over to the theater for a while."

Dad hurried off and returned with a cat carrier whose two hissing occupants seemed less than thrilled to be confined together. But instead of taking off immediately, I hauled the carrier inside and put it in the front hall while I ran upstairs to take the long, hot shower I'd been fantasizing about. I felt lighter when I finished, as if I'd washed pounds of cat pee and dander down the drain.

I wished I had time for the nap Michael had suggested. But it was already one o'clock. Rehearsal would have been going on without me. Not that Michael needed me there every second, but there were things I needed to get done. Maybe after I delivered Niva's cats. . . .

Coming downstairs I ran into Rose Noire. She was smudged with flour and smears of chocolate, which lifted my spirits almost as much as a nap would have, since it meant she had been baking.

"Meg, I know the rehearsals are off limits to everyone except cast and crew and invited guests—"

I felt a pang of guilt, and prepared to apologize for not inviting her already.

"But I was wondering—if I take the boys to rehearsal, can I stay and watch for a bit?"

"Of course," I said. "But why aren't they at rehearsal now?"

"Michael's doing a kid-free run-through first," she said. "He doesn't want to overtire them. Child actors are to report at three."

"Good idea," I said. "And if you really want to watch, no problem. I'd have invited you already if I'd known you were interested."

"Oh, I didn't want to see it until it was almost ready," she said. "But I figure it must be fairly close to ready if you're opening tomorrow."

"God, I hope so," I muttered.

"Another thing—there's a potluck supper tonight at Trinity."

"Which happens to coincide with the actual dress rehearsal."

"And you and Michael will be working hard all through it, I know," she said. "So if I stay and watch rehearsal, when it comes time for the boys' dinner break—I assume they will

get one—I could take them over to the church just long
enough to fuel them up and then bring them back for the
dress rehearsal."

"That would be fabulous," I said. "Speaking of the boys—"

"Napping," she said.

"How did you manage that?"

"I told them if they didn't nap, I wouldn't try to talk you
into letting them go to the potluck, and what's more they'd
probably have to leave rehearsal before the rest of the cast
because of their bedtimes."

"And that worked?"

"It might not have," she admitted. "But then I took them
sledding for a couple of hours and wore them out. That's why
I'm getting such a late start on my baking for the potluck."

"You're a genius, and I will get out of your hair and let you
bake in peace." As I hurried out to my car, I reminded myself how fortunate Michael and I were to have Rose Noire
still occupying yet another of our many extra rooms. And
uttered a small prayer that it would take her a few more years
to decide which of her many admirers she wanted to settle
down with.

As I drove back to town with Christmas music playing
softly on the radio, occasional low growls emerged from the
carrier. Once, when we were nearly at the bed-and-breakfast,
open combat broke out. I pounded on the carrier until the
two subsided into irritated growls again and they remained
quiet until I parked in front of our destination.

"Behave yourselves," I told the cats as I hauled their carrier out of the passenger seat. "I just might be about to crack
the riddle of Weaseltide."

Chapter 26

Niva Shiffley's bed-and-breakfast was a huge three-story Victorian house that had started life as the Methodist parsonage, back in the late nineteenth century. She'd been one of the first people to see the potential in her cousin Randall's efforts to increase tourism in Caerphilly, and had scraped together enough money to buy the house and convert it from a warren of run-down student apartments into a showplace.

And she'd had the good sense to hire Mother as her decorator, and give her a free hand to turn the place into a high Victorian fantasy. They'd outdone themselves this year with the Christmas decorations. An enormous Christmas tree completely filled the front window, so covered with decorations that you almost had to take it on faith that there was evergreen underneath. And while the decorations were all reproductions, they had been carefully aged until they had the patina of antiques that had been handed down for generations. I knew this for sure because I was one of the people Mother had drafted to help out with the rush aging job when Niva had complained that the tree looked too new.

I set the cat crate down and gazed through the windows for a few moments, admiring my handiwork and pondering the fact that Melisande Flanders was staying here. Learning this didn't exactly make me revise my opinion of our rabid fan, but it did make me a lot more curious about her. Niva's bed-and-breakfast wasn't cheap. People didn't stay here because they couldn't afford the Inn—they stayed here because they preferred Victorian luxury to its modern and

more institutional cousin. And maybe because they wanted
to be within easy walking distance of the heart of the festival.
If Melisande really was staying here she wasn't just a rabid
fan, she was an affluent one.

Time to see what Niva had to say.

I rang the old-fashioned Victorian twist doorbell and
picked up the cat crate again.

"Merry Christmas, Meg! Come and warm yourself!" Niva
was dressed in a high-necked velvet gown with a starched
lace collar—not quite a Victorian costume, but definitely intended to suggest the era. She flung the door wide and mo-
tioned me in with vigorous, almost frantic gestures, as if a
blizzard were raging outside and I were in dire need of a cup
of wassail. "What can I do for you?"

"I come bearing cats," I said. "Long-haired ones. Clarence
said you'd be willing to foster a couple."

"Ooh!" Niva peered into the carrier. To my relief, the cats
just stared back at her instead of hissing or spitting. "Let's
take them into the parlor and have a look."

The parlor—I'd have said living room, but to each his
own—was also decorated to the hilt. Several trees' worth of
evergreen with red velvet bows draped the mantel, the chair
rail, the window sills, and the crown molding. And Victorian
toys were piled not only under the tree but in the corners
and on the tables and just about anywhere else she and Mother
could find a few square inches of space. Old-fashioned dolls
in dainty, lace-trimmed gowns. Carved and painted wooden
animals—dogs, cats, horses, and even elephants. A Victorian-
era bicycle with an enormous front wheel leaned in one corner. A brightly painted rocking horse posed in another.
Miniature drums and trumpets were scattered about. On
the mantel were several jack-in-the boxes, including one
whose jack bore a curious resemblance to the widowed Queen
Victoria. Regiments of painted toy soldiers marched across
the sideboard, and a long line of tiny animals waited patiently

to board a wooden Noah's ark by the hearth. And there were enough tops, hoops, balls, building blocks, alphabet blocks, yo-yos, checkerboards, and mechanical metal banks to fill a hundred stockings.

While I was gawking at the scenery, Niva had opened the crate door and was extracting the first of the cats.

"What a beautiful kitty you are!" she exclaimed as she reached in and lifted out what looked like a limp pale gray fur stole.

I'd have gone for "what an enormous kitty you are!" myself—the thing must have been three feet long, and twenty-five pounds if it was an ounce. But to my relief, it didn't claw or yowl—it just looked back unblinking as Niva cooed over it.

"Rowr?" The other cat, no doubt feeling ignored, stuck its head out of the crate and looked around. Two more different cats would be hard to imagine. The second cat, though also long-haired, was a mere puff of black fur—only a kitten. While the gray cat lolled contentedly in its new human's arms, the black kitten skittered across the soft oriental carpet and pounced on one of the dolls.

I winced, but Niva seemed undisturbed.

"You are a caution, aren't you?" she said to the kitten. "Here, hold this one for a moment."

She handed me the gray cat—I upped my estimate of its weight to thirty pounds—and went to chase the kitten. The gray cat and I eyed each other, and it made no protest when I gently deposited it into a large, shallow cat basket sitting to one side of the hearth. At least I hoped it was a cat basket— why else would anyone have that large a wicker basket sitting around empty save for a cushion on the bottom? The gray cat sniffed it suspiciously then, apparently satisfied, carefully settled its considerable bulk more comfortably on the cushion and appeared to go to sleep.

Meanwhile Niva was chuckling as she tried to extract the

leg of a vintage stuffed bear from the kitten's sharp little claws and teeth.

"Yes, I think these two will do nicely," she said. "I do hope you're not really expecting to get them back."

"If you're serious, you can handle the adoption paperwork with Clarence," I said. "I'd give him a few days until he sorts out all the fostering."

"Can do."

"And that will give you time to see if you really want him or her." The kitten, deprived of his stuffed bear, had gone after Niva's dangling earrings and had snagged his claws in her lace collar.

"Oh, don't worry. He—hmmm." She abruptly flipped the kitten over, inspected his hindquarters, and nodded matter-of-factly as she turned him right-side up again. "Yes, he. He's just a kitten. He'll settle down. And they'll both bring a little life to the place. Amuse the guests."

"Speaking of guests, you have a Ms. Flanders saying here."

"Yes—Melisande Flanders—Milly for short."

"Is she in?"

"For the moment. She doesn't spend much time here."

"If it's the person I'm thinking of, she spends most of her time over at the theater."

"That's the one." She glanced over her shoulder as if to make sure Ms. Flanders wasn't in the hallway. "You should see what she's done to my blue room." She'd damped down her normally hearty voice to a mere murmur. "Turned it into a shrine for that actor. The one who's appearing in Michael's play. I almost had a cow when I first saw it—posters all over the walls! But she was very considerate, really—no tape on the walls or anything destructive like that. She hung all the posters with strings from curtain rods or sprinkler heads. It's obviously not the first time she's done this to a rented room. Well, it takes all kinds, doesn't it?"

"Do you think I could talk to her?"

"She hasn't shown her face yet this morning," Niva said. "Not surprising, considering how late she came in last night. Nearly three o'clock!"

"And woke you up, evidently."

"I can't rightly say she did. I was up and down all night, worrying about the storm. She came in real quiet-like—can't complain about that. But what with hearing the snowplows going by, and worrying about whether the guests who were leaving would be able to get away, and whether the ones due in might cancel—well, I was up and worrying most of the night. Lord, I hope tonight's guests don't need anything after dinner, because I'm already dead on my feet."

Suddenly she switched back into hearty hostess mode.

"Good morning!" She beamed at someone over my shoulder. "Milly, wait till you see the cats Meg brought me. Are you hungry? It's past our usual breakfast service time, but everything's out of whack with this snow. I could whip you up something."

"No thanks." Milly/Melisande was standing a few steps from the bottom of the stairway. She was already wearing her coat and hat, and was pulling on her gloves. "I'm heading out."

"Be careful," Niva said. "The roads will be slippery."

"It's okay," Melisande said. "I'm walking."

"If you're going to the theater now, I could give you a ride," I offered. "I'm going that way anyway, and it's beastly cold out there."

"They say we're going to have a high of eleven today," Niva exclaimed. And the wind chill's below zero."

"Well—thank you," Melisande said.

Niva showered us with admonitions to stay warm and safe on our way out, and waved as we climbed into the Twinmobile.

I was just starting the engine when the phone rang. The caller ID showed the police station.

"I should take this," I said, turning the engine off again. "What's up?" I said into the phone.

"The chief is releasing Mr. Haver," Kayla said. "At least for the time being. He has no idea where his car is, and it's probably buried under the snow anyway. Any chance you could pick him up? Or should I call him a cab?"

"Tell Mr. Haver I'd be happy to take him to the theater." I watched Melisande's eyes light up. "I'm only a few blocks away, so it should only take me a few minutes."

"Oh, my," Melisande said, as I started the car again. "I've never gone anywhere with Malcolm before. But are you sure it will be okay?"

"If he's having one of his fits of artistic temperament, you can wait at the police station, and I'll circle back and get you as soon as I've dropped him off."

"I hate to put you to all that trouble."

"You wouldn't be the one putting me to trouble," I said. "And I appreciate your flexibility."

Haver was pacing up and down the stretch of sidewalk in front of the front door of the police station when I pulled up. He didn't object to Melisande's presence—I wasn't even sure he noticed her. He stomped up to the back door of the Twinmobile and hopped in.

"What took you so long?" he said. "I was freezing out there."

"You could have waited inside," I pointed out. "I'd have come in to find you."

"I didn't want to spend another second in durance vile," he said. "They've had some squalid little murder at the far end of the county, so of course they're looking to pin it on the outsider."

"Doesn't look as if they're trying all that hard to pin it on you," I said. "After all, they let you go pretty quickly."

"Because my lawyer pointed out that they have neither a time of death nor a weapon, and that I am alibied for most of the evening. To say nothing of the fact that they cannot come up with a plausible motive for me to kill a man I barely knew."

Knowing the chief, I thought it a lot more probable that he was turning Haver loose only to lull him into a false sense of complacency. And maybe to give him scope to do something to incriminate himself.

"I expect as soon as rehearsal starts they'll march in with their jackboots and haul me off for another round of the third degree."

"Ridiculous!" Melisande burst out. "I know perfectly well that you couldn't have done this—and I'm sure all your fans will be outraged. We believe in you, even if the police don't. We'll organize a demonstration."

"Not necessary, my dear," Haver said. "Not yet, anyway," he added in an undertone. "But that was an experience! I shall have to use these emotions in my performance! 'I have almost forgot the taste of fears. / The time has been, my senses would have cool'd / To hear a night-shriek; and my fell of hair / Would at a dismal treatise rouse, and stir, / As life were in't.'"

Macbeth, I noted, as he continued to soliloquize the whole way back to the theater. *Macbeth* gave way to *Hamlet* and eventually to *Richard III.* I more than half suspected that his lawyer had ordered him to say as little as possible in the interrogation room and he was babbling to relieve the unaccustomed stress of having to be silent. Ah, well. Melisande was enchanted, and I was just as happy not to have to make conversation with him.

When we got to the theater, the lights were on in the box office in the lobby, so I pulled up to the front steps. Haver generally preferred going in the building that way whenever possible—it made for a grander entrance.

To my surprise, after hopping out of the back seat of the Twinmobile, Haver opened Melisande's door with a dramatic bow. She sat frozen.

"Oh, I couldn't," she murmured. "I just usually wait by the stage door."

"And it's much too cold for that today," Haver said. "You should come in to keep warm, and watch the rehearsal. If you sit quietly in the back, no one will mind."

She looked at me.

"If it's okay with Mr. Haver, it will be fine with Michael," I said. "Go on."

I paused for a moment, watching her float up the broad marble steps on Haver's arm. I hoped his gracious mood lasted at least a little while. And that he snarled at someone other than her when what I'd come to think of as the real Haver emerged.

Chapter 27

"She's been a fan for over three decades," I muttered as I drove around to the back to park. "If he hasn't managed to disillusion her in all that time, I doubt if he'll do it today." And there was nothing I could do about it if he did. I parked my car, and slipped in through the back door. Which was propped open again. I confiscated the bit of wood someone had put in it as a doorstop and added an item to my notebook to research alarms for the door, and meanwhile to put up a stern sign.

Two o'clock. If things were going well, they might already have finished the first run-through. Probably better if they hadn't. Michael could just step aside and let Haver take over. Haver often managed to disappear before the fifth act, and it had probably been a while since he'd done the fourth or the fifth wholly sober.

In the corridors, I ran into O'Manion. He seemed to be coming from Haver's dressing room.

"Where the hell do the local cops get off, arresting my client?" he said.

"They haven't arrested him," I said. "They were questioning him. He was one of the last people to see the murder victim alive."

"Says who!"

"Says me," I snapped back. "Shortly after we talked yesterday I followed him from here to the farm where the murder subsequently took place and watched him buy alcohol from the man who was later killed."

O'Manion blinked, and it was a good ten seconds before he found his tongue again.

"That doesn't mean Malcolm killed him," he said. "Ridiculous." But he said it with much less conviction.

"You were out looking for him till very late, I heard," I said. "A pity you didn't find him."

"A pity, yes," O'Manion said. "Not only didn't I find him, I got stuck in a snowbank."

"You too?" I said. "The same thing happened to Mr. Haver."

"Yes, although I managed to dig myself out. Took several hours, and by the time I was finished, I just went back to the hotel to get out of my wet clothes and warm up."

Not quite the story Sammy had told. And Sammy's story might well be confirmed by other deputies, or by the Shiffleys driving the snowplows. I wondered if the chief had talked to O'Manion yet.

"And then I was awakened by a call from Malcolm, demanding that I find him a defense attorney," O'Manion went on.

"And you found him one with admirable speed," I said.

"I already had some names," he said. "Something I do for all my clients when they're making any kind of protracted stay in a strange place, incidentally," he added, seeing the look on my face. "Because I know how much prejudice there is in small towns against outsiders, and particularly actors. And my list also includes a dentist, a dry cleaner, and an all-night pizza delivery in towns civilized enough to have one. Do you know you don't even have a Starbucks in this godforsaken place?"

"I'm sorry you're not getting any pleasure out of your visit to Caerphilly," I said. "But maybe things will pick up soon."

He gave me a sharp look—perhaps a guilty conscience was making him wonder if there was a double meaning in my words. A guilty conscience or just a well-developed sense of propriety?

"You know the police impounded Malcolm's rental car," he said.

"No, but I'm pleased to hear it," I said. "He doesn't need a car."

"Is that why the owner of the rental agency isn't returning my phone calls?" he asked. "Have you got him in on the plot along with all the bars and liquor stores?"

"No, but it's a small town. He probably knows all about the murder. Maybe he's squeamish about the possibility of having one of his cars used by someone who might stash a body in the trunk."

"And he's the only agency in town."

I nodded.

"I could call one of the big chains and have them deliver a car," O'Manion said. "Or I could let him use my car."

"That's your prerogative," I said. "If you really want to undermine our efforts to keep him sober so he can go onstage tomorrow night."

"You want to be the one to tell all this to Malcolm?" he asked.

"I'd be happy to. The sober companion we've hired is on his way here—he should be here by the time rehearsal is over. He can drive Mr. Haver anywhere he needs to go. To and from rehearsals. To and from meals, if Mr. Haver chooses to eat someplace other than the Inn. On personal errands. Anywhere we actually want him to be able to go."

"He won't like it."

"He doesn't have to like it. He just has to put up with it until the play is over."

O'Manion shook his head, and his anxious face suggested he might be just a little afraid of his client.

"You did tell him about the sober companion, didn't you?" I asked.

"I did. He told me to . . . he expressed his distaste for the idea."

We stood looking at each other for a few moments.

"He's your client—maybe even a friend—after all, you've been together for what—forty years?"

O'Manion nodded. I wasn't sure if he was agreeing to the friend part or just the forty years.

"Help us help him," I said. "Or if you can't or won't help, just don't get in our way."

He closed his eyes and nodded. Then he opened his eyes again and shook himself.

"I'm going to watch the rehearsal." He strode off toward the stage.

I went around and made my entrance through one of the doors the audience would use.

To my relief, rehearsal had begun, and Melisande was sitting quietly in the very back row. She was beaming with delight, so I gathered Haver had held fire while in her company.

"I'm so excited!" she whispered. "Thank you—I owe this to you. And I promise I'll stay back here and be quiet as a mouse."

"If it's okay with Mr. Haver it's fine with me," I said. "Just remember that if his mood changes—"

"Of course!" she said. "The minute he says he wants his creative space, I'll leave."

Creative space? More likely he'd tell us to get her the hell out of here. But I kept the thought to myself.

I turned my attention to the stage where Michael and Haver were sorting out some tricky bit of blocking. Haver's owlish solemnity suggested he might not be entirely sober, but at least he was, for the moment, here, vertical, and cooperative.

I wondered if the presence of Mr. O'Manion, now sitting in the front row with folded arms, had anything to do with it.

Melisande and I watched in silence for a few minutes. At least she was watching. I was focused more on coming up with a suitably subtle way to ask her about Weaseltide. But before I'd come up with anything she leaned over and whispered to me again.

"Do you know if the college ever lets people use any of their rooms for community events?"

Bingo!

"They've been known to on occasion," I said. "You generally have to go through the proper bureaucratic channels, of course, and it helps to know someone at the college. What's the event?"

"Well, a lot of Haverers are coming to town for opening night," she began.

"Haverers?"

"That's what we call ourselves—Malcolm's most devoted fans. I'm the one who thought that up." She actually simpered as she said it. "And don't believe anyone who tells you otherwise. And we'd like to have a little party together. The landlady at my bed-and-breakfast is very nice, but I can tell she really wouldn't like the idea of having it in my room— and she's probably right, we do stay up late and get a little silly. And it's such a small room that there might not be room for all of us. I remember at Worldcon one year we had over two hundred people! Of course, that was when the show was still running in prime time—a lot of people seem to lose interest after a show goes off the air."

She frowned, and shook her head slightly as if the fickleness of these former fans both saddened and puzzled her.

And the show had been off the air for nearly thirty-five years. To me, the puzzling thing was not that some fans had fallen by the wayside but that any had remained so devoted.

"I asked at the Inn, but like most hotels, they wouldn't let us bring our own food in, and their prices were astronomical, and they weren't exactly encouraging."

I tried for a moment to imagine her dealing with Ekaterina and shuddered at the thought.

"So I've been asking around town, and I haven't had much luck," she said.

"You asked at the Episcopal church, didn't you?"

"Yes, but they never got back to me."

"Probably because you never really explained what you wanted," I said. "Although the fact that you didn't leave them a phone number or an email might also have something to do with it."

"Oh!" Her hands flew to her mouth. "I didn't—but I thought. Oh, goodness. Yes, I probably did forget to give the minister my number. I was so nervous, and she was so . . . imposing."

Imposing? I'd heard Robyn called many things. Deeply spiritual. A fierce advocate for the underdog. A passionate crusader for peace and justice. An inspiring preacher, an excellent organizer, and a serious contender in town's unofficial contest for best maker of chocolate chip cookies. But imposing? She was about as imposing as Niva's new kitten.

"Did she really not understand?" Melisande asked.

"All you said was that you wanted to hold a Weaseltide celebration," I said. "At least that's what she thought you said—maybe she misunderstood you. And if you tried to explain it—"

"Oh, dear," she moaned. "Did I do that again? Yes, Weaseltide is what we call our little celebrations."

"Not that it's any of my business—but it's an odd sort of name. Where did it come from?"

"From an episode of *Dauntless Crusader*," Melisande explained. "Episode thirteen of season two, called 'The Lady in the Lake.' Sir Tristan—that was Malcolm's character—Sir Tristan was supposed to guard a group of nuns who are going on a pilgrimage, and one of them turns out to be the widow of a man he served with in the crusades, and she wants to meet him alone so he can tell her what really happened to her husband. Do you remember the actress who played

Sue Ellen on *Dallas*? J. R. Ewing's wife? She was—but you don't want to hear about that, I'm sure. Anyway, at one point in the evening Malcolm bows and says, 'My lady, I will meet you in the herb garden at eventide.' Only for some reason it came out garbled, and 'eventide' sounded more like 'wea-seltide.' So that's what we started calling our little gatherings. Weaseltide."

I found myself wondering if Haver's alcohol problem dated back to his years on *Dauntless Crusader*.

"I wish you'd explained that to Robyn," I said. "The rector. I have no idea if she'd agree, even if the parish hall is free—"

"Oh, and could you tell her it's really a very quiet gathering?" Melisande said. "We absolutely forbid any alcoholic beverages, because we all know about Malcolm's struggles over the years, and if he should decide to come—which he doesn't usually, but we always try to let him know that we would love to have him! We usually do a potluck dinner, with soft drinks and iced tea, and if we can get a television and a VCR we might watch a few favorite episodes—they've never come out on DVD, more's the pity, although Lady Constance, one of our members, keeps saying she's going to convert them to DVD but she never has. And sometimes we read fanfic aloud, or have a trivia contest. But mostly we just get together and reminisce and enjoy each other's company. We've all known each other for thirty-five years now."

"I'll tell Robyn," I said, "and see what she says."

We watched the rehearsal in silence for a minute or two.

"Tell me," she asked. "Is it true that the man who was murdered out at that farm was the one who was supplying Malcolm with drink?"

My, how word gets around.

"It looks that way."

"Good riddance, then."

Chapter 28

I turned to glance at her, startled by the degree of anger in her tone. She glanced up at me.

"Oh, I know it's a terrible thing to say about another human being—but he was poisoning Malcolm. He's always struggled bravely with all the difficulties that come along with having a creative personality. I'm not glad that awful man is dead, but I'm glad he's out of Malcolm's life."

She turned back to watching the rehearsal, and I made a mental note to share this conversation with the chief.

"You're welcome to come to the Weaseltide celebration if you'd like," she said after a few moments. "Of course you're probably already very busy opening night."

"I'll keep it in mind," I said.

"If there is an opening night for Malcolm," she said softly.

On stage, Michael and Haver were having a discussion. Not an argument, but clearly they were disagreeing over something. But politely. Maybe Haver didn't need a minder. Maybe he just needed his agent in the front row, staring daggers at him.

But then I glanced over at Melisande, her face wore a look of naked hatred.

I had a bad feeling about this. Even if Melisande hadn't killed Willimer, she was not playing with a full deck, mentally speaking. She wasn't just a fan; she was a fanatic, in the truest sense of the word. And right now this arguably unbalanced woman was glaring daggers at my husband, just because he was having a small disagreement with her idol.

I decided to see what I could do to defuse her anger.

"I do hope Michael doesn't have to go in to argue with the college authorities again," I said. "So far he's been able to convince them to keep Mr. Haver in the play, but you know how bureaucrats are. Absolutely no understanding of the creative mind."

She seemed to digest that for a moment, looking back at the stage with a puzzled frown.

"Bureaucrats." She shook her head in commiseration. "They're the ones trying to get rid of Malcolm?"

"And Michael's fighting it," I said. "That's why he steps in whenever Malcolm doesn't feel up to rehearsing. That way it's just the director filling in. If the college bureaucrats got their way they would force him to hire an official understudy, who could very easily turn into a replacement—well, we don't want that, do we? And Michael's decided to hire someone to help Mr. Haver." Actually, he didn't know he'd decided this yet, but I'd tell him about it as soon as I got a chance.

"Help Malcolm? How?"

"Someone to be with him all the time, and make sure he chooses positive ways of coping with the pressure," I said.

"A sober companion." Melisande nodded. "That's a good idea. He always hates it when they do that to him, but it makes it so much easier for him to work."

Okay, maybe she wasn't completely out of touch with reality. And why was I surprised that we weren't the only group to have considered a minder for Haver?

"If only someone had warned us," I said. "We'd have had someone with him from day one."

"Probably his agent's fault." Now her steely glance was aimed at the agent.

"Maybe," I said. "But he's doing his best now. Helping Michael fight the bureaucrats."

She nodded, her expression suggesting that she'd given O'Manion at least a temporary reprieve.

Should I follow this up with a complaint that the bureaucrats in question had all gone out of town for the holidays? If she did turn out to be the killer—or a killer—I didn't want her targeting random members of the college administration.

"But all's well for now," I said. "The sober companion should be here soon—possibly by the time rehearsal's over, and it should be clear sailing from now on."

Which was as close as I could come to saying "please, if you killed John Willimer in some misguided attempt to help Malcolm Haver get sober, you can stand down now."

"Well, I still need to talk to the police," she said. "To tell them I can alibi Malcolm."

"Alibi him? How?"

"I was at the Caerphilly Inn, making another attempt to see if I could cut a deal with them to rent a party room there," she said. "And just as I was leaving, I saw Malcolm drive away. So I jumped into my car and caught up with him. I followed him to a house in a really fancy part of town. He parked there and went in. I waited for a while. In fact, quite a while—I didn't mind, because I had my iPad and I could read a book. The snow was really coming down, but I wasn't too worried, because the plows kept coming by regularly, but still, I was just about to give up and go back to my bed-and-breakfast when he came out. I followed him back to the Inn, and then after he went inside, I went back to the bed-and-breakfast."

I pondered this for a while. It didn't match up at all with what we'd learned from Mrs. Hammerschmidt. But it was the chief's job to sort that out, not mine. Though I did ask one question.

"I don't suppose you happened to notice the time during any of this."

She frowned slightly.

"I can't be sure of the time I left the Inn," she said. "Maybe eight? Or maybe even later. Although I'm sure the lady manager at the Inn could tell you. She's very . . . Teutonic, isn't she?"

"Slavic, not Teutonic." I hoped she wouldn't say that to Ekaterina's face. I remembered her telling me that her grandfather had died in the Battle of Kursk—or was it the Battle of Kharkov?—so I didn't think she'd appreciate being mistaken for German. "But yes, she's very efficient."

"Anyway I know he left to go back to his hotel at one forty-five," she said. "I remember it distinctly, because I was wondering if my landlady would be upset with me for coming in so late, and just then Malcolm got in his car and took off. And I have the address, too—I'm sure whoever Malcolm was visiting can confirm his alibi." She rattled off an address that I recognized as being in Westlake. I jotted it down in my notebook.

"Unless the person he was visiting is the person who is supplying him with Demon Rum," she said. "That was the main reason I didn't want to leave until he did. I thought perhaps if he was driving erratically, I could try to get him to pull over so I could take him back to the hotel. But his driving was perfectly fine, I'm relieved to say."

"I'm sure the chief will find your information very interesting," I said. She smiled, and returned to watching the rehearsal.

"Got to go," I said as I stood up. "Work to do."

She barely acknowledged my departure. The run-through had begun again, and she had eyes only for Haver.

I paused at the door and looked back. The anger had left her features and she was once more happy and enthralled. I'd seen looks like that on my sons' faces—less often, as they grew older. Watching a favorite movie. Awaiting the opening of the ice-cream maker. Contemplating the loot they'd gathered from trick-or-treating.

I pulled out my phone and sent a quick text to Robyn.

"Mystery solved," I said. "Weaseltide = a gathering of Malcolm Haver's fan club. Seems mostly harmless."

I was about to put my phone back in my pocket, but Robyn texted back almost immediately.

"We can probably fit them in the afternoon of your opening night. Let's talk tomorrow. Got to go—camels running amuck."

I was glad I knew that the camels in question were the six teenagers who'd been recruited to don hairy costumes and shamble down the nave in the wake of the wise men during the pageant. I tucked my phone away and hurried down to the costume shop where, as I hoped, I found Mother conferring with one of her costume crew minions.

"I think we're just going to have to make another one," she said. "Meg, do you have any idea how Mr. Haver is managing to ruin his nightgowns so quickly?"

I was about to shudder and disavow any knowledge of Haver's nightwear when I realized she was holding up one of the ornate Victorian nightgowns Haver wore during his nocturnal expeditions with the three Christmas ghosts. Running down the left front of it was a large stain. Startling for the moment, but thanks to all of Dad's dinner table talk of gruesome crimes and medical misadventures, I knew that a moderately fresh bloodstain would be reddish brown, not the purple-red I saw on the nightgown.

"Red wine, do you think?" Mother asked.

"Looks more like beet juice," I said. "I have no idea why he would be drooling beet juice on himself while in costume, but the next time I search his dressing room I'll keep an eye out for the stuff and confiscate it. By the way, have you found a minder for him? Actually, I guess we should say a sober companion—I found out that's the official name for what we want."

"Your cousin Maximilian should be here this evening," she said. "Luckily, he's between jobs—though he isn't all that fond of working as a sober companion. He prefers personal protection assignments—much less stressful."

"I'm glad you talked him into it, then. Thanks."

"You're welcome, dear." And then she turned back to her minion. "I really think we will have to make at least one spare. Would you be an angel and get that going? I'm going to consult my stain expert to see if there's any way to treat this, but if it really is beet juice, it could be rather hard to get out."

I left them to their consultations and took the elevator up to the floor with Michael's office. There I used his computer to print a stern warning sign that I could put on the back door. Then, once I'd tucked it into my tote, I leaned back in Michael's desk chair and called the chief.

Chapter 29

"You will be delighted to know that thanks to you, I now know what Weaseltide is," I said when I had him on the line. "It's a gathering of Haverers. Which is what Malcolm Haver's most avid fans call themselves. Apparently a bunch of them are coming to see the show on opening night and want to have a party afterward. Or beforehand. Melisande was a little vague on the details."

"Dear Lord," he murmured. "Do you have any idea how many of these . . . Haverers we should be expecting?"

"No idea. To hear Melisande talk, quite a bunch, but I wonder if she's overly optimistic. I mean, after thirty-five years, how many people are really going to be that gung ho? And in case you're worried, they don't sound like a particularly wild bunch. I expect they're mostly women in their fifties or sixties, and according to Melisande, their idea of a high old time is drinking soft drinks while watching old VHS tapes of his television show. Robyn's probably going to give them the green light to have their celebration in the parish hall."

"The world is a curious place. I should probably talk to this Ms. Flanders."

"And she's eager to talk to you," I said. "She claims she can alibi Haver. Apparently she shares our concern over his tippling, and was out doing some surveillance of her own during last night's snowstorm." I related the gist of my conversation.

"That's interesting."

"Yeah, very interesting," I said. "Considering that what we

already know about Haver's movements last night bears no resemblance to her story. He didn't come back to the Inn at all, he stayed at the Bluebird. And for that matter, he took off from the Inn a lot earlier than eight or nine o'clock."

"They're positive?"

"They were on high alert. Checked his room every hour or so. So even if he snuck out of Mrs. Hammerschmidt's bed-and-breakfast, he didn't go back to the Inn. But in case you're worried, I didn't tell her that I already knew her story was a complete crock. I figured you'd want to do that."

"I appreciate your restraint."

"Of course, it's possible that she's not really lying."

The silence on the other end of the phone seemed to suggest that the chief was thinking this over.

"I'm not sure I follow you," he said finally.

"Haver and O'Manion are both driving silver Honda Accords from Van Shiffley."

"You think she followed the wrong car?"

"It's possible, isn't it?"

"Wouldn't she have noticed that it wasn't Haver getting into the car?"

"Maybe she only spotted the car from a distance and assumed it was Haver's," I said. "It was after dark, and in the snow. Or maybe she left the Inn following Haver, lost him, and thought she'd found his car again when she'd actually run across O'Manion."

"Clearly I will need to check out both those possibilities. Thank you."

"Then again, I'm not sure how that theory fits in with what the staff at the Inn have to say," I went on.

"And that is?"

"That O'Manion spent most of the evening with a . . . lady of the evening."

Silence on the other end. A rather long silence. Knowing the chief, I found myself wondering if he were blushing.

"Did your fan indicate the address at which she was ob-serving what she believed was Mr. Haver's car?" he asked finally.

"Yeah," I said. "An address in Westlake." Hadn't he heard that part? I wasn't fond of Westlake—most of its residents were snooty and pretentious. But if I were thinking of setting up shop as a prostitute, I didn't think I'd pick Westlake.

"Yes," the chief said. "And the address was?"

Now this was interesting. Maybe I was wrong about West-lake's potential for harboring a den of iniquity. I opened up my notebook and read him the address. The chief sighed slightly.

"And you heard this from?"

"Staff gossip." I didn't want to get Sammy in trouble, so I added, "Some of them were trying to help out with the search for Haver."

Which wasn't entirely a lie. They were helping, by search-ing both the building and the grounds repeatedly. But if the chief got the impression they had been prowling the streets of the town . . . "Keep this to yourself," he said finally.

"Do you mean there actually is a prostitute in Westlake?"

"We have received anonymous reports to that effect," he said. "We have no solid evidence to indicate that this is so. We do have some indication of . . . difficult interpersonal relationships between some of the residents."

"I've had neighbors I wasn't fond of, but I didn't call the cops and accuse them of being hookers," I said. "So you think it's just a nasty rumor?"

"It's possible," he said. "And also possible that some of the residents disapprove of the degree to which a recently di-vorced neighbor may be enjoying her newly single status. For the moment, the important thing is that my deputies have been keeping a very close eye on that part of Westlake, and their duty logs may contain evidence that corroborates or casts doubt on the alibis some of these witnesses will be giving me."

"But in the meantime, I should shut up about all of this so I don't mess up your investigation."

"I would appreciate your discretion, yes."

After we hung up, I grabbed a couple of strips of tape for the sign. I locked up Michael's office again and headed downstairs to post the sign on the inside of the back door. Then I went into the theater and stood near the back, watching the rehearsal.

Up on stage they'd reached the scene where Scrooge and the Ghost of Christmas Past eavesdropped as the twenty-something Scrooge got his walking papers from Belle, his one-time fiancée.

"Another idol has displaced me; and if it can cheer and comfort you in time to come, as I would have tried to do, I have no just cause to grieve."

"What idol has displaced you?"

"A golden one."

Haver was in one of what I called his torpid moods, appearing to zone out whenever he didn't have any lines of his own, as if nothing of the slightest interest could happen onstage if he wasn't speaking. Which was annoying, but actually preferable to his scene-stealing moods, when he'd react so dramatically to anything the other actors said or did that the audience couldn't focus on anything but him. And both very different from what Michael would have been doing—he had an uncanny ability to take the audience's attention and direct it wherever it should be at any given point of the play. I wasn't sure if there was even a name for it—maybe it was just called being a team player—but whatever it was, Haver either didn't have it or didn't often bother to use it.

But he came alive again when his next line came round, and made you feel the pathos of Scrooge's ordeal.

"Spirit! Show me no more! Conduct me home. Why do you delight to torture me?"

"One shadow more!"

"No more. I don't wish to see it. Show me no more!"

Just then I felt my phone buzzing in my pocket. I was tempted to ignore it—why couldn't the world let me enjoy just one scene in peace?

But it wasn't in my nature to ignore a ringing phone. I stepped out into the lobby and answered it.

"Hello?" My guarded tone probably didn't sound too welcoming.

"Meg? Meg Langslow?"

"Speaking. Who's this?" I realized I probably sounded rather brusque, so I softened my tone. "And how can I help you?"

"Um . . . this is Manoj? At the zoo?"

He sounded unsure of his own name. Then I remembered him.

"Hi, Manoj. You head up the aviary, right?"

"Yes, although we are short-staffed today, and I am the senior keeper on duty. Do you know how we can find Dr. Blake? There is a situation that is urgently needing his attention."

"I don't know offhand, but I can try to round him up. What's the problem?"

"There is a man here from the U.S. Fish and Wildlife Services who is trying to confiscate the new animals."

Chapter 30

"Confiscate the new animals?" I repeated "On what grounds?"

"He says they are important evidence in an animal smuggling ring he is investigating. He is threatening me with all kinds of legal problems if I do not hand over the tiger and the apes and the finches. Charging me with illegal possession of a wild animal."

"You're a zookeeper, for heaven's sake." I said. "Wild animals are your job. What does the jerk think you keep in the zoo—parakeets?"

"I have no wish to defy the United States government," Manoj said. "But I have even less wish to disobey your grandfather."

Nice to know he had his priorities straight.

"Look, tell him you don't have the authority to release the animals, but you are making every effort to find someone who does," I said. "I'll send up a few flares and track down Grandfather."

"Flares? What good will flares do?"

I was remembering Manoj now. Very earnest, and very literal-minded. But a good keeper.

"That was a metaphor," I said. "What I am actually going to do is tell everyone I can think of to tell everyone they think of that Grandfather is urgently needed at the zoo. The grapevine should track him down pretty quickly."

"That would be excellent." He still sounded anxious. "I only hope I can hold the fort until he arrives."

"Want me to come out and give you some moral support?" I said.

"I would be forever grateful!"

I hurried downstairs, left word with the stage manager where I was going, and dashed out the back door to the parking lot. But before I started the car a thought came to me. I dialed the police station and asked to be put through to the chief.

"Something important?" the chief asked when he got on the line. His tone suggested that it had better be.

"Remember that officious Fish and Wildlife agent who was sniffing around here a few days ago?"

"I do."

"Pretty sure he's out at the zoo right now, trying to confiscate the animals we confiscated this morning."

"On what grounds?"

"No idea," I said. "Grandfather's not there, and Manoj, the acting duty keeper, is very young and more than a little spooked by the whole thing. I'm heading out there to provide moral support."

"Good! Point out to this overreaching bureaucrat that the animals there were confiscated during a duly authorized animal welfare investigation and entrusted to the care of a certified wildlife rehabilitator."

"Roger."

"And moreover that they are potential evidence in an ongoing homicide investigation!"

"I think I'm going to enjoy this moral support thing." I didn't try to hide the laughter in my tone.

"Meanwhile I will put out a BOLO on your grandfather and dispatch an officer to assist you in your efforts to preserve the chain of custody on my evidence."

"Perfect," I said. "Thanks."

I felt so much better after my conversation with the chief that I turned on my radio so I could sing along with Christ-

mas carols on my way out to the zoo. The college radio station, normally my favorite, was having one of their Christmas
carol request days, but even the knowledge that someone
within the station's tiny broadcast area had called in a request for Justin Bieber's "Mistletoe" didn't bring me down. I
just changed channels to the other local station, which, to
my delight, was playing the Mediæval Bæbes' *Mistletoe and
Wine* album.

I was humming along with "A Coventry Carol" when I
pulled up at the zoo's main gate. A truck was parked right
in front of the gate, in the fire lane. Not an official government truck—a large, nondescript panel truck whose muddy
green top coat of paint was peeling off to reveal that it had
once been dark brown. The license plate was so dirty that it
was unreadable from more than a couple of feet away.

I parked directly behind the truck and snapped a couple
of pictures of it before I got out of my car. And then a quick
shot of the license plate on my way past.

I saw only a few tourists, and those seemed to be hurrying from one indoor exhibit to another. But given the sub-
freezing temperatures, I was amazed to see any tourists at
all. I suspected the special holiday season "Animals of the
Bible" exhibit was working its magic, since the few visitors I
saw all seemed to be carrying the special little guidebook
that let you check off all seventy-four creatures on exhibit,
in a kind of zoological scavenger hunt. No doubt by the
time the exhibit closed, Grandfather would have convinced
himself that it was all his idea instead of Caroline's, and
would be planning an even grander number of animals for
next year.

Still, right now it was probably a good thing attendance
was low. Just inside the front gate I found Manoj arguing
with a tall, burly man in faded jeans and a camouflage hunting jacket that he almost certainly couldn't zip over his sub-
stantial potbelly. Well, Grandfather had mentioned that the

Fish and Wildlife agents did a lot of undercover work. Still—I wasn't impressed.

"I'm telling you, I have no authority to release so much as a garter snake!" Manoj was saying, quite loudly. The agent was standing very close to him, and Manoj only came up to his chin. I could tell he was nervous, but he wasn't retreating.

Actually, he couldn't easily retreat—his back was against the wall of the administration building. Two other keepers were lurking nearby, but obviously trying to keep out of the agent's way.

"Hey, Manoj," I said. "How's it going?"

"Hello, Meg!" Manoj looked delighted to see me. The agent turned and scowled at me.

"Are you the person who's authorized to sign off on the transfer of my animals?" he asked.

Someone needed lessons in charm and tact. "My animals" indeed.

"I just came to meet with Dr. Blake," I said. "He's not here yet?"

Manoj shook his head.

"Meg Langslow." I held out my hand, and after a beat, he took it. His hand was flabby and sweaty.

"U.S. Fish and Wildlife Service," he said. "How much more time am I going to have to waste in this godforsaken hick town before you people get with the program?"

"Yeah, we must seem pretty slow to you important government officials," I said. "Speaking of which—mind if I ask for some ID?"

He glared at me as if my request was unbelievably stupid. Then he reached into his pocket, pulled out something and held it in front of my eyes for a couple of seconds. Yes, it seemed like a Fish and Wildlife photo ID badge, but his fingers obscured most of the name and a good bit of the photo.

"Now let's get this show on the road. I gave Manuel here the paperwork. What's the holdup?"

"We cannot release any animals without approval from Dr. Blake," Manoj said.

"You're also going to need a release from the chief of police," came a voice from behind me.

We all turned to see Aida standing in the gateway. Aida was an impressive figure at any time in her well-tailored deputy's uniform. At five ten, she was as tall as me, but on her it looked even taller. And when you added in her stern expression, her alert stance, and the way her right hand rested near her gun—if I were a bad guy, I wouldn't stick around. Even an undercover Fish and Wildlife agent should be reasonably impressed.

"Sir, those animals are evidence not only in a local animal cruelty investigation but also in an ongoing homicide investigation," Aida said. "I think you'll find that the homicide case takes precedence over whatever you're planning to do with them."

"This is preposterous," the agent exclaimed. "I'm going to report this to my superiors."

He gave up looming over poor Manoj and headed for the exit.

"You people are going to find out what it means to mess with the feds," he said, as he strode through the gate.

Aida followed him. I scurried to keep up with her, and Manoj and the two other keepers followed suit, though they remained inside the gate peering out. Interesting. Aida had driven into the driveway the wrong way, through the exit. Her car was parked diagonally in a way that blocked the whole road, and so close to the truck that he was effectively trapped between her cruiser and the Twinmobile.

"You've blocked me in," the agent snarled. "Move your stupid car."

"I need to see some ID first, sir." Aida might have looked relaxed, but we'd taken martial arts classes together. I could recognize her ready stance when I saw it.

"I'm not going to stand for police intimidation!" the agent shouted.

"No one's trying to intimidate you, sir," Aida said. "I just need to see your ID."

The agent took out his photo ID and tried to pull the same thing he'd done to me—flash it in front of her for a few seconds, then tuck it away again. She snatched it out of his hand.

"Hey!" He grabbed at the ID, but Aida had taken a couple of steps back.

"Stay where you are, Mr.—" She glanced down at the license. "Ruiz."

"Ruiz?" I muttered. I'd heard that name before.

Aida shot me a quick warning glance and I realized she wanted me to shut up.

And I remembered who Ruiz was—Laurencio Ruiz, Grandfather's friend in the U.S. Fish and Wildlife Service. Hard to imagine Grandfather tolerating, much less befriending, a jerk like this.

"This seems to be in order, Mr. Ruiz," Aida said.

I bit my tongue. In order my eye! Was this sniveling creep actually a friend of Grandfather's? Or was he impersonating the real Ruiz?

"Don't think I won't report this harassment," he muttered.

"That's your prerogative, sir," Aida said. "Just one question. You want to explain to me how a dead body over in the Clay County morgue happens to be wearing your fingerprints?"

The fake Ruiz made a break for it. Aida pulled her gun, but Manoj and the other two zookeepers sprinted after him, so she holstered it again and she and I joined in the chase. Fortunately the zoo staffers were a lot younger and faster than the imposter, and probably had a lot of experience subduing escaping wildlife of all sorts.

"Meg," Aida said as she handcuffed the imposter. "You mind calling the chief and letting him know we have the guy? I'm going to be busy for a few minutes arresting him and Mirandizing him and seeing if I can figure out who he really is. I'll call him when I've done that."

I figured Aida would be safe—not only was the fake Ruiz handcuffed, but one of the keepers had run back into the zoo and returned to stand over the prisoner, armed with a stun gun and one of the long sticks they used for handling poisonous snakes. I strolled a few yards away and called the station.

"Aida has the guy," I said. "So the dead guy in Clay County is the real Agent Ruiz?"

"Yes," the chief said. "Apparently AFIS had no difficulty finding a match for the partial prints Horace took—and there was a flag on the file to notify Fish and Wildlife if they got any queries about him. There wasn't a BOLO out, because he was working undercover—infiltrating a particularly vicious gang of smugglers. He'd missed a check-in, but apparently that happens sometimes, and they didn't want to blow his cover."

"So does this tie in with your murder case?" I asked.

"Quite probably. Laurencio Ruiz was almost certainly killed by someone in the smuggling ring he was investigating. Our search of Mr. Willimer's house turned up no documents to provide any clue to where he got the exotic animals we seized. Maybe he was part of the ring, or maybe he bought animals from them for resale. We don't know yet, but I expect it will turn out that our fake Ruiz or one of his criminal associates killed Willimer for some reason connected with the smuggling operation."

"That could be complicated to figure out," I said.

"It could." Curiously, the chief didn't seem to find that discouraging. "But it looks as if we'll have a lot of help figuring it out. Genuine Fish and Wildlife agents are already on their way here, along with FBI agents, DEA agents, ATF agents—the smugglers have diversified into all kinds of illicit substances. Yes, before long we'll have every kind of federal agent you can think of underfoot."

"Doesn't sound like fun," I said.

"No," he agreed. "But they should be willing and able to provide all the resources I need to get my murder solved. I can live with the federal invasion if it gets me that."

"Aida's trying to figure out who the imposter really is," I said. "She'll call you when she has that. Or maybe just bring him in."

"Thanks."

After we hung up, I realized that, like the chief, I was suddenly feeling rather . . . *cheerful* wasn't quite the word. After all, Laurencio Ruiz was dead—a good man, doing important and dangerous work. And a friend of Grandfather's.

Maybe *optimistic* was the word for what I felt. Not just because the chief was close to solving Willimer's murder— although that was certainly something to celebrate. But if the fake Ruiz and his nasty animal smuggling ring had killed Willimer, then everyone connected with *A Christmas Carol* was innocent. Haver, O'Manion, Melisande—they might be annoying, uncooperative, or even crazy, but they weren't killers. And the chief probably felt much the same at the thought that the killer wasn't local.

But my feeling of optimism faded a little when I spotted Dad's car racing up the lane toward the zoo. He pulled up just behind me, blocking what was left of the fire lane in front of the zoo, and he and Grandfather leaped out.

Chapter 31

"What in blue blazes is happening?" Grandfather demanded. "Chief Burke said I was needed over at the zoo to keep someone from stealing the new animals."

"Does he look familiar?" I asked, pointing at the imposter, who was now upright, being escorted to Aida's police cruiser.

"Never saw the blighter in my life."

"He's claiming to be Laurencio Ruiz."

"Nonsense." He glared at the imposter. Then his face fell. "Does this have anything to do with Ruiz not getting back to me?"

"Dad," I asked. "Did you happen to take a picture of that John Doe you and Horace examined over in Clay County?"

Dad looked stricken for a moment, then nodded. I knew he would have. Like me, Dad had gotten into the very twenty-first-century habit of snapping a cell phone picture of anything he thought might later be useful. He pulled out his phone and began pushing buttons.

"This is going to be bad news, isn't it," Grandfather murmured.

Dad held up the phone. Grandfather looked at the screen and nodded.

"Yes. That's Laurencio. Damn."

We all stood in silence for a few minutes. And then we watched as Aida loaded the imposter into her cruiser.

I decided it would be a good thing to distract Grandfather.

"So enlighten me," I said. "Why would this smuggler guy

even try to steal back the animals? Was he stupid enough to think we'd let him get away with it?"

"Criminals are often rather stupid," Dad said.

"And greedy," Grandfather added. "I expect it was greed that motivated him."

"Were the animals that valuable?"

"Oh, yes," Grandfather said. "Between the chimps, the ocelot, and the tiger, and the Gouldian finches that have become so inexplicably popular lately—well, black market prices fluctuate wildly, but I expect he could get anywhere from fifty thousand to two hundred thousand for them. Worth a little risk, I should think. Especially if the tiger turns out to be what I think it is. Come on, I'll show you."

"It's not just a tiger?" I muttered as I followed him and Dad at a near run to the tiger's new quarters.

The tiger was inside, sulking in the warm tropical atmosphere of a small enclosure in the big cat house. Nearby, in the large main enclosure, Tiberius, Livia, and Vipsania prowled restlessly and seemed less than enchanted to have a new resident.

"Notice the difference between him and the others," Grandfather said. "The narrower skull, the longer muzzle, the rhomboid stripes, and that bright orange color."

Yes, he did look a bit different, though I wouldn't have noticed if he hadn't pointed it out. Or if I'd noticed, I'd have assumed the differences were typical of an adolescent tiger.

"I'm not sure yet, but I think he could be a South China tiger," Grandfather said.

"And that's rare?" I asked.

"All tigers are rare," Grandfather said. "But the South China tiger is functionally extinct in the wild. There are thought to be less than a hundred of them in captivity. So if this smuggling ring Laurencio was trying to infiltrate has got hold of one of them—this could be enormous."

Dad and Grandfather seemed to have settled in to contemplate their rare tiger for the time being. I decided it was time for me to get back to the theater.

"I was trying to decide whether to name him Nero or Caracalla," Grandfather was saying as I headed for the door. "But then I realized—why am I naming all the tigers after villains? From now on, I'm giving them heroes' names."

"Good plan," Dad said.

"And I think I'll call this fellow Laurencio."

Grandfather wasn't looking my way, but I gave his idea a thumbs-up anyway.

Time for me to get back to the theater. Rehearsal would have started. And although I could contribute little or nothing to what was actually happening onstage, the closer we came to opening night the more little practical problems arose offstage to distract Michael. Those I could deal with just as well as he could. Often better. Time to leave crime solving to the chief.

I was halfway to the theater when my phone rang. I glanced over at the seat where I'd tossed it. Ekaterina. I was tempted to let it go to voice mail and call her when I got to the theater. But if something dire was happening, I wanted to know.

I grabbed the phone and answered it as I steered my car into the nearest place where the snowplows had created a little bit of a shoulder.

"In the last few days I think I've talked to you more than to my husband," I said. "What's up?"

"Meg, do you know if there was a reason for the police to confiscate the bird?"

"Bird?" My brain drew a blank for a moment. "You mean Haver's finch? Not that I know of. Is it missing?"

"Yes. Mrs. Frost is hysterical."

"Mrs. Frost?" Something didn't add up. "Why would she be upset? For that matter, why would she even know it was missing?"

"Apologies," Ekaterina said, "I omitted to give you the

necessary context. You recall that I put Mrs. Frost in the same hallway as Mr. Haver and Mr. O'Manion."

"The better to keep an eye on all three," I said. "I remember. Go on."

"Apparently while passing Mr. Haver's door, Mrs. Frost heard the finch singing, and became agitated for the bird's welfare. She said she was fond of all the pretty birds. So I instructed Lupe, the housekeeping associate who cleans that hallway, to notify me when she was ready to clean Mr. Haver's room. My plan was to collect the old lady and take her in to see that the bird was in fine shape. And she *was* in fine shape—I did a video consult with Dr. Rutledge over the phone this morning, and he was very satisfied with her condition, and promised to come by to inspect her in person tomorrow."

Poor Clarence. On top of everything else he'd been dealing with since this morning's raid, he was having to make house calls at the Inn.

"But that was this morning," Ekaterina said. "Just now, when I went in to display the bird to Mrs. Frost, she was gone."

"Just the bird, or was the cage gone, too."

"The cage, too. And to the best of my knowledge, Mr. Haver is still at rehearsal. I have not yet checked with every single staff member, but so far no one I have spoken to has seen Mr. Haver, and no one admitted anyone else to the room."

"Then why would you think the police had confiscated the finch? They couldn't have gotten in without one of your staff."

"They are the police. They have resources we ordinary civilians do not."

Actually, I suspected the chief would be envious of some of Ekaterina's resources.

"I think they'd clear it with you first," I said aloud. "They know you've been helping us on this."

"If it is not the police, then perhaps Mrs. Frost is right," she said. "Perhaps the finch smugglers infiltrated the hotel to reclaim the bird."

"Mrs. Frost said that?"

"Actually, what she said was that the man must have taken the finch. And when I asked what man, she said, 'The man who comes to take the animals.' She was very agitated. It took two frozen daiquiris to restore her to a state of calmness."

The man who comes to take the animals. That did sound rather ominous.

"I think you need to tell this to the chief," I said.

"What if he does not approve? Of our searching Mr. Haver's room?"

"You don't have to mention the searching," I said "You could just let him assume housekeeping noticed the absence of the bird when they went in to clean."

"Perhaps you could tell him?"

Was it a generic Russian thing, this disinclination to talk to the police? Or a daughter of a self-proclaimed Russian spy thing?

"Let's make sure the bird's really missing," I said. "I'm on my way over to the theater. Haver should be there, rehearsing. I'll ask him about the finch. Or maybe I won't need to ask. It's always possible Haver decided to take the bird over there."

"If Mrs. Frost becomes agitated again, I will suggest as much. I will let you know if we discover anything."

"Likewise."

I pulled back onto the road. And quickly realized I was driving much too fast. I forced myself to slow down to a little under the speed limit. I checked the clock on my dash. Three o'clock. Theoretically, the second run-through should start any minute, although who knows what Haver's arrival had done to the schedule.

I'd find out soon enough.

Chapter 32

I was relieved to see that the parking lot was full. Good! They needed all the rehearsal time they could get.

Although when I peered into the theater, I found Michael and most of the cast sitting in the first row of seats or on the edge of the stage, devouring pizza while Michael told them what they'd done right or wrong during the act they'd been rehearsing when the pizza had arrived. This, I'd learned, was called "giving notes."

"Grab a slice," Michael said, waving at the boxes from Luigi's that were lined up along the apron—the front part of the stage that curved out into the audience.

I wasn't waiting for permission. A few minutes earlier, if anyone had asked whether I was hungry, I might have shrugged and said "not really." But my stomach growled at the smell of the pizza, and I tried to remember the last time I'd eaten. I'd had a doughnut at the police station before this morning's raid, and nothing since.

I grabbed two slices. Luigi's pepperoni and sausage was my favorite at any time, but now—ambrosia.

As I ate, I scanned the assembled cast and crew, looking for Haver. And not spotting him.

"Okay, at the beginning of the Fezziwig scene," Michael said, looking at his notebook. "No, never mind; that's for Malcolm."

I sidled over to the nearest crew member—who happened to be Jake, the set designer.

"Haver's not here?" I asked in an undertone.

"His fan club took him to lunch." Seeing my puzzled look, he elaborated. "Haver said his stomach couldn't handle pizza this close to opening night, especially after the local police gave him the third degree, and I gather they also took away his car keys. So the fan lady offered to take him someplace where he could get whatever he wants instead."

"I bet she was excited."

"Over the moon." He grinned and shook his head. "No idea what she sees in him, but if she's willing to chauffeur him around and stroke his ego, it makes it much more pleasant for the rest of us."

Not to mention the fact that she was well aware of the importance of keeping Haver sober.

And, at least by the sound of it, they'd run through the first two acts before breaking for lunch. Given Michael's good mood, I suspected Haver had been reasonably well behaved and cooperative. So although I was still mildly annoyed that I'd have to wait to ask him about the missing finch, more important things were going right.

Things in the theater seemed to be under control, so I decided to see what else needed doing.

Jamie and Josh were sitting with their fellow juvenile cast mates and seemed reasonably attentive to Michael's notes. So I waved at them and at Rose Noire, who was sitting in the back row, clearly enjoying her look at what went on behind the scenes as much as the play itself.

Then I quietly slipped out of the theater and into the busy world of backstage.

Prop shop, costume shop, scenery shop—I had errands in all three. But I decided that first, while Haver was out, I'd glove up and give his dressing room a quick search. Not the kind of exhaustive search I'd done when I'd found the gun— just a quick check to see if the finch was there, and maybe a peek into the places where he'd been in the habit of hiding bottles.

And it occurred to me that the space above the ceiling tiles was plenty large enough to hold a bottle. Maybe that could explain the couple of times when, even though I hadn't found a bottle, Haver had still gotten progressively more inebriated as the rehearsal wore on. So I climbed up and checked that space, too.

My hand met something.

The gun was back.

"Deja vu all over again," I muttered. "And this time I am not putting it back." Hadn't the chief himself said he wished I'd confiscated it last time?

I grabbed a clean hand towel, wrapped the gun in it, and stuck it in the bottom of my tote.

I was about to retreat to someplace more private so I could call the chief when a crazy thought hit me. I stuck my head out of the dressing room and checked to make sure no one was in sight. Then I dashed down the hall to the closet where the janitorial supplies were kept, in search of the equipment I'd need to lay a snare for Haver.

I didn't find quite enough mousetraps to make a complete ring around the opening in the tile, so I alternated the mousetraps with sheets of flypaper. And then I carefully eased the tile in place with the tips of my fingers to make sure all the mousetraps and flypaper sheets stayed in place, so no matter which direction Haver groped after pushing away the tile he'd encounter something he wouldn't enjoy.

Then I ran down to my car and called the station.

"Meg, what's wrong?" Debbie Ann said. "You sound out of breath."

"I just ran all the way to my car," I puffed.

"Is something wrong?"

"No, something's right," I said. "I found Haver's gun."

"Let me get the chief."

It didn't take long.

"You found the gun? Where?"

"Same place I found it before," I said.

"Did he reload it?"

"I didn't check." The thought that I might have been running around the theater with a loaded gun rattling around in the bottom of my tote shook me a little. I put my gloves back on, unwrapped the gun, and toggled the switch to open the magazine.

Empty. I let out the breath I'd been holding.

"No, it's still unloaded," I said. "I thought it felt light."

Actually, it had never occurred to me to wonder if he'd loaded it again, but I wasn't about to admit that.

"I realize that you probably aren't as interested in it now that you've got the phony Agent Ruiz," I began. "But I would still like to get it out of the theater, so is there any chance you could confiscate it anyway?"

"Actually, I'm still very interested in examining Mr. Haver's gun," the chief said. "I'm a little shorthanded right now, so it could take a while to send someone over there."

"Want me to bring it in?"

"That would be very kind of you."

"Kind, nothing," I said. "I don't care if this thing is unloaded—I will still feel a lot better when it's out of my hands."

We signed off, and I started the car. I was already starting to feel a sense of relief. Within minutes, Haver's gun would be safely locked up in the police department's property room. And knowing the chief, I was sure he'd find a way to keep it there until Haver left town. And while in theory he could buy another gun—well, any time now, Cousin Maximilian would be arriving to take up his sober companion responsibilities. Mother and I could make it part of his job description to see that Haver stayed not only sober but disarmed.

As I threaded my way through the downtown tourist traffic to the police station—even my shortcuts were jammed today—I found myself thinking that if I were elected Queen of the Known Universe, I would issue a decree that made it possible to declare certain people in need of constant adult supervision. Haver, for example, would arguably be a happier, healthier, and more successful human being if he had someone looking after him. Not just a sober companion but a sanity companion.

"And most of you would benefit as well," I said, under my breath, as I watched a party of tourists stop dead in the middle of the street to consult their map. But I smiled as I said it. I didn't want anything to upset them and distract them from spending their money in the brightly lit and tinsel-laden stores. As Randall was fond of saying, "Be nice to the tourists—they're keeping your taxes down."

There were a couple of unfamiliar cars in the parking lot of the police station. I spotted a sedan with the ATF logo on its door, and two Clay County police cruisers. And since you didn't often see Crown Victorias in civilian use, I suspected at least one other law enforcement agency had arrived in Caerphilly.

Interesting. It had only been about twenty-four hours since the chief had sent in the fingerprints Horace took from the man we now knew was Laurencio Ruiz. Given the speed with which these various interested agencies were showing up, whatever the fake Ruiz had been involved in must be something pretty big.

I parked at the far end of the lot and bustled into the station—the temperature was still hovering in the single digits.

Inside, I found Kayla sitting at the desk. She started and looked guilty when I came in, and I noticed her surreptitiously pressing a button on her phone. I'd probably caught her using the intercom to eavesdrop on something in the chief's office.

"I brought Haver's gun," I said, putting my tote down on

the desktop and pretending not to notice what she'd been up to.

"The chief will be glad to get that." She looked around to make sure no one else had snuck into the room, and then stage-whispered to me. "Mr. Brickelhouse has an alibi."

"Brickelhouse?" I repeated. "Is that the guy who was pretending to be a Fish and Wildlife agent?"

She nodded.

"How good's his alibi?"

"About as good as it gets," she said. "He was in police custody in Rockingham County last night. The Rockingham County Sheriff *and* the FBI were questioning him about the disappearance of the real Fish and Wildlife agent. They let him go eventually—I guess they had to because they didn't have a body or anything. But now they know where the body is, so I bet he'll be staying behind bars. Maybe not here, though."

"Is that why the Clay County folks are over here?"

"Yes—they're being complete jerks, by the way. Trying to assert jurisdiction. You'd think they'd be glad to be rid of a John Doe that was taking up space in their morgue. But the point is—Mr. Brickelhouse couldn't have killed Mr. Willimer. And by the time they arrested Mr. Brickelhouse, Horace had already gone over to process Mr. Haver's room, and luckily the chief figured it would be just as well to let him finish, just in case. And he found something."

"Something incriminating?"

She nodded, and then her face took on a look of faux innocence.

"Chief, Meg's here with Mr. Haver's gun," she said over my shoulder.

Chapter 33

I turned to see the chief. He didn't seem as cheerful as he had sounded when I'd called to tell him of the phony Ruiz's arrest.

"I suppose Kayla told you that Mr. Brickelhouse—your fake Fish and Wildlife agent—couldn't have killed Mr. Willimer."

"Sorry, chief," Kayla murmured.

"So you really *do* want Haver's gun," I said. "I thought you were just humoring my desire to keep it out of the theater."

"It's entirely possible that Mr. Willimer's murder will turn out to be the handiwork of one of Mr. Brickelhouse's criminal associates," the chief said. "But in the meantime, Mr. Haver remains very much a suspect. So yes."

I reached into my tote, pulled out the towel-wrapped gun, and handed it to the chief.

"Did you touch it?" he asked.

"Because if I did, you'll need my fingerprints for comparison," I said, nodding.

"Actually, now that you're a town and county employee, I think your fingerprints are on file," he said with a smile. "Just wondering if we'll need to access them."

"I only touched it with gloves on," I said. "Given the state of Haver's dressing room, gloves probably aren't enough— I'm wondering if I should escalate to a hazmat suit."

"That's good," he said. "That you wore gloves, that is. Sorry about the need for a hazmat suit."

"I suppose you'll be sending it down to the crime lab in Richmond for testing," I said.

"Actually, as soon as Horace gets back from the Inn, I'll have him fire a couple of rounds so he can do his own test," the chief said. "And then we'll send it down to the crime lab. Horace's word is good enough for me, but juries and defense attorneys are always much more impressed with the state crime lab folks."

"By the way," I said. "Did Ekaterina call you? I mean, lately—within the last couple of hours."

"No." He smiled slightly. "She still doesn't quite believe that we are rather different from the KGB."

"She was under the impression you'd confiscated Haver's finch," I said.

"Is it missing?"

I nodded, and relayed what I remembered of Mrs. Frost's comments.

"'The man who comes to take the animals away.'" The chief frowned. "I don't like the sound of that. Thank you. I will consult the ever-growing collection of colleagues fighting over the guest chairs in my office and see if any of them will own up to nabbing the finch."

"Yeah," I said. "From the look of the parking lot, I figured you must have your hands full with the visiting law enforcement."

"Not as full as they will be." He cast a baleful glance at the corridor that led to his office. "But it's in a good cause." He sounded as if he were reminding himself. He nodded to me, and headed back to his office.

"And I'd better get back to the theater." I waved good-bye to Kayla, wrapped myself up, and strode out into the bitter cold.

On the way out I passed a brace of state troopers coming in. Poor Chief Burke.

And a vehicle was just pulling into the handicapped space.

A very unusual-looking vehicle. A pickup truck whose front end looked huge, almost inflated, and dwarfed the tiny cab, with a modest cargo area bringing up the rear. It appeared to have started life as a black truck, but had received a right rear fender transplant from a sea-foam green sibling, and its owner had not bothered to paint over the many places where dents or rust spots had been repaired and painted with reddish primer. Definitely not a modern pickup truck—I suspected it was older than I was. In fact . . .

I did a quick search on my phone and confirmed that the truck could very well be a 1956 Ford pickup.

The owner—an elderly man in a bright green John Deere cap—was hanging a well-worn handicapped parking tag from his rearview mirror. He saw me looking at him and rolled down the window.

"Is Henry Burke in there?"

"Yes, sir," I said.

"Tell him to come out here."

"Wouldn't you rather come in?" I asked. "It's below freezing out here and—"

"I know how cold it is, girlie! I can't come in—I have a sick sheep in the back and I need to get her home to the farm."

"I'll go and ask him to come out," I said. "May I tell him who's calling on him?"

"Mort Gormley."

As I suspected. I walked inside, where the chief was standing at Kayla's desk, talking to her.

"And I'm sorry," he was saying. "I know it makes more work for you but—"

"Chief," I interrupted. "Mort Gormley wants to talk to you. I invited him to come inside, but says he can't leave his sick sheep alone in the truck."

"What the Dickens," he muttered. But he strode over to the rack just inside the door, put on his heavy coat, and went outside. I followed.

"Mr. Gormley—" the chief began, as he approached the truck.

"Where the blue blazes do you get off, siccing the state troopers on me!" Gormley bellowed. "Like to give me a heart attack when they pulled me over."

"I didn't sic the state troopers on you," the chief said. "When one of my officers went over to your farm this morning, we couldn't find you, and no one had any idea of your whereabouts. We were concerned."

"Concerned that I'd bumped off my next-door neighbor and fled the jurisdiction, eh?" Gormley erupted with wheezy laughter. "Well, I'm here. And I didn't kill John Willimer. Took one of the Cotswolds down to Blacksburg to see a specialist at Virginia Tech. You want to waste your time checking my alibi, I can give you the name of the vet techs who stayed up all night with us."

He fumbled inside his coat and eventually pulled out a sheet of paper. The chief stepped closer to the truck to take it.

"Thank you," he said. "You ever see anything strange going on over at the Willimers?"

"Nope." Mr. Gormley shook his head. "I keep myself to myself. And after your Deputy Shiffley spoke to Willimer about those dogs of his, he did the same. Been meaning to say I appreciated that."

The chief nodded.

"What about the old lady?" Gormley asked. "She need anything?"

"She's staying here in town for the time being," the chief said. "We're hoping she'll turn out to have some kinfolk. Is your sheep going to be all right?" He nodded to the bed of the truck, where the placid white face of a sheep emerged from a small mountain of ratty blankets and tattered old quilts.

"She should be now." Gormley's voice softened slightly.

"Not doing her any good sitting around out here, though. I'd like to get her home and bedded down, if it's all the same to you."

"I appreciate your dropping by," the chief said. "Drive carefully."

Gormley pulled the handicapped placard off his rearview mirror and stowed it in the glove compartment. Then he looked back at the chief.

"Did you really think I might be your killer?" he asked.

"Mort," the chief said. "To tell you the truth, yes—I was worried that Willimer might have given you some new provocation. And I know how angry I'd feel toward someone I thought was responsible for the death of a helpless animal in my care. But when we couldn't find you, I was even more worried that the killer might have gotten you, too."

"I may be old, but I'm ornery," Gormley said. "Take a lot to kill me. And I'm right partial to my sheep, but I wouldn't kill a man over them. You can believe that or not—makes no never mind to me."

"I believe you, Mort," the chief said. "Drive carefully."

Gormley looked at the chief for a few moments, then nodded. The chief and I stood watching as he backed, inch by inch, out of the parking space, slowly pulled out of the lot, and disappeared, gradually, into the distance.

"Blast," the chief said. "I'm relieved to see he's not another victim, but I was hoping he'd have noticed something. Not a whole lot more potential witnesses out in that part of the county. But I shouldn't complain. The case is moving rapidly."

"Unlike Mr. Gormley."

"Yes." He chuckled softly. "Hard to believe we only found Willimer this morning."

"I know," I said. "Seems like at least a week."

"At least," he agreed. "Meg, I hope you're right about Michael being ready to step into Mr. Haver's part on a moment's notice."

"You're going to arrest him?"

"I'm going to bring him in for more questioning. I might end up detaining him."

"I thought the latest theory was that the killer would turn out to be someone from the smuggling ring."

"That was before Horace processed Mr. Haver's room. Vern's on his way over to the theater to collect Mr. Haver."

"Damn," I said. "I'd probably better get over there to help Michael deal with the fallout."

But when I slipped into the theater and found a vantage point backstage, I could see Michael onstage, where Haver should have been—standing beside the Ghost of Christmas Yet to Come, eavesdropping on the two actors who played Scrooge's fellow businessmen. That meant they were in the third act. I checked my watch. Three forty-five. Good— they were only running an hour or so late on the first run-through.

"*When did he die?*"

"*Last night, I believe.*"

"*Why, what was the matter with him? I thought he'd never die.*"

"*God knows.*"

"*What has he done with his money?*"

"*I haven't heard. He hasn't left it to me. That's all I know. Bye, bye!*"

Had Vern come and gone already, taking Haver with him? I know the play must go on, but . . . so quickly? Maybe Michael was just . . . showing Haver how he wanted him to do something?

I couldn't see much without barging out onstage and interrupting the rehearsal. So I ducked back into the hallway, followed it out to the lobby, and went in the main doors. I could see not only the stage but also the whole house.

Some of the actors who weren't on in this act were sitting in the first few rows. I saw Rose Noire sitting just behind the small clump of child actors, including Josh and Jamie.

No sign of Haver.

"Meg?"

I started, and turned to find Vern Shiffley standing beside me.

"Do you happen to know when this Haver fellow goes on?" he asked.

"He should be on now," I said. "The part Michael's playing—that's his part."

"Then where is he?"

"I'd like to know myself." I led the way backstage. Haver wasn't in his dressing room. Or the costume shop. Or the bathroom. Or in the wings. Several of the actors onstage spotted us when we were poking about backstage and their concentration suffered.

"Let's take a break, people," Michael said. "Meg, is something wrong?"

"Haver's not here?" I asked.

"Never came back from lunch. So I finally said the hell with it." He looked as if he wanted to say more than that, but after a glance at the section where the child actors were sitting, he just set his jaw.

"So he's flown the coop," Vern said.

Chapter 34

"Maybe he's flown the coop," I said. "Maybe he's just taking his own sweet time getting back from lunch."

"Any idea where he went for lunch?" Vern asked Michael.

"No idea," Michael said. "The chief confiscated his rental car, so the Rabid Fan was going to drive him somewhere. Sorry—I don't actually know her real name."

"Melisande Flanders," I said, to Vern. "She's staying at Niva's bed-and-breakfast."

"She hasn't come back, either," the actress playing Mrs. Cratchit said. I noticed that I wasn't the only one to glance at the aisle seat on the back row where Melisande had been sitting.

"Any chance one of the other deputies already picked him up?" I asked Vern.

"Unlikely." He shook his head. "Chief didn't put out a BOLO, just called to tell me to pick him up and keep it discreet."

"Good riddance, I say," Bob Cratchit muttered.

"Well, when he's on his game, he's pretty damned good," the Ghost of Christmas Past said.

"But when was the last time he was on his game instead of on the sauce?" Bob Cratchit replied.

"Okay, folks," Michael said, cutting through these and similar murmurs elsewhere in the crowd. "Let's get on with the run-through. Vern, you're welcome to stay and wait for Haver. Or we could call you when we see him."

"I'll check and see what the chief says." Vern went out through the doors to the lobby. I followed.

"Am I correct in assuming that once you find him it's unlikely we'll get Haver back today?" I asked.

"I'd say unlikely you'll get him back, period," Vern said. "I haven't heard what Horace found over in his room at the Inn, but it's got the chief all fired up."

"Damn," I said. "I was hoping—"

"Meg?"

I turned to see Melisande appearing from behind one of the tinsel-laden potted evergreens that dotted the lobby.

"You're back," I said. "Great! Where's Mr. Haver?"

"I don't know."

"You don't know," I repeated.

"I know, I know," she said. "I thought it would be such fun to take him out for lunch, plus I could keep an eye on him and make sure he didn't . . . overindulge in anything that would hurt his ability to rehearse when he got back."

"Your willingness to serve as a volunteer sober companion is duly noted," I said. "But—"

"And Malcolm was good as gold!" she exclaimed. "He directed me to this barbecue place he'd heard about—just a little hole in the wall, it even called itself 'The Pit'—and it was so rough-looking I'm not sure I'd have dared go inside by myself."

"I know the place," I said. Rocky, The Pit's owner, was well-known for offering free food to anyone who was down on his luck, and Clarence's biker friends tended to hang out there in between charity rides, playing pool while keeping a weather eye out for drunks, druggies, homeless people, runaways, stray kittens—anyone who might wander in needing rescue or rehabilitation. Later on, maybe, I'd tell her how very safe she had been in The Pit. For now, I put on my stern face. "So where is he now?"

"We were back here, and about to go into the auditorium

with our carryout bags, when he realized he'd left his script in my car," she said. "And I said I'd run down and get it, and he said nonsense, he wouldn't think of inconveniencing me because of his absentmindedness. So I gave him my keys and he hasn't come back. And I went down to look and my car isn't in the parking lot."

"He stole your car."

"He may have borrowed it."

"How long ago was this?"

"Um . . . fifteen minutes? Maybe half an hour?"

Vern, who had been eavesdropping nearby, stepped forward.

"Ma'am, can you give me the make, model, and license number of your car?"

"Why? He didn't steal it!" Melisande yelped. "He absolutely has my permission to drive it!"

"Yes, ma'am, I understand that." Vern had adopted his best "aw, shucks, ma'am" manner. "But we urgently need to talk to Mr. Haver and—"

"I won't help you persecute him! He didn't do anything!"

Melisande turned and fled through the glass front doors of the lobby, nearly bowling over a pair of tourists headed for the ticket office.

"I don't know the license number," I said. "But it's a bright red Ford Focus. I've seen it in the parking lot often enough."

"Thanks," he said. "Shouldn't take too long to get the license number from the DMV, but the guy already has a head start on us. Got a name on her?"

"Melisande Flanders."

While Vern made phone calls—first to the chief, to report on what Haver was up to, and then to The Pit to see if Rocky remembered what time the pair had left—I kept an eye out for Melisande. The temperature was only in the teens and she'd taken off without her coat. If she didn't come back soon, we'd need to send someone out to look for her. Possibly with an ambulance.

But about the time Vern was finishing up his second phone call, she slipped back in through one of the glass front doors—the one farthest from where Vern and I were standing. I gathered she was hoping to escape our notice.

"If you want to have another go at Melisande, there she is." I nodded toward where Melisande was darting from one potted evergreen to another, trying to make her way unseen to the door that led to the backstage area.

"You think she's likely to tell me anything?" Vern's expression showed how unimpressed he was with Melisande's attempts at stealth.

I looked over to Melisande's current hiding place, behind the finch cage. She seemed not to realize that its mesh sides provided very little cover. She peered out, saw that I was looking in her general direction, and ducked back behind the cage.

"No." I shook my head. "I think if she saw Malcolm Haver commit murder in cold blood, it wouldn't take her more than an hour or two to convince herself that he'd been acting out of self-defense. If she thinks you're going to arrest him, there's no way she'll help to find him."

"Then we'll rely on your information till the DMV comes through," he said. "I'd better get out there and help look for him."

He strode back out to his car. As he exited, a tall, muscular young man in his twenties came in. What I could see of his face between the knit hat and the scarf wrapped around his nose and chin was cheerful, freckled, and vaguely familiar. His eyes lit up when he saw me.

"Meg!" He hurried over with an outstretched hand. "I recognize you from the family reunions."

"And you must be Maximilian." He had a good handshake and a nice smile.

"Just Max," he said. "Only our mothers call me Maximilian. So where's my charge?"

It took me a while to convince Max that it wasn't his fault Haver had fled before he arrived. And I didn't try to talk him out of going in search of the red Ford Focus. In fact, once Max had departed, I called Stanley Denton to ask if he could join in the search.

Then I slipped quietly back into the house and sat in the back row of seats. They'd resumed the run-through while I'd been gone, and had reached the scene where Scrooge was buying the enormous Christmas goose to send to the Cratchit family.

Do you know the Poulter's in the next street but one, at the corner?
I should hope I did.

An intelligent boy! A remarkable boy! Do you know whether they've sold the prize turkey that was hanging up there? Not the little prize turkey,—the big one?

What, the one as big as me?

What a delightful boy! It's a pleasure to talk to him. Yes, my buck!
It's hanging there now.

Is it? Go and buy it.

Pull the other one.

No, no, I am in earnest. Go and buy it, and tell 'em to bring it here, that I may give them the direction where to take it. Come back with the man, and I'll give you a shilling. Come back with him in less than five minutes, and I'll give you half a crown!

Not for the first time, I found myself imagining the mixed feelings the goose must have inspired in Mrs. Cratchit. Yes, of course, she would have been delighted to have so much food to feed a family that probably survived all too often on lean rations. But on the other hand, what kind of an idiot sends an enormous raw bird to a woman who's just about to serve her much more modest but already fully cooked goose and needs to turn her attention to the complicated job of cooking the plum pudding?

Just then my phone buzzed—buzzed, rather than rang, because it had become second nature to turn off the sound when I walked into the theater.

Robyn. I decided I should probably take it, so I stepped outside into the lobby.

"Just so you know, I'm having second thoughts about whether hosting Weaseltide is a good idea," I said. "Since the organizer thereof is currently aiding and abetting Malcolm Haver's flight from the law."

"Oh, dear. Well, I always put everything on the calendar in pencil. If you decide it's a bad idea, I can suddenly remember that we have a meeting of the Ladies of Saint Clotilda that afternoon. Actually, I was calling about something else. Could you possibly bring Mrs. Frost to Trinity tonight for the potluck supper?"

"I'm not coming, remember? I'll be at the theater. Dress rehearsal."

"Oh, I know—and you'll be terribly busy! But you're one of the few people Mrs. Frost actually knows, so it would be much easier if you could coax her into coming—"

Should I tell Robyn exactly how little I cared whether Mrs. Frost came to the potluck dinner?

"And also, we've packed up a feast for the cast and crew—Michael told me how many people there would be—and if you drop by with Mrs. Frost, we can load it all into your car."

I suddenly felt like a jerk.

"Okay—for a bribe like that I'll do it," I said. "But I warn you, I can't guarantee that I can talk her into coming if she balks."

"Well, if she turns up her nose at us, you can still come by for your food. The supper starts at six, but if you need to drop her off a little earlier, we have plenty of people here to take care of her, and the food for the theater's all ready."

I glanced at my watch. Four thirty. It would be nice to get this over with.

"I could bring her now," I said.

"Splendid."

So I dashed down to my car and headed for the Caerphilly Inn.

Chapter 35

The college radio station was back to more palatable Christmas fare—soothing piano versions of Christmas carols. And at five o'clock they'd be continuing their quest to play every known recording of Handel's *Messiah* before the end of the holiday season. Today's offering, the announcer burbled, would feature Dame Kiri Te Kanawa and the Chicago Symphony Orchestra. He rattled on breathlessly, giving the entire cast list.

"Just get back to the Christmas music," I muttered. But by the time he did, I was pulling up in front of the Inn.

As I was walking into the lobby, I ran into Horace about to make his exit, with his forensic bag in hand. He looked tired—no wonder, given how early he'd been up and how much he'd had to do today.

But he didn't just look tired—he looked . . . grim?

"How was your search?" I asked.

"Meg, you know I can't tell you that," he said.

"Sorry," I said. "I figured that was a little less impersonal than asking 'how was your day?' Especially since I already know you've had an exhausting and crazy busy day."

"Didn't mean to snap at you," he said.

"And I shouldn't be prying. Truce." I held up my hands as if in surrender.

That got a smile out of him.

"Truce," he echoed.

"Am I allowed to ask if anyone has found Haver yet?"

"You're allowed to ask, but as far as I've heard he hasn't been found. Sorry."

"Not your fault the jerk decided to go on the lam," I said. "And frankly, at this point I don't care if he's guilty or not. I just hope you've found something that definitely either incriminates him or absolves him. This business of not knowing whether he'll be still free to go onstage opening night is shredding all our nerves."

"What happens if he can't go on?" Horace asked, shifting his bag to his other hand. "Does the play get canceled and you have to give all the people their money back?"

"No," I said. "If Haver can't go on, Michael will take his place."

"And he can do that, no problem, right?"

"No problem. In fact, I think Michael gave up on him when he didn't come back after lunch. They've been doing run-throughs during the day, to make up for not being able to rehearse, and if Haver's still AWOL Michael will play his part at dress rehearsal tonight. And at opening tomorrow night."

"Good." Horace nodded, and set out across the parking lot toward his police cruiser.

Had Horace just dropped me a rather large hint?

Time would tell.

I went inside the Inn. Ekaterina was standing by the registration desk. She did not look happy.

"I gather Horace found some evidence in Haver's room," I said.

"Did he say what?"

I shook my head.

"But this is not acceptable! We have a guest who may turn out to be a homicidal maniac, and the police tell us nothing!"

"I don't think he's a homicidal maniac," I said. "Just a common or garden murderer."

"Oh, and that is so much better. Well, I will see what I can find out."

"If you find out anything, let me know," I said. "Meanwhile, I am going to see if Mrs. Frost wants to go to the potluck dinner at Trinity."

"Good. She needs distraction. Distraction of a sort that does not come with a paper parasol in it." Ekaterina dashed off, looking preoccupied. I took the elevator up to the third floor and followed the hallway to Mrs. Frost's room.

As I knocked, I glanced farther down the corridor. The doorway to 314, Haver's room, was blocked off with several lengths of crime-scene tape whose gaudy yellow color clashed with the subdued lavender and moss green of the corridor.

"Yes? Who is it?"

Mrs. Frost's door opened the few inches allowed by the security chain, and she peered up at me through the opening.

"It's me. Meg Langslow." No reaction. "I was the one who drove you over here."

"Oh, yes, dear. That was very kind of you."

"Reverend Robyn Smith asked me to come by and see if you'd decided to accept her invitation to come to the potluck dinner tonight at Trinity Episcopal," I said.

"I'd only be in the way," she said.

"Of course not," I said. "There's always plenty of food— way more than needed—and people would enjoy meeting you. Robyn, in particular, is looking forward to it. She's a big animal lover—I'm sure she'd love hearing about your cats."

"Well . . . if you're sure it's not an imposition."

"Robyn's worried that the snow might keep people away," I improvised. "We really do need people to swell the crowd and eat up all the food."

"Give me a minute, then."

She shut the door, and I could hear rustling inside. Then silence. Then more rustling. I felt a surge of impatience and irritation, so I took a couple of deep breaths and reminded myself that she was an old lady. And old lady in a wheelchair. Doing things took longer for her.

Then I heard the security chain rattling. And the dead bolt being turned.

"All right, dear. The door is unlocked."

She was sitting about two yards inside the door, smiling at me. I mentally kicked myself for my impatience. She wore a red flowered hat—what Mother would call a church hat—a blouse printed with a bold red poinsettia pattern, and bright green stretch pants. Her coat was draped across her lap and she was clutching a well-worn but still presentable navy-blue purse with both hands.

"I hear it's bitter cold out there—will my coat be enough?" She held up the sleeve of a navy-blue cloth coat.

"It wouldn't be if we were going to walk, but you should be okay," I said. "My car heater works fine, and you won't be out in the cold more than a minute. Shall I push your chair?"

"Let me just make sure I have the key card for my room." She peeked fruitlessly into two of the purse's outside pockets before spotting the card in the third.

"Ready to go!" she chirped.

I wheeled her down the long hallway to the elevator. The Inn's thick, cushy carpet felt wonderfully soft underfoot, but it didn't make pushing a wheelchair very easy. I wondered if I should ask Meredith if there was any way of getting an electric wheelchair for Mrs. Frost. So much easier not only for her but for anyone who was helping her.

I'd worry about that later. All I had to do was get her to the potluck. Once we reached Trinity, there would be plenty of helping hands to take care of her, and I could go back to the theater bearing goodies in plenty of time for the dress rehearsal.

In fact, the helping hands kicked in as soon as I hit the

lobby. One bellman insisted on taking my place behind Mrs. Frost's chair while another took my keys and ran to fetch my car. All I had to do was watch while they carefully hoisted Mrs. Frost into the passenger seat and stowed her wheelchair in the back of the Twinmobile.

Just as the bellhops were closing the doors, my phone rang. Robyn. I answered with some trepidation—what if she was calling with some change in plan?

"Meg—are you still planning to bring Mrs. Frost to the potluck?"

"She's sitting here beside me and we were about to head your way," I said.

"Wonderful! I'm so looking forward to meeting her! But tell me—could you run a small errand on your way?"

"What's the errand?" Not that I didn't want to help Robyn in whatever way I could, but if, for example, her small errand involved a quick trip down to Richmond, or up to Dulles Airport, I would need to weasel out. "And remember, I don't have my usual cargo space—Mrs. Frost's wheelchair is pretty big." On top of weighing a ton.

"Well, there are going to be such a lot of people at the buffet, and they should all be in a festive holiday mood, so I thought it might be a splendid time to show off some of the golden retriever puppies and see if we can place a few more. So could you possibly drop by your house and bring along a few?"

"Hang on." I looked over at Mrs. Frost. "Would you mind if we made a short detour on our way to the church?"

"Of course not," she said. "I'm enjoying the chance to get out and see the scenery."

"I think I can manage that," I said to Robyn. "Anything to reduce the animal population of our barn. How many?"

"I'd say half a dozen, including some of each sex if they're old enough that you can tell which is which."

"One coeducational half dozen puppies coming up."

"Wonderful! I so look forward to seeing them!"

I wondered if Robyn was in the market for a puppy herself. I was about to ask if I should bring along a cat or two while I was at it, but stopped myself in time. Of course not. Mrs. Frost was going to be there, and the sight of people taking away some of her cats would be bound to upset her. Doubtless Robyn had already thought of that.

So I merely said good-bye and started up the Twinmobile.

"My goodness," Mrs. Frost said, as we started down the Inn's gently curving mile-long driveway. "I am getting to see the sights these days."

Her voice sounded cheerful enough, but her smile looked tremulous, and I reminded myself that she'd just lost a family member—though I hoped not the only family she had left. Then I saw her yawn, delicately.

"Oh, dear," she said. "It's not your company, dear; it's about my nap time. Is this one of those seats that leans back?"

I explained how to find the lever and she exclaimed with delight at how comfortable the seat was to nap in.

I wasn't sure it was a good idea, letting her fall asleep in my car. Even including the detour out to our house, the trip to Trinity wasn't that long. But the poor old soul looked so droopy. In fact, her breathing had already slowed by the time we hit the main road, and not long after that she began snoring softly.

Well, at least I'd have peace and quiet on the drive. I hadn't been looking forward to another stream-of-consciousness monologue. I'd had a hard enough time listening to it this morning on the way into town, and that was when we were all actively trying to glean every possible bit of information about her and Willimer.

I thought of turning on the radio to hear a little soft Christmas music—but no; it had just turned five o'clock, which meant the college radio station would have started playing the *Messiah*. I'd save that in case we needed something to jolt Mrs. Frost out of her nap when we arrived at the church.

When we were about halfway to the house, I felt my phone buzzing in my pocket.

Chapter 36

"I should get this," I murmured. Mrs. Frost snored softly as I pulled into the mouth of a neighbor's driveway, fished out the phone, and answered it.

"Ekaterina here. I have obtained the information you requested."

The information I requested? It took a minute for the light to dawn.

"You mean you figured out what Horace found in Haver's room?" I asked.

"Yes. But something does not compute."

"Like what?"

"When Deputy Hollingsworth arrived, I assigned one of my best operatives to observe his activities."

"One of your best whats?"

"Operatives. Lupe Esparza. One of my housekeeping staff. To look at her, you would think she is nothing but a sweet little old *abuelita*, and with the guests, she prefers to pretend that she has no English."

Yes, I was pretty sure I'd met Lupe.

"Lupe managed to overhear a phone call between Deputy Hollingsworth and the chief. Apparently his find was a wallet belonging to Mr. Willimer."

"I can see how that would be somewhat suspicious."

"Especially since it was stained with blood, and contained a receipt from the Clay County ABC store that was dated at eight forty-seven p.m. yesterday."

Damn. A good thing Michael was rehearsing as Scrooge,

since the chances of his having to take over from Haver just reached near certainty.

"Well, I guess that explains why the chief wants to talk to Haver," I said. And why both Vern and Horace hinted that he might not be sending Haver back to rehearsal.

"Yes, but it does not make sense. How did the wallet get there?"

"Presumably Haver left it." I was catching on. "Which would be a pretty stupid thing to do, I admit. He may not know *who's* searching his room and confiscating his booze, but by now he's absolutely figured out it's happening. Why leave such incriminating evidence in his room, where the searchers are sure to find it? Why not wipe it clean of prints and toss it into a storm drain, or a trash can, or even just a big snowbank?"

"Yes, very good questions—although people do strange things under the influence of strong drink," Ekaterina said. "But the question is not why he would do it, but when could he possibly have done it?"

"Oh," I said. "I see. You mean the wallet wasn't there this morning—because I think you'd have noticed a random wallet suddenly appearing in a drawer, even without the bloodstains. So he must have hidden it sometime this afternoon."

"Which is impossible," she said. "As you perhaps have begun to detect, I have been becoming increasingly provoked with Mr. Haver. Especially after the disappearance of the finch. So I rekeyed his room."

"You what?"

"Rekeyed his room. So the next time he tried to get in, his card key would not work and he would have to come down to the front desk to get a new one. And then before I left his room, I did a quick search, just to make sure he had not hidden any more bottles there while stealing the finch. There was no wallet in the room at that time. And I instructed all the staff to notify me immediately if Mr. Haver showed up, and to delay him at the front desk until I could speak to him. He has not appeared."

"So even if he was stupid enough to have wanted to hide the wallet there, he had no access."

"No legitimate access," Ekaterina corrected. "If he is a member in good standing of this sinister smuggling gang, perhaps my rekeying the room did little to deter him."

"Or maybe he's just the innocent dope we think he is, and a real member of the sinister smuggling gang planted the wallet in his room. You need to tell the chief about this."

"Yes, but—he will perhaps be displeased with me. When I told him about the disappearance of the finch, he told me to keep everyone out of the room and let him know if Mr. Haver came back. It did not occur to me until later that perhaps when he said everyone he meant to include me. Perhaps he will be enraged that I searched the room."

"He may not be happy, but if the wallet was planted, he'll want to know that."

"Are you sure?"

I glanced over at Mrs. Frost, who was still fast asleep and snoring slightly.

"Yes. Look, I have to drop some puppies and Mrs. Frost off at Trinity Episcopal. When I finish doing that, I'll drop by the police station."

"Let me know when you are there," she said. "And I can meet you there. I would appreciate your assistance when I approach Chief Burke."

"Yes," I said. "Talk to you later."

I hung up and pulled back onto the road.

A few lights were on in the house. Some of the visiting cousins settling in, no doubt. If I were a better person, I'd go in and welcome them, but I was anxious to get Mrs. Frost and the puppies over to Trinity and return to the rehearsal. So instead of parking in front of the house, I pulled into the lane that led to the barn and parked right outside its doors. I got out of the car, shutting the door quietly so I wouldn't wake Mrs. Frost.

I felt a pang of worry about her. She looked so peaceful, and her future was so uncertain. What if the chief had no luck finding any relatives? Or what if the relatives wouldn't or couldn't take care of her? I was sure Meredith would find some place that could take her, but it might not be anywhere she'd like to be. And it probably wouldn't allow her even the one cat we'd let her take with her to the Inn.

I should talk to Robyn. She might have some good ideas about where Mrs. Frost could go if no loving family showed up to claim her.

But I could worry about that later.

When I stepped out of the Twinmobile, the cold air hit me all the harder because I'd jacked up the heat to make sure Mrs. Frost wouldn't feel chilled. A good thing we wouldn't be staying here long. It was bitter cold. In the teens? I pulled out my phone to check as I opened the barn door—the human-sized door, not the one you could drive a truck through. Yikes, not even in the teens—it was nine degrees Fahrenheit. Probably a record.

I was relieved when I stepped into the relatively balmy air inside the barn. I knew it was only sixty or sixty-five, but it felt like a sauna after the outside. I stood for a moment, flexing my fingers. Should I open the big door and drive the car in? To keep Mrs. Frost warm? Not necessary. All I had to do was run into my office and grab a couple of puppies—the larger ones that Clarence had declared ready either for adoption or for fostering away from their mothers. I could hear a few of them yipping even now. And then we'd be off.

And besides, probably a bad idea to bring her in here, I reminded myself as I pulled the door closed. There was still a wall of cats along one side of the open central space. About a third of the cats I'd seen before were gone, and there was no longer a break in the middle of the row. This was a good sign, wasn't it? It meant that all the cats Clarence, Dad, and Grandfather had chipped and vaccinated had already found foster homes. And surely the rest would follow suit once they'd had their turn in the makeshift clinic.

I had just turned left, heading for my office, when I heard a noise behind me.

"Meg?"

I whirled to find Haver, standing near the other end of the barn. Evidently he'd been hiding behind some of my blacksmithing equipment.

"What are you doing here?" I asked.

"Looking for you, actually," he said. "I need your help."

He wasn't holding a gun. Of course, I'd turned the one from his dressing room over to the chief, but there were plenty more guns where that had come from. But he wasn't holding one right now—that was a good sign, wasn't it? In fact, he was holding out his hands as if pleading with me.

"You need my help?" I repeated. "With what?"

"I'm going away," he said. "The cops are about to arrest me for murder. Arrest *me*—for *murder*! Are they crazy?"

"Maybe they've eliminated all their other suspects."

"Then there must be some other suspect they haven't thought of," he said. "Anyway, I'm not going to stick around to be railroaded. I'm going to blow this pop stand. Stay hidden till they figure out who really did it. Michael can have my part. He's better at it anyway. Better at it the way I am now—sober, I could give him a run for his money. Maybe I will someday. But not now."

"So you're leaving." Clearly he was an actor, not a scriptwriter—even I could have scripted a punchier farewell speech.

"Yeah, but there's just one thing I need you to do for me. I want you to take care of Fiona."

"Fiona?"

"Here—I'll show you."

He turned and took a few steps back toward where he'd been hiding and ducked behind my forge. I was curious to see what he wanted to ask me, and he sounded harmless enough. Still, I began backing slowly toward the door, with an eye to making a break for it if he emerged from hiding again with the gun.

But instead he emerged carrying the Gouldian finch in its cage.

"This is Fiona," he said. "I can't take her with me. It's not fair. Hell, I don't know what came over me. I'm not fit to take care of a pet. Not right now. When I got her home, I was so excited—I love birds anyway, but there's something about these finches that really speaks to me—the beautiful plumage, the sweet singing. But then I realized I had no idea what to feed her. I gave her some crackers and granola, but she didn't seem too crazy about either of them. I tried to call Willimer to ask what she should eat, but he wasn't home, and I figured I'd go out and find a pet store and ask, but I only found one in the whole town and it was closed by that time, and after that I got stuck in the snow. Never got home again that night. And by the time I did get there, the next morning, I guess the hotel staff had figured out what she needed. Whole sack of birdseed was there waiting for me. Which was nice of them, but it just made it more obvious how unfit I was to take care of her."

The whole time he'd been talking, he was staring at the bird with the sort of dopey-eyed half smile you'd see on the face of a middle-school boy in the throes of his first crush. Not just staring at her, but scratching her feathers gently with one finger. Fiona seemed to like that and chirped melodiously.

"Take care of her." He pulled out his hand and shoved the cage toward me. "I know if you can't keep her yourself you'll find her a good home."

"I'll consider it," I said. "If you answer a couple of questions."

"Anything." He set Fiona's cage down in the space between us and drew himself up to his full height.

"So you say you didn't kill Willimer—do you know who did?"

"No." He shook his head violently. "Why would I want to kill the only man in town who would sell me a drop to drink?"

"Maybe because you realized he was ruining your chances of a comeback," I suggested.

"You're assuming I'm still sober enough to care about the comeback." He gave a hollow laugh. "I'm pretty close to not caring about anything but my next drink. I'm sure Vince O'Manion would like to throttle him about the comeback, but—"

He stopped short and suddenly looked ashen.

"You don't suppose it was Vince, do you?"

"Could be. Chief Burke's probably still checking out his alibi. But the chief tends to pay a lot more attention to people who run away when he tries to talk to them."

"Damn." Haver seemed stunned at the possibility. "If they lock Vince up, I'll never get another agent. You have no idea what he's put up with from me over the years."

Actually, I had a pretty good notion, but I didn't think it would help if I told Haver that. Instead, I asked the question that had really been bothering me.

"What about your gun?" I asked. "Where is it?"

"Gun?" He looked genuinely surprised. "I didn't kill him. I told you that. And I don't have any gun."

"What about the gun that was hidden behind the tile ceiling in your dressing room?"

"Are you crazy?"

"You didn't hide your gun there?"

"I don't have a gun, so how could I hide one in my dressing room? Are you—oh, my God. Vince!"

"Your agent?"

"It could be his. It has to be his."

"Does he normally travel with a gun?" It sounded pretty farfetched to me.

"Yeah." Haver shook his head as if this baffled him. "He basically thinks there's no civilization outside of L.A., New York, and maybe London. If he has to go anyplace else, he gets totally paranoid, like it's someplace out of *Deliverance* and brings his peashooter. And yesterday we got into it a bit about my drinking—he was telling me if I got pulled over for drinking here, he would have no way to fix it, much less keep it out of the papers, and did I want to see headlines like 'Hollywood Has-Been in DUI.' And I was trying to get back at him, so I said that maybe he should be careful himself, because 'Over-the-hill Agent Arrested with Concealed Weapon' wasn't much better. And then I had to go to rehearsal, so I stormed out."

"And you think O'Manion hid his gun in your dressing room while you were out?"

"I have no idea—I wasn't there. But he could have. That's the only way I can think of that there'd be a gun there."

It sounded plausible enough. I'd pass it along to the chief. Maybe he could confiscate O'Manion's gun and see if it was the murder weapon. And—

"How nice," came a voice from behind me. "Just the two people I wanted to see."

Haver's head jerked toward the voice, and he didn't look happy. I turned to see what was up.

Mrs. Frost was standing in the doorway pointing a gun at us.

Chapter 37

"Who's that?" Haver asked.

"John Willimer's mother," I said.

"The old bat in the wheelchair?"

I winced. Haver had a lot to learn about not ticking off people who were pointing guns at him. But Mrs. Frost seemed to find his words amusing.

"Yes, the old bat in the wheelchair." She chuckled. "Funny, isn't it, how everyone overlooks old people. Especially old women. You were so hell-bent on getting your bottle you probably didn't even notice me."

"I noticed you." Haver shook his head. "Don't remember much about you, though. I was kind of distracted by the seven million damned cats."

My mind was sorting through the possible implications of Mrs. Frost's unsuspected mobility. Sorting through them and not liking them one bit. I decided at least to pretend to assume she was pointing the gun at Haver because she thought he'd killed her son-in-law and wanted revenge.

"Look, Mrs. Frost, there seems to be some doubt about Mr. Haver's guilt, after all," I began. "Please don't shoot him until we find out for sure. There's some very good evidence to suggest that Mr. Haver's agent shot Johnny."

"His agent! Don't be an idiot," she said. "I shot the bastard."

"Oh, God, no," Haver moaned.

"But why?" I asked. She liked to talk. Now was a good time

to keep her talking until I could figure out some way to get us out of this.

"He was a jerk," she said. "He'd been sponging off me for years. Couldn't hold down a job. Drove my Becky to drink— she might be still alive if it wasn't for him. And he was threatening to turn me in."

"Turn you in?" Did she mean to Social Services? "For what—having too many cats?"

"Too many cats!" She seemed to find that funny. "Did you really think Johnny was the brains behind the animal business? He was terrified of anything bigger than a puppy. Hell, sometimes I think he was scared of the puppies."

"But he was the one who sold me Fiona," Haver said.

"The finch?" Mrs. Frost snorted. "Not without running into the house to ask my permission and find out what price to ask. And he overcharged you, you know. Doubled what I told him to ask for and kept the extra cash for himself."

Haver blinked in surprise. He looked at Fiona mournfully. I hoped knowing she wasn't as expensive as he'd thought she was didn't cool his enthusiasm for her.

"Johnny always was a sneak," Mrs. Frost went on. "But I figured if he was starting to pull stupid stuff like that, it was time to get rid of him."

"So you shot him? With that?" I nodded at the gun she was holding. "But how did you ever get it out of your house?" Surely perky Meredith hadn't obligingly packed it for her.

"I didn't, honey—you did. In the litter box. In a plastic bag, so the litter and the cat pee wouldn't get to it."

"So all that fuss about bringing your favorite cat and his special litter box was just a ruse to get the gun out of the house. And the wallet, too, I suppose. How did you manage to plant that in Haver's room?"

"Got the maid to let me in to see the bird," she said. "And

hopped out of the wheelchair for a few seconds when she went into the bathroom to scrub the john."

"If you hadn't come in here, we'd probably still be trying to figure that out," I said.

"Yeah, right," she said. "I overheard you talking to that nosy Russian bitch. The two of you were getting way too close. And planning to go to the cops. I knew I'd have to arrange accidents for the both of you. Didn't expect you to give me such a perfect opportunity so soon, but I do appreciate it. Now—let's see how we're going to arrange this."

My mind was scrambling, trying to come up with a plan. She was standing just inside the barn door, which was by far the closest exit, and probably the only unlocked one. She had her back to my office door—what if I pretended to see someone behind her, so she'd whirl around and—

No. What if she not only whirled around but fired in the direction I'd been looking. She'd be firing at the door of my office. The office that was filled with puppies. I could hear their faint whining and yipping still. A glance to my right wouldn't be any better—it could induce her to fire into the wall of cat carriers. And she was keeping too close an eye on the barn door to fool her into suspecting a threat from that direction.

"I really should shoot you first," Mrs. Frost said. "The scenario I'm going for is that Haver here shot you, and then committed suicide."

"If only I'd gone for the dinner theater job," Haver moaned.

"You'll have a hard time making it believable," I said.

"Well, they might guess it was a double murder instead of a murder/suicide," she said. "But they won't have a clue it was me. I'll be sitting in the front seat of your car, feebly calling for help."

"I could be doing *Mousetrap* in Fort Myers." Haver wasn't

even watching her, just standing there with his eyes closed, awaiting his fate.

Maybe I could manage to fake with eyes left, to the barn door. She might fall for it. If only I could count on Haver to do something useful when I made my break.

Just then I heard a slight creaking noise. I looked over Mrs. Frost's shoulder to see that the door to my office was open a crack. Hope surged. Was someone in there?

"And do you really think I'm going to fall for that old trick, dearie?" Mrs. Frost said. "The eyes widened in concern for something you see behind my back? Nonsense!"

No, it wasn't nonsense. Suddenly my office door swung open and a tidal wave of golden retriever puppies spilled out into the barn, yipping with delight.

Mrs. Frost's gaze wavered for a moment, and I decided this was our chance.

"Take cover!" I shouted to Haver.

I gave him a shove in the right direction before following my own order and darting behind one of the tall metal storage cabinets that held my tools and supplies. I armed myself as well as I could, grabbing a half-finished fireplace poker in one hand and a ball peen hammer in the other.

"Cry 'Havoc' and let slip the dogs of war!" Haver proclaimed. Instead of taking cover, he'd climbed on top of my worktable, as if the puppies were the danger rather than Mrs. Frost.

A few of the puppies were running toward him, or me, or exploring the far reaches of the barn, but most of them had converged on the first human being they'd encountered. They were leaping on Mrs. Frost's legs, barking at her, and grabbing the cuffs of her bright green stretch pants with their sharp little teeth.

"That this foul deed shall smell above the earth / With carrion men, groaning for burial," Haver continued. Still quoting *Julius Caesar*, I noted mechanically.

Mrs. Frost was kicking at the puppies, and using language that most little old ladies of my acquaintance either didn't know or refrained from using in public. Fortunately, she didn't seem inclined to use up any of her ammunition on the puppies. Also, fortunately, her kicking wasn't hard enough to hurt the puppies. In fact, they seemed to think she was playing with them, and more and more of them joined in the exciting game of tugging on her pants legs, trying to topple her.

"Get these monsters away from me!" she shouted.

"I gin to be aweary of the sun / And wish the estate o' the world were now undone." Haver had snatched up a three-foot iron rod that had been lying on the table, awaiting its turn to become a poker, and was waving it wildly overhead. I wondered if there was any significance to the fact that he'd switched from *Julius Caesar* to *Macbeth*.

I'd worry about that later. Seeing that Mrs. Frost was starting to lose her balance, I crept out from behind the cabinet, hammer and poker at the ready, and began sidling along the side of the barn, preparing either to jump her or make a bee-line out the door, whichever seemed possible.

She toppled over suddenly, and fell over backward into the throng of puppies. A few puppies, who didn't get out of the way fast enough, yelped in pain as they wriggled out from under her, but most yipped and began enthusiastically licking her face. Or her neck. Or whatever part of her body they could reach.

I dashed over, pinned her wrist to the ground with the poker, and scooped up the gun.

"Ring the alarum-bell! Blow, wind! come, wrack!" Haver exclaimed, waving his arms wildly. "At least we'll die with harness on our back."

He jumped down from the table with a wild yell that was no doubt intended as a war cry. But he landed unsteadily, shouted "ow!" and was easily toppled over by a contingent of puppies that had grown bored with chewing Mrs. Frost's shoelaces and were looking for new challenges.

"Are you okay?" I asked.

"Get those horrible things off me!" Mrs. Frost screamed.

"I may have sprained my ankle," Haver announced. "That was the sort of thing that I would have left to the stunt men, even in my callow youth."

"Do you think you can still go on?" I asked. "Onstage, that is."

"Of course I can," he said. "If you still want me. I think Scrooge would work with a limp."

"There should be some duct tape over on the table you leaped off of," I said.

"I'd rather have my ankle bandaged by qualified medical personnel if it's all the same to you."

"The duct tape is for Mrs. Frost, not you," I said. "See if you can limp over to get it, and make sure she can't so much as move a finger."

"To hear is to obey," he said.

"Mommy?"

I looked up to see a head peering out of my office door.

"Jamie? What are you doing here?"

"We came out to play with the puppies while Aunt Rose Noire finished packing up her dishes for the potluck supper," Jamie said. "When we heard the little old lady saying nasty things to you, Josh climbed out the window and went to the house to call the police. And I let the puppies out so they could rescue you."

"You did splendidly," I said. "Both of you."

"Everything's okay now, isn't it?"

"Of course," I said. "Everything's fine."

"Should I go tell Josh to call 911 again and tell them not to come?"

"No." I was keeping my eyes on Mrs. Frost. "I think Chief

Burke would like to talk to both of these people. You go back to the house and tell Josh and Rose Noire to stay there until I'm finished here. And you stay and make sure they do it."

"Okay." The prospect of bossing his twin around did a lot to relieve his anxiety.

Though it was probably too late to keep Rose Noire in the house. I could hear her voice outside, coming rapidly closer.

"Meg? What's going on? Meg?"

And in the distance I could also hear sirens.

"Do you think the police can finish with us in time to get to rehearsal?" Haver asked.

"Odds are good," I said. "The chief knows how important the dress rehearsal is to the success of the play."

"Excellent! Because now that I'm vindicated, I can't wait to go onstage. 'Spirit! hear me!'" He struggled to his knees, carefully brushing the odd puppy aside, and assumed the pose he used when Scrooge finally repented at the feet of the Ghost of Christmas Yet to Come. "'I am not the man I was. I will not be the man I must have been but for this intercourse. Why show me this, if I am past all hope? Assure me that I yet may change these shadows you have shown me by an altered life.'"

"Damn, I hope they put me in solitary," Mrs. Frost grumbled.

Just then my phone rang. Michael.

"We're starting rehearsal again in an hour," he said. "Are the boys with you?"

"Yes," I said. "And I can bring them over in an hour."

"Great," he said. "Since we're giving up on Haver, and I want to get in at least one complete run-through with me in the role."

"Actually, we may not have to give up on Haver," I said. "I might be able to bring him along with the boys."

"Are you sure the police won't just show up to arrest him?"

"No, I think they've found the real killer," I said. "I'll fill you in when I get there."

"Fabulous," he said. "Now all I need is for someone to figure out why Haver's agent is running around the theater with his hands covered with mousetraps and flypaper."

Chapter 38

"So this is Weaseltide!" Robyn stood just inside the doorway of Trinity's parish hall, surveying the celebration in progress.

"They probably could have held it in Melisande's bed-and-breakfast," I noted. "They wouldn't even have been very crowded."

"But this is so much more festive—and if they'd held it at the bed-and-breakfast, we wouldn't have been able to join in the fun." Robyn beamed approval at the twelve Haverers in attendance. And at the several times as many locals who'd showed up to bring food and stayed to help celebrate. In Caerphilly, people perked up their ears at the mere mention of a potluck event. If you added in the fact that certain people were bringing their specialties, you could guarantee standing room only. And as Caerphilly potluck events went, this was a winner. Muriel, from the diner, had brought three different kinds of her prize-winning pies. Minerva Burke, the chief's wife, had brought her meatballs in grape jelly and chili sauce, usually one of the first dishes to disappear. Randall had brought several hams from one of his cousins who raised free-range, organic heritage-breed pigs. Some of the non-cooks had chipped in to get large pizzas and pans of lasagna from Luigi's, everyone's favorite Italian restaurant. Even Rose Noire's Tofu Surprise was a hit—the surprise being that she'd managed to make the stuff not only edible but reasonably tasty. And there were three kinds of green bean casserole, four kinds of pasta salad, mashed potatoes with and without skins or garlic, vegetarian and carnivore stuffed shells, corn on the cob, fresh baked rolls and biscuits, huge tubs of Greek and tossed salad—I gave up trying to make a complete list. The only thing we didn't have was wine or beer, because we didn't want to expose Malcolm Haver to any more temptation than necessary.

"The buffet is definitely a hit," I said. "But I think they could have gotten along without that." I pointed to the VHS tape player we'd scrounged up. It was hooked up to the large TV screen at one end of the parish hall, but except for a ceremonial playing of the blooper reel—which I learned was a compilation of silly mistakes the cast had made during the filming of *Dauntless Crusader*—the VHS player had been largely ignored.

"I think its importance is mostly symbolic," she said. "With all due respect to Mr. Haver, I don't think Weaseltide is entirely about him anymore. Or the television show. I think it's about friendship. Think of it—these women have been part of this group since their teens or twenties—nearly four decades of friendship."

I nodded. They were a diverse group. Ten white, one black, one Asian-American. I found myself wondering how the latter two had become such devoted fans of a short-lived television show about medieval England—and 1980s Hollywood's version of medieval England at that. To each her own.

Some of the Haverers were staying at the Inn. Some had found bed-and-breakfasts with less rarified room prices. They must have planned this excursion months in advance to have gotten rooms in town at this time of year. Three were bunking in a dilapidated travel trailer parked beside our barn. Some looked spry enough to run a marathon. Several leaned on canes. One cruised around on a mobility scooter. Some were dressed in their Sunday best. Some in jeans.

And while they were all delighted to have Malcolm Haver attending their party, I could tell that most of them weren't bowled over or intimidated by his presence. Melisande was pretty excited, and one other was hanging on his every word, but the rest were treating him with kindness, with deference—but definitely without hero worship.

Still, they were here, not just attending Weaseltide but spending good money to stay in Caerphilly and attend *A Christmas Carol.* Haver was visibly pleased.

He even seemed to be enjoying the homely yet festive atmosphere of the parish hall. The various children's Bible classes had made most of the decorations, and Haver seemed as charmed as the parishioners with the results—particularly the various nativity scenes that dotted the walls between the construction paper wreaths and popcorn garlands. I took a few pictures myself: the wise men carrying gifts wrapped in red paper with big gold bows on the top. The wise men carrying gifts in giant sacks like camel-riding Santas. The shepherds whose flocks looked less like sheep than llamas. The angels flying over the manger with their comic-book-style superhero capes billowing behind them.

"So this is Weaseltide." Chief Burke was sipping a glass of ginger ale punch and looking a lot more relaxed than he had twenty-four hours previously. "Nice bunch of people, these Haverers."

"How are things over at the station?" I asked.

"Still crazy," he said. "I've got people there from Federal agencies I've never heard of before, all fighting over who gets the next crack at Mr. Brickelhouse. Who is already singing like a canary and implicating all his criminal associates. Including Mrs. Frost. In fact, especially Mrs. Frost—to look at her, who'd imagine she was the criminal mastermind behind a major smuggling ring. With any luck, by this time tomorrow we'll have sorted out who I'm extraditing Brickelhouse to and things can get back to normal around here."

"What about Mrs. Frost?" I asked. "Don't they all want to extradite her, too?"

"They're even more interested in extraditing her, but they

all understand that our murder investigation takes priority. Although it might not take too long before we can get rid of her—the district attorney is working on cutting a deal with her attorney."

"But will her attorney accept a deal?" I'd been worrying about this. "What if he tries to get her off with an insanity plea? All he has to do is show a few pictures of the cat infestation and the jury would know she's a few ants short of a picnic. But that doesn't mean she should get away with murder."

"An insanity defense is a lot harder to pull off than you'd think," the chief said. "And regardless of what he says to the press, Mrs. Frost's attorney knows that."

"And what if the jury falls for her sweet little old lady act?" I asked. "She's very convincing, and it's not as if I got any video of her kicking the puppies."

"We have a couple of witnesses to that."

"Only me, I'm afraid," I said. "Haver was too busy having Shakespearean hysterics to notice the puppies were there."

"You and Jamie," the chief said. "He made a point of telling me about the mean old lady who kicked the puppies. Don't worry," he added, seeing my face. "I think it's very unlikely this will come to trial, and even if it does and we have to call Jamie as a witness—"

"Just promise me that if it does go to trial and you do need to call him, you call Josh as well," I said. "To testify about how he went to call 911. Because otherwise there will be no living with either of them."

"Understood," he said. "But as I said, unlikely it will come to trial, but the threat of your testimony and that of the twins should help the DA reach a satisfactory deal. One that involves a non-trivial prison sentence. And after that, all those other agencies will be standing in line to prosecute her."

"At least Meredith Flugleman can stop worrying about finding someplace for her to live."

"Yes." The chief smiled slightly. "I expect she'll be housed somewhere at the taxpayer's expense for the rest of her life. Now if you'll excuse me, I'm going to have a smidgen more of that ham Randall brought before it all disappears."

He lifted his plastic punch glass to me in salute and headed for the buffet. I was about to follow suit when Stanley Denton appeared.

"Evening." He looked around to make sure no one was nearby before adding. "All clear. At the hotel and the theater. Not sure I would stake my life on it—alcoholics can be diabolically clever. But if he's managed to hide a bottle someplace that neither Ekaterina nor I can find, then maybe we should tip off the CIA to recruit him."

"Excellent." I raised my ginger ale and we clinked plastic cups.

"Of course, I put a lot more faith in your cousin Maximilian," Stanley said.

"And even more faith in Haver's own change of attitude," I said. "I think the last two days gave him a wake-up call, and he's genuinely trying to change."

"May it last for the whole run of the play," Stanley said.

"May it last the rest of his life," I countered.

He nodded and we clinked plastic cups again. Then he headed for the buffet, just as Vince O'Manion strolled over to my side.

"You must try one of these." O'Manion plopped something on my plate—a small object impaled on a red toothpick with little fronds of gold tinsel at the top.

"What is it?" I peered at the object, which looked rather like a fried dumpling.

"Just try it." He picked up the object by its toothpick and aimed it at my mouth.

"I'm not asking out of pickiness," I said, forcing his hand back toward the plate. "The last time I let someone feed me something that looked like that it turned out to be Crab

Rangoon, and I'm allergic to crustaceans. I have no desire to spend opening night in the ER." Actually, my allergy wasn't all that severe—a Benadryl had been enough to quell the Crab Rangoon side effects. But I was well aware that repeated exposure to an allergen could increase my sensitivity to it, and on top of that I simply disliked the taste of crab.

"Pork gyoza," O'Manion said. "Japanese version of a fried dumpling. I can ask Marcy for the complete list of ingredients if you like."

"As long as it's not crab, shrimp, or lobster." I picked up the gyoza and took a small bite. And then a larger one.

"This is good." I popped the last bit into my mouth. "In fact, it's great," I added when I could no longer be accused of talking with my mouth full.

"I told you so." He held out another gyoza. I nodded and snatched it as soon as it hit my plate.

"There's a dish full of them on that table," he said, pointing. "If you want any, I'd go soon. I suspect they won't last long once people taste them."

"I will. Who's Marcy, anyway?"

I assumed he'd point out the cook so I could go and thank her. I was surprised—and more than a little curious—to see him turn beet red.

"She's a friend of mine," he said.

"Here in Caerphilly?"

"I see you've heard the invidious rumors—yes, Marcy was the . . . friend I was visiting the night of the murder."

I only nodded.

"And I'm overjoyed that I've been able to help her find her real niche in life. I mean, it was pretty obvious that she wasn't really cut out to be . . . um . . ."

"A lady of the evening?" I suggested.

"Yes. It was . . . well, never mind. But somehow we got to talking about food, and she offered me a piece of the apple cobbler she'd just made—ambrosia! And what that woman can do with a simple dish like shepherd's pie! We stayed up till two in the morning, cooking and eating—she was doing the cooking, of course, though she pitched in a bit on the eating. And when I woke up the next morning—well, the next afternoon, actually—it occurred to me that she was wasting her talents here. And I happen to have a client who could use a cook. So I made a few phone calls, and in a day or so she's flying out to California."

"To Hollywood? Or someplace more like Beverly Hills?"

"Pacific Palisades," he said. "Much trendier than Beverly Hills these days, if you have a few million to spare. There she is."

He pointed to the food table where a woman was putting out a steaming new tray of gyoza. She was a little shorter than me and about my shape—not fat, but comfortably padded and in no danger of being mistaken for an anorexic. She had a soft, round face and a pleasant smile. Not anyone I'd have ever picked as a call girl. But for a cook—definitely good casting.

"Is this a client you dine with regularly?"

"He will be from now on. Look, I wanted to thank you. This whole thing could have been a disaster, but I think it's going to turn out all right. Malcolm's got a whole new sense of purpose. He's excited about a role for the first time in ages."

"I'm glad to hear it." I was studying the last gyoza on his plate, wondering if he'd pitch a fit if I swiped it.

"And whether he knows it or not, I am well aware that we have you to thank." He seemed to notice my interest in the gyoza and took a bite out of it.

"So has the chief given back your pistol yet or are you facing the wilds of Caerphilly unarmed?" Maybe it was a mean thing to ask, but he didn't have to eat the gyoza right in front of me with quite so much lip-smacking ecstasy.

"Alas." He shook his head. "He'd already shipped it down

to the state crime lab by the time you determined that the old lady was the killer. Apparently there's a lot of red tape involved with getting it back."

"Frankly, I'm relieved to know we'll have one less person packing on opening night," I said. "What was the reason for hiding it in the ceiling, anyway?"

"Malcolm had me convinced I could be thrown in jail just for carrying it around in Virginia," Haver said. "And he was so furious with me that I was sure he'd turn me in, just to cause trouble. So I thought I'd hide it in his dressing room, where it'd be handy if I needed it, but the only person likely to get in trouble over it would be him. I have to admit, I was pretty terrified when I came back and found it missing."

I studied his face. I wasn't rabidly anti-gun, but I did feel pretty strongly that anyone who did own a gun needed to be responsible about it. Bringing a gun someplace without checking into the legality of it, and then leaving it lying around where anyone could find it—as far as I was concerned, the longer the crime lab kept O'Manion's lethal little security blanket away from him the better.

"If coming here really makes you that anxious, hire a bodyguard," I said. "I'm sure Mother could recommend one."

"I might just do that," he said. "After all, for such a small place, you have had an awful lot of murders lately." He popped the rest of the gyoza into his mouth. "Mmph-vreow," he said— at least that's what it sounded like through the gyoza. He waved and drifted off—in the direction of the buffet.

I had every intention of following suit, but I had only taken a few steps toward the buffet when I ran into Haver himself.

"Will you join me?" Haver handed me a plastic glass of punch. " 'The cups that cheer but not inebriate.' "

"Not Shakespeare," I said. "He was a 'give all my fame for a pot of ale' kind of guy."

"William Cowper." Haver sipped his punch. "You know what's the toughest part of this sobriety thing?"

I shook my head.

"Insomnia. That's one of the ways I've always tended to fall off the wagon. The insomnia gets so bad, I take just one drink to help me doze off."

"Talk to my dad," I said. "He's a doctor, and I'm sure he'd be glad to help."

"And have him prescribe me some pills instead of booze?" Haver shook his head. "Not sure that's any better."

"Dad's big on natural treatment for insomnia," I said. "He and my cousin Rose Noire. Talk to both of them while you're in town."

He nodded. Although he didn't look convinced. I'd have a word with Dad and Rose Noire myself.

"I bet the first thing they tell me to do is get rid of Fiona. My finch," he added, as if he thought I might not remember. "And I suppose they'd be right. She is a bit of a challenge."

"You could always rehome Fiona at the zoo," I said. "Grandfather has plenty of finches there to keep her company. She'd soon settle in."

"I suppose I should," he said. "But dammit—I love her. She's so beautiful, and she sings so sweetly. I've sort of come to see her as a symbol of my new sober life."

For my part, I'd have put more faith in Cousin Max, or whatever sober companion O'Manion could find when Haver left Caerphilly. But if Haver thought the finch helped, I wouldn't argue with him.

"I just wish she'd shut up at night," Haver said, sounding more plaintive than resentful. "I think she sleeps all day when I'm away and sings all night."

"You can fix that easily enough," I said. "Just put the cover on her cage. She'll get used to sleeping when you do."

"Cover?" He looked startled. "You mean the cage was supposed to come with a special cover that makes them shut up?"

"It's not a special cover," I said. "Just throw a blanket over it. Or an afghan. Anything that keeps out light and lets in air."

Did the man know nothing about birds?

"And Fiona will go to sleep?"

Evidently not.

"Look," I said. "I gather you're a first-time pet owner. How about if I arrange for Clarence to give you a few lessons on bird care."

"Do you think he would?"

"Of course. And what's more—"

"Meg, dear."

We both turned to find Mother standing behind us. Haver's face took on a look of fear and anxiety.

"Happy Weaseltide," I said.

"And a very merry Weaseltide to you both," she said, lifting her cup of tea. "Mr. Haver."

He stood at attention, and from the look on his face, you'd think that at any moment he expected her to shout "Off with his head!"

"We're having a little family dinner on Christmas Eve," she said. "A sort of midnight supper, because of how many of the family will be either appearing in or watching the show. If you're not otherwise engaged, we'd be delighted if you'd join us."

Haver's jaw literally fell open, and it took him several seconds to pull himself together.

"I'd be honored," he said. "Truly honored. Thank you!"

Mother clinked her plastic glass again his, and then against mine and sailed off.

"I'm overwhelmed," Haver said.

"Don't be too overwhelmed," I said. "Mother's idea of a little family dinner means only a hundred people or so."

"But including me as one of the hundred is so kind of her," he said. "Wonderful. People here can be so nice. I wish things had been like this the whole time I was here. I know it's all my own fault. Damn planes anyway."

"Planes?" I wasn't sure I understood what planes had to do with his behaving like an utter jerk for the first several weeks he was in town, but I was curious to hear his explanation.

"They give me migraines," he said. "Ghastly migraines. And I guess I take it out on other people when I feel bad. By the time I felt better enough to be civil to anyone, I'd been typecast as . . . well, a real-life Scrooge."

"May I suggest something?"

"Does your dad also have a lot of natural remedies for migraine?" Haver sounded skeptical.

"He probably does," I said. "And we have several migraine sufferers in the family, so he keeps up with the cutting edge of what conventional medicine is doing in that area. But actually, what I was going to suggest was that next time you arrive someplace with a raging migraine—just tell someone."

"Yeah." He nodded. "I just hate having people think I'm weak."

"If they think you're weak because of a medical issue, shame on them, but even if they do—isn't having people think you're weak better than having them think you're a complete and utter jerk?"

"Good point." He lifted his plastic cup in salute. "I will definitely take it under advisement."

"Hey, Malcolm." Cousin Max strolled up, holding Haver's coat, hat, scarf, and gloves. "Time for me to drive you over to the theater."

"So soon!" He didn't sound pleased. For a moment, I found myself worrying that he might be one of those actors who suffered from horrible stage fright. He must have seen my anxious look.

"Oh, don't worry," he said. "I'm like an old fire horse when I hear that 'places, everyone.' I'm just sorry to leave such a lovely party. But there will be other parties! In fact, I'm going to check with the Inn and see if I can throw one tonight, after the show. Or perhaps tomorrow—soon, anyway!" He threw his scarf over his shoulder for emphasis as he spoke, nearly smacking Max with it. Then he trotted over to say good-bye to the Haverers before he left. And the ladies tending the buffet table. And Robyn. And Chief Burke.

I was relieved when we finally dragged him away from the Weaseltide festivities and got him installed in his dressing room.

Backstage would have looked like chaos to an outsider, but with my newfound and hard-won insider status I could see the order and purpose of it all. Actors struggled into their costumes, did their vocal warm-ups, and performed whatever superstitious rituals they believed would ward off stage fright and ensure a good performance. The tech crew did last minute checks and double checks on all the sound and lights. The set crew went around testing to make sure nothing was about to fall apart. Rose Noire, who'd volunteered to wrangle the child actors, was leading them through a calming yoga routine.

I peeked out from behind the curtain to see the audience. The Haverers formed a small block in the middle of the second row, surrounded by Mother's family. Should I tell the boys how many aunts, uncles, and cousins were here to watch them, or would that make them more nervous?

No time anyway.

"Places!" called the stage manager. Haver and Bob Cratchit took their places in Scrooge's counting house. I slipped back into the wings as Michael, representing Charles Dickens, strolled onstage, carrying a quill pen and pretended to be writing on a sheaf of paper as he spoke the play's opening lines.

"Once upon a time—of all the good days in the year, upon a Christmas Eve—old Scrooge sat busy in his counting-house. It was

cold, bleak, biting, foggy weather; and the city clocks had only just
gone three, but it was quite dark already.

As he spoke, the curtain rose to reveal Bob Cratchit, bent
almost double over his ledger, shivering in spite of his over-
coat and scarf, while behind him Scrooge slowly counted a
stack of shiny gold and silver coins, glancing up occasionally
to make sure his clerk was still hard at work. The door flew
open and Scrooge's nephew entered, carrying with him a
gust of fake snow.

"*A merry Christmas, uncle! God save you!*"

"*Bah, humbug!*"

Haver was good. Not better than Michael would have
been, of course—I don't think it was bias making me think
so. But maybe as good, though in a very different way. He
was quite definitely a "squeezing, wrenching, grasping, scrap-
ing, clutching, covetous old sinner," but underneath it all,
even in the first scene, you could see something—a hint of
vulnerability? Or maybe just a thread of wry, self-deprecating
humor—that would make his eventual repentance believable. He barked out "are there no prisons? No workhouses?"
with a savagery that made a few in the audience gasp. And
yet I could tell that they were starting to feel sorry for him
when the clanking noise that heralded Marley's ghost re-
sounded through the theater.

Mother joined me in the wings to see how the audience
reacted when Marley's ghost entered. She'd had his costume
and makeup done in fish-belly-white and streaked with a re-
pellent yellow-green luminescent paint, making him look
like a cross between Boris Karloff as *The Mummy* and an extra
from *The Walking Dead*. Mother beamed with pleasure at the
audience's collective gasp.

I was relieved when the Ghost of Christmas Past's torch
worked as it was supposed to, but I tensed up during the
scene between Scrooge and the ghost, because I could see
Josh waiting on the opposite wing to make his entrance. His

cue came, and he slipped onstage, ready to be revealed when Scrooge and the ghost approached him

"The school is not quite deserted. A solitary child, neglected by his friends, is left there still."

Josh looked appropriately solitary and neglected. But he also managed to look uncannily like a much younger version of Haver. It was the facial expression, I decided—that, and the way he lifted his chin and extended his neck, as if already rebelling against the stiff collar his older self so resented.

I hardly breathed during the whole scene, and let out a long—but silent—sigh of relief when young Scrooge's sister Fran came to fetch him home and Josh made his triumphant exit.

And then I could breathe again, at least until the Ghost of Christmas Present led Scrooge to the Cratchits and Jamie, as Tiny Tim, made his entrance on Bob Cratchit's shoulder. I'd been a little skeptical about casting him as Tiny Tim, since he was tall for his age—taking after both Michael and me—and as healthy as a little horse, but he managed to appear so frail and wan that I hoped no one from Social Services was in the audience. And yet when he uttered his quavering "God bless us, everyone," I was sure they could hear him just fine in the back row.

Chips off the old block, both of them.

I thought I could breathe now, with both of the boys' main scenes successfully completed. But I found myself caught up in Haver's performance. Not better than Michael would have done, and I could definitely see areas where Michael had influenced him—but still. Very different from Michael. And very compelling.

Especially the scene where Scrooge, after seeing the tombstone with his name on it, falls to his knees before the Spirit of Christmas Yet to Come and begs for a reprieve.

"Am I that man who lay upon the bed? No, Spirit! O no, no! Spirit! hear me! I am not the man I was. Why show me this, if I am

past all hope? Assure me that I yet may change these shadows you have shown me by an altered life. I will honor Christmas in my heart, and try to keep it all the year. I will live in the Past, the Present, and the Future. The Spirits of all three shall strive within me. I will not shut out the lessons that they teach. O, tell me I may sponge away the writing on this stone!"

I could hear sniffles from the audience, and I was willing to bet there wasn't a dry eye in the house. I felt a little choked up myself, and not just from how moving his speech was: bless his heart, he'd fallen to his knees to repent in the absolute dead center of his spotlight. I glanced up at the tech booth to see that the crew member who ran the lights was doing a fist pump and silently cheering. After that the show seemed to race to its conclusion. Scrooge sending the Cratchits the prize turkey. Scrooge dropping by to wish his estranged nephew a merry Christmas. And in a departure from the book that made for a more theatrical ending, Scrooge showing up in time for dessert at the Cratchits' house, giving Jamie a chance to reprise his "God bless us every one!" And then as Scrooge and the Cratchits reveled silently in the background with cups of punch and slices of pie and plum pudding, Michael stepped back on stage to close the play.

Scrooge was better than his word. He did it all, and infinitely more; and to Tiny Tim, who did NOT die, he was a second father. He became as good a friend, as good a master, and as good a man as the good old city knew, or any other good old city, town, or borough in the good old world. Some people laughed to see the alteration in him; but his own heart laughed, and that was quite enough for him. And it was always said of him, that he knew how to keep Christmas well, if any man alive possessed the knowledge. May that be truly said of us, and all of us! And so, as Tiny Tim observed, God Bless Us, Every One!

The audience was on its feet even before the curtain closed. They applauded through seven curtain calls, and then kept applauding while Haver dragged the backstage crew on stage—Mother and her costume crew, Jake and the set crew, the lighting and sound crew, the stage manager . . . even me and Cousin Max.

The Haverers began a cry of "Speech! Speech!" and before long the entire audience took it up. Michael gestured to Haver, who stepped forward, blew kisses to the crowd, and made hushing gestures.

"Damn," Jake murmured. "He called their bluff."

For a moment I was worried. Haver looked a little like his old self, proud and irascible, and I braced myself to see what he'd say. But just as he was opening his mouth, he happened to glance over at Josh, who was imitating his stance, his facial expression—even the haughty way he arched his neck. He burst out laughing and threw up his arms in a gesture of surrender.

"For once, I'm speechless," he said. "God bless us, every one! Merry Christmas to all, and to all a good night!"

"Melchior! Give Caspar back the frankincense! And Baltha-zar, if you don't stop throwing myrrh at the shepherds, I'm demoting you to junior sheep!"

I gazed sternly at the three middle-schoolers who were playing the wise men in this year's church Christmas pageant. Wise persons, actually, since we'd given the role of Caspar to one of the girls. Melchior and Balthazar assumed implausible expressions of innocence, and Caspar wisely postponed any vengeance she'd been planning against her rowdy fellow Magi.

I turned my gaze on the shepherds, who quickly pretended that they hadn't been about to start yet another fencing match with their crooks. And then on the Virgin Mary, who was chewing gum again. Her jaw froze, and then she swallowed hard.

"We only have three more rehearsals left." I spoke calmly, but with the precise enunciation that should warn any child who was even halfway paying attention that they were all on very thin ice. "If anyone has decided that appearing in the Christmas pageant is too much work, just speak up and I'll find someone to replace you."

The faces of the younger cast members—the ones playing sheep, assistant shepherds, or junior angels—took on an eager, hopeful look as they glanced around to see if any of the older children with larger roles were having second thoughts. The older children all assumed expressions of injured dignity.

Well, except for my own twin eleven-year-old sons. Both of them regularly appeared in children's roles in local theater productions and prided themselves on being young professionals in the dramatic arts, well on the way to following in their father's footsteps. Josh, who played Joseph, was doing a fair imitation of my stern parental manner. Jamie, the angel Gabriel, was contemplating his fellow cast members with an expression that tempered melancholy disappointment with celestial forgiveness.

I stared at the cast for a few more moments, letting my words sink in. Then I gave them a brief, approving smile and clapped my hands.

"Places, everyone!"

The children swarmed to take their starting positions. The sheep and shepherds milled stage right. Joseph, Mary, and the angel Gabriel formed a semicircle around the manger. The wise persons clustered stage left, followed by the half-dozen children who'd be playing their camels. The camels had been behaving quite angelically ever since I explained to them that the three best-behaved among them would get to wear the camel heads while the remaining three would play the camels' rear ends. I needed to find similar leverage over the rest of the cast. Since my notebook-that-tells-me-when-to-breathe, as I call my giant to-do list, wasn't within reach, I made a mental note to brainstorm on the matter.

Mary knelt beside the straw-filled manger and bent tenderly over it. Then she snapped her head up and shuffled backward a foot or so, still kneeling.

"Baby Jesus needs a new diaper," she said, wrinkling her pert, freckled nose.

Josh bent over, sniffed, and nodded.

"We don't need Baby Jesus," I said. Several shepherds tittered. "I mean, we don't need to have him lying in the manger this early in the rehearsal. We don't want him getting tired and cranky."

The central role of Baby Jesus was to be played by four-month-old Noah, the son of the Reverend Robyn Smith, Trinity Episcopal's rector. At least that was Robyn's idea. I was more of a pragmatist when it came to children. Noah might be cherubic-looking, but he was also colicky. I didn't think the congregation was ready for the spectacle of a red-faced infant Messiah shrieking loud enough to drown out the choir. I planned to make sure we didn't lose track of Noah's understudy, a highly realistic life-sized baby doll.

And since Noah had neither lines nor blocking to learn, we certainly didn't need him at rehearsal.

"Robyn?" I turned and scanned the sanctuary. "Has anyone seen Reverend Robyn?"

"Right here." Robyn bustled in through a side door. "Do you need Noah now?"

"We don't need him at all today," I said. "Could you take him back to your office?"

"Of course." She turned to leave.

"Robyn, wait."

I was about to ask why she was leaving without Noah. Then I realized—she was holding Noah. And bouncing him up and down while he uttered a few of the choking noises that usually signaled his intention to begin howling like a banshee.

I turned back to the stage. If Robyn was holding Noah—

"That's not Noah," Jamie said, shaking his head hard enough to make his halo bounce.

"What child is this?" Josh proclaimed dramatically.

I could see the shepherds and wise men starting to inch closer to get a better look.

"Everybody, stay where you are," I ordered.

I hopped up onto the stage and swept aside the thick

tangle of straw to peer down at the infant. Definitely not Noah—this child was blond. Although I estimated he was probably about the same age, four months, give or take a little. He, or more probably she—the baby was wearing a pink onesie. Not that the color necessarily meant anything. When Josh and Jamie were infants, Michael and I had received a few pink and purple hand-me-downs. Michael had initially turned up his nose at these, but the week both boys came down with a stomach bug—and shared it with us—even he had given up his objections to the girly clothes when we'd run out of more masculine outfits.

I could figure out the baby's gender when I did the diaper change, which was definitely needed. Though the child was happy at the moment, smiling angelically, the way many infants do once they've accomplished a particularly smelly bowel movement.

Also unlike Noah, who could be heard out in the hall, screaming his lungs out.

"Look." Jamie, who was leaning over the back of the manger, pointed to something—a note attached to the baby's clothing with a large safety pin. It was folded once, and there was nothing written on the outside, but presumably there was a message inside.

I lifted up the top flap of the note with the edge of my finger, something I realized I'd picked up from my cousin Horace, a trained crime scene investigator. Probably overkill in this situation, but still.

I read the note and froze.